The Adventures of Henry and Eulalie

D1216259

Mushin Knott

Illustrations by Kalpart

Strategic Book Publishing and Rights Co.

Strategic Book Publishing and Rights Co., LLC
USA
www.sbpra.net

For information about special discounts for bulk purchases, please contact Strategic Book Publishing and Rights Co., LLC. Special Sales, at bookorder@sbpra.net.

ISBN: 978-1-68235-711-8

Dedication

To John Hendrix:

My heart, my hope,
my inspiration for a hero.

Table of Contents

Part I

Chapter I
Blackout

"Crack!" went the bat as Tommy McCorkle hit a pop fly to right field. Henry Harris, squinting in the afternoon sun still high in the cloudless sky, watched the ball fall easily toward him and prepared to catch it. All eyes, shaded by the green caps of the Colonials Little League baseball team, were on Henry, hoping for the third out that would close the inning and signal the end of practice. Henry held up his gloved hand to catch the ball, and as its arced path crossed the sun, he blinked hard.

Nobody moved except Tommy as he rounded first base and headed for second, preparing to slide in the event Henry failed to catch the ball. A moment later, Tommy reached the bag and stopped to look around him, only to find the infield strangely vacant. As he wondered where everyone had gone, Kyle, the catcher, walked past him, pulling off his facemask to reveal a look of curious concern. Tommy turned to see a crowd gathering in right field.

"What happened?"

"Where's the ball?"

"Did it hit him?"

"Henry, are you okay?"

Murmured questions spread through the team as the puzzled boys stood over Henry's motionless body. Seconds later, when Henry did not get up, Mr. Waddleman jumped up from the sideline bench and raced out to check on the young boy.

"Henry, can you hear me?" the man asked sheepishly, as fear crept into his voice and beads of sweat formed on his balding head.

Mr. Waddleman was not the team's usual baseball coach, nor did he look the part. He was rather a short, plump man whose primary responsibility was in the role of assistant principal. He was an amiable fellow and happy to step in when a teacher fell ill, or to volunteer as coach or chaperone at a moment's notice, like today when Mr. Kent was off enduring emergency dental work. On occasion, you might even find him behind the wheel of the big yellow bus driving the children to school.

Mr. Waddleman squatted beside Henry and gently removed the baseball cap from his head. Henry's head lolled gently to the side as if he were in deep slumber.

"It must have hit him," said Kyle, looking down at his unconscious friend sprawled out on the grass, but no mark of injury supported his assumption. Instead, Henry looked peaceful, spread out like a snow angel on the cool green grass, as the clear spring day burned blue and gold around him.

"It didn't hit him," said Mr. Waddleman nervously wondering what to do next.

"How do you know?" asked Tommy who had joined his teammates encircling the unconscious boy.

"Because the ball is still in his glove," replied Mr. Waddleman with a shaky voice. "He caught it."

"Third out!" yelled Kyle.

Chapter II
The Scientists

"Aha! He's here! It's working! It worked! I told you it would!"

Excited whispers roused Henry from his daze. He rubbed his eyes, trying to discern the shapes above him in the gray-lit room. He was not in the schoolyard any longer, and these were not his teammates surrounding him with eager, shining eyes.

"Don't be frightened, son. You are safe and among friends," said a tall white-haired man, his thin frame draped in a long white lab coat.

Two more people in lab coats stood next to the tall man. One, a small woman with frizzy salt-and-pepper hair that gave an air of unruliness to her otherwise tidy appearance, smiled at Henry, with eyes crinkling generously at the corners. The other, a man much shorter than the first, grinned and nodded excitedly, his round eyes set in a circular face.

"My name is Dr. Finnegan," continued the tall man. "And this is Dr. Scala and Dr. Hector," he said, indicating first the wild-haired woman and then the round-faced man. "Welcome home, Henry."

"H-Home!" stammered Henry. "What do you mean? Where am I? Who are you? I've never seen this place before!" He was frightened, certain now he did not recognize these strange people.

"No, this has not been your home for some eleven years now," said the woman. "Not since you were but a few days old."

"We have a lot to tell you Henry!" said the small man enthusiastically. "But first, you must tell us how you are feeling. Are you dizzy? Can you walk?"

"Of course I can walk," said Henry with suspicion. "Why wouldn't I be able to walk?"

Henry hopped off the cushioned slab and surveyed his surroundings. Humming machines with blinking sensors lined the walls of the dimly lit room. In the corner, a printer jerked wild patterns onto large paper that piled in heaps on the floor. Henry noticed he no longer wore his green and white baseball uniform but instead was clothed in a comfortable, blue body suit.

"Where are my clothes? Where's my baseball glove?" asked Henry irritably.

The tall one, Dr. Finnegan answered. "This suit keeps your body warm on this end when it is not in use. We are, or course, able to bilocate material objects, but we only had need to call forth your consciousness, at least this first time. Consciousness, unlike objects, cannot be multipresent. We have maintained your first body here all these years as a vehicle to bring you back to us."

"Bilocate? Multipresent?" asked Henry. "What does that mean? I don't understand!" Henry grew anxious as he searched his memory for his last conscious thought. The last thing he remembered was squinting through the sunlight at the baseball, calculating its descent and preparing for the catch. Then everything went blank. He could not recall the satisfying thud of the ball in his glove. What could have happened?

"Henry?" Dr. Hector interrupted his thoughts. "Did you mention a baseball glove? What time was it when you left the Earth?"

"Left the Earth!" exclaimed Henry with growing agitation.

"That is a very good point Dr. Hector," said Dr. Finnegan hastily. "Henry, please tell us what were you doing when you ... uh, right before you arrived here?"

"I was practicing with my baseball team after school," said Henry.

"What time was it?" asked Dr. Finnegan.

"About four thirty in the afternoon," replied Henry.

"We must have miscalculated the time," said Dr. Scala. "We should get him back as soon as possible. People might ask questions."

"Yes, yes, I agree," said Dr. Finnegan. "We have friends there, but still, it will no doubt arouse suspicion, or at least unnecessary curiosity. I am sorry, Henry. We will call you back this evening while your world sleeps. Explanations must wait until then. Please, come back and lie on the table. We will leave the room while you translate."

"Translate? I don't understand what you are saying. What will you do to me? Where am I? What do you mean 'when I left the Earth'?" Henry had never before doubted his own senses, but this conversation with the scientists left him deeply muddled.

"Please Henry," said Dr. Finnegan. "You must trust us. If we do not get you back presently, there could be trouble. We will explain everything tonight when we call you back. Please, will you trust us?"

Henry sighed and resignedly lay back down on the slab as the scientists left the room and gently closed the door behind them. He closed his eyes and clenched his teeth in anticipation as he listened to the whirring machines, wondering what could possibly happen next.

Chapter III
Nurse Edna

Henry opened his eyes to a square-patterned tile ceiling checkered with fluorescent lights. The smell of antiseptic signaled he was in the school nurse's office. The room smelled clean and white like cotton balls. He had been here once before when he scraped his knee bloody sliding into home plate. Then, he had torn his pants clean through and the nurse had put a stinging, orange medicine on the cut.

Nurse Edna's giant head came into view and blocked out most of the overhead light. She loomed over Henry and smiled at him through thin, wrinkled, red-painted lips. Her small eyes, adorned with brightly colored lids and mascara-laden eyelashes, showed concern. She was a full-bodied woman with big orange curls arranged closely around her pudgy face. Her hair was the color of iodine. She wore too much makeup and always smelled of talcum powder.

"Henry, honey, how are you feeling?" rang out her shiny voice. "You gave us all quite a scare. You have been out cold for ten minutes now." Nurse Edna was one of those people who seem to sing words instead of merely saying them, no matter what the topic of conversation.

"I'm fine," said Henry as he eased himself into a sitting position on the white cot. He took a deep breath and realized he meant it. He felt refreshed as if he had had a short but invigorating nap. He wondered if his strange encounter had been no more than a lucid dream.

Mr. Waddleman knocked quickly on the door and poked his head inside.

"Is everything alright in here?" he asked Nurse Edna. Seeing Henry awake and alert, he smiled with obvious relief.

"I'm alright now," said Henry. "I should be getting home, though. I don't want my parents to worry about me."

Nurse Edna replied, "Well, dear, of course we telephoned your parents at the first sign of concern and they should be arriving any moment."

"I'll call them now and let them know I'm alright," said Henry. "They would have to leave work to come and get me. I live only a few blocks away. I can walk home from here."

"Oooh, I'm sorry Henry," began Nurse Edna in her singsong voice. "There are forms to be filled out and rules to be followed and ..."

"It's okay, Edna," interrupted Mr. Waddleman. "There's no need for all that. The ball didn't hit him. There is no injury so the school will not be liable. He just fell asleep for a few minutes. Right, Henry?"

"Well, sir," Nurse Edna continued, "it is not normal to just fall asleep in the middle of baseball practice. Plus, the appropriate protocol is to ...."

"I will sign whatever forms you need," said Mr. Waddleman, waving off her tuneful objections with an air of authority unusual for the timid man. "Come on Henry. I'll see you home."

Glad to escape, Henry jumped off the cot and followed Mr. Waddleman out of the nurse's office. Together they walked down the cold, shiny, linoleum hallway leading to freedom on the other side of the heavy double doors. Henry was eager for some time alone to think about the strange encounter with the scientists. It had seemed so real, but his memory of the scene was quickly fading, as a dream lost in the distractions of morning light.

Henry and Mr. Waddleman emerged into the afternoon sunlight on the front side of the school opposite the baseball field. Henry was relieved when Mr. Waddleman said goodbye to him at the door, reminding him to call his parents so they would not worry further about his sudden spell. Henry nodded, a little befuddled by so strange an afternoon, and turned his steps toward his neighborhood, a couple of blocks east.

"Henry, wait," Mr. Waddleman called out. Henry stopped and turned, squinting against the sun descending toward the horizon. Mr. Waddleman's face was in shadow as it eclipsed the burning orange ball. Dancing sunbeams shot light rays around the top of his shiny head. He looked like a strange angel with a statue of liberty halo who was about to give profound advice to his guardian charge.

"Don't forget your glove," he said.

Chapter IV
Mr. and Mrs. Harris

Henry had been home for nearly a minute when his mother and father rushed in through the front door.

"Henry, sweetheart, are you sure you're okay?" his mother exclaimed.

As promised, Henry had called his parents before walking home. He assured them he was fine, but his mother would not be satisfied until she conducted her own examination. Mrs. Harris knelt in front of him, held him out at arm's length, and began a series of quick motions meant to determine his physical well-being. First, she looked into his eyes, pulled wide between her fingers and thumbs, then checked his wrist for a pulse rate, and finally pushed back his hair to feel his forehead for elevated temperature all in the span of about five seconds. Then, deciding that hugs and kisses fix most ailments, she hugged him tightly and repeatedly kissed his face until Henry broke away with an "Aw, mom, I'm fine, really. I'm too old for all that stuff."

"Eleven isn't too old to still need your mother from time to time," she teased. Since Henry seemed healthy, his parents eventually agreed to let him be. They decided to remain watchful for any disturbing symptoms, but in the meantime, life was allowed to return to normal. Mrs. Harris started dinner while Henry and his father headed to the backyard where, the previous summer, they had built a half-pipe skateboard ramp. Mr. Harris was an avid skateboard enthusiast and was thrilled when his son had shown a liking for the sport. He loved these afternoons with Henry as they practiced new tricks together.

Mr. Harris was a tall, attractive man who somehow managed to keep his youthful spirit despite the fact that he was nearly fifty years old. He was well into his thirties when he and his wife adopted Henry. They had both wanted children, but none had come until the morning they literally found a baby on their doorstep. They searched for the child's parents without success and the authorities fared no better. Yet, the child thrived in his new home and there was no one to object to the quiet adoption that soon followed. To this day, Henry's origins remained a mystery.

Henry had a happy childhood and he loved his adopted parents as his own. His father was an inquisitive man who loved the Discovery Channel and spent his free hours tinkering with his own inventions. He sold the most useful ones in his store that specialized in unusual and hard-to-find gadgets. Mr. Harris did most of his business on the internet, but he kept a storefront to warehouse his goods and provide a meeting place for like-minded enthusiasts. He enjoyed his customers and the quaintness of an oddity shop that specialized in weird and wonderful objects. The name of his store was *Someone Should Invent That!* and he kept a suggestion board on this same topic. His customers submitted ideas for useful gadgets, and Mr. Harris designed and developed the most promising of them to sell in his store.

Mr. Harris had met Henry's mother while conducting research for one such invention. She was working part time, as a librarian's assistant, when she noticed an intriguing young man scouring the technical and scientific journals. Whispered conversations bred a certain intimacy that blossomed under their mutual love of learning.

Mrs. Harris's love of books and their wisdom inspired her career as a digital archivist, which is something like a modern-day librarian. She worked in the preservation of digital information, as well as the transfer of ancient texts to technologically advanced and less fragile media. Computer files do not turn yellow and brittle with age, and cyberspace provides an excellent refuge from would-be censors and book-burners.

Mrs. Harris loved to cook and play crossword puzzles, but her favorite pastime was telling Henry and her husband unending stories about worlds beyond. She knew tales from long ago and stories from distant lands. She knew legends from the sea and the myths of forgotten cultures. She could recall with amazing clarity the fairy tales she read as child and would relate with thrilling possibility those nonfiction accounts she often came across in her work that were stranger than any author's imagination.

This evening went by quickly enough in the usual whirlwind of weeknight chores. By the time Henry ate his dinner, finished his homework, and took his bath, he had almost convinced himself that the afternoon's events were no more than a dream. He could imagine no more plausible explanation than that he had simply fallen asleep on the field like Mr. Waddleman had said. As odd as it is to fall asleep on a baseball field in the middle of practice, it is odder still to wake up among scientists who describe the Earth as a place you have just left. Henry figured the best thing to do was to go to bed early and see what happened. After all, if he *had* fallen asleep, he obviously needed more rest. If it was something else, well, the scientists did say they would bring him back tonight. By the morning, he should know whether it had just been a dream. Henry climbed into bed and buried himself in the covers, not certain for which of the two outcomes he was hoping.

Chapter V
The Garden

Henry once again opened his eyes to a gray-lit room. He lay flat on his back, staring up at a dull expanse of shadowed ceiling. At first, he thought was still in his bed with the first rays of sunrise softening the darkness. Then, he heard whirring machines and muffled voices. His heart quickened with anticipation as he propped himself up by his elbows for a better look around.

"He's back, Doctor," said a now-familiar voice. The three scientists whom Henry had met earlier that afternoon—Dr. Finnegan, Dr. Scala, and Dr. Hector—gathered around him, each of them looking pleased.

"Welcome back, Henry!" said Dr. Finnegan with a bright, toothy smile. "I do hope we got it right this time. You were in bed asleep at this hour, correct?"

"Yes sir. Yes, I was," replied Henry.

"Good! Wonderful!" said Dr. Finnegan. "By our estimations, it should be near midnight your time, so we have hours before anyone should attempt to awaken you. When you go back, we will send with you a tiny clock. Please set it precisely and bring it back here on your next visit. Then, we will know exactly what time it is in your world."

"You mean I can take objects with me when I ... when I ..." Henry stammered trying to remember the word the scientists had used.

"Bilocate," said Dr. Finnegan, finishing Henry's sentence. "And yes, you should be able to convey inanimate objects with you. Simply, hold the device in your hand and concentrate on it as you return home. You will find that it goes with you. In fact, the next time you come you could bring along the clothes you are wearing if you prefer. If you will it, it should work."

"But come," he continued, "more of that later. I'm sure you have many questions for us, which we will do our best to answer."

Dr. Finnegan led Henry out of the room and down a long corridor. The tall scientist then opened a door and ushered Henry into a large open room with a massive glass window. The room resembled an airport lobby, except instead of asphalt and airplanes on the other side of the glass, an enormous outdoor garden bloomed—the most beautiful garden Henry had ever seen. It was daytime here, wherever here was. From the position of the sun, it appeared to be late afternoon. Towering sunflowers swayed in a gentle breeze, their stalks surrounded by lush green vegetation and gorgeous flowers in vibrant colors. Henry had never seen anything so lovely. He put one hand longingly on the glass barrier and leaned forward until his forehead touched its cool surface. He could almost smell the sweet fragrance of the flowers and feel the perfumed breeze on his cheek.

"This was your mother's garden," said Dr. Scala, breaking Henry's daydream. "I should say your birth mother. She was a gifted gardener. She was also my friend."

"My birth mother?" Henry asked, spinning around on his heels. Her statement affected him physically and he looked for somewhere to sit down. He walked over to a large, overstuffed, oatmeal-colored couch and sunk into its welcoming cushions. Dr. Hector came in with a tray of hot cocoa and warm cookies and set them on a table near Henry.

"Yes, Henry," said Dr. Finnegan. "Please make yourself comfortable. Have something to eat. We have a long story to tell you."

"My birth mother," Henry repeated softly. Henry rarely thought about his birth parents. He knew the Harrises had adopted him as an infant, but to him they were his real mom and dad. They were the only parents he ever knew and he was fine with that. He had never wished for any parents other than the ones who had raised him. Yet, he had to admit, the possibility of uncovering his obscured beginnings intrigued him.

Henry looked up at the scientists with quiet expectation, wondering if their story would compare to the exciting adventures his mother often told. Looking around this strange room at his three new acquaintances, and then beyond the glass into the magnificent garden outside, Henry had a feeling it would.

Dr. Finnegan sat down in a chair facing Henry. He rested his elbows on his knees, leaned forward, and clasped his hands together. With his chin on his hands, he looked thoughtfully off to the side as if trying to remember something he once knew. After a moment, he straightened his posture and leaned back in his chair. "Well," he sighed, "I suppose we should start at the beginning."

Chapter VI
Sun-Rhea

"The place where you now find yourself is called Sun-Rhea," Dr. Finnegan began. "We are a planet distant from, yet similar to, Earth. We here are members of the Federation of Free Minds, the last free vestige of a once enlightened society dedicated to the pursuit of truth inherent in the wonders of the universe. Our peace was destroyed when our great enemy Mocarsto came from the Wildlands and made his home among us. The Wildlands is a strange place, full of magic and unexplained wonders; it is not a world wholly compatible with our own. In fact, the two worlds rarely meet.

"As the legend goes, Mocarsto was tricked in love by a woman named Thera. She sent him out of the Wildlands on a fool's errand meant to prove his love and win her heart. Upon discovering her deception, he also learned he was unable to return to the Wildlands. Thera had cast a spell on him to bar his reentry to his homeland. Indeed, the path to the Wildlands is elusive to most, but one born and bred within its borders can make the crossing. Few of our kind ever find the path to the Wildlands, and those that do seldom return. Your mother, Henry, was unique in this ability. She was born in the Wildlands, and she alone among us could travel, at will, the path that links these two worlds.

"Mocarsto was furious when he realized Thera's trickery. His enduring rage fueled a merciless quest for power and an unwavering determination to subjugate all life. Over the years, both his power and his anger have grown. He is a tremendous liar and an artful deceiver who promises his minions freedom from worldly cares in exchange for their sworn devotion. He began with a small band of weak-minded followers, but his numbers grew quickly as he gained control over the resources of the land. Mocarsto feeds his followers a substance he calls "hypnofood," the metabolic properties of which reduce independent thought and lower resistance to authority. He has been breeding an army of zombies who have traded their free will for a life of predictable ease. The poor fools work in his factories to produce the very substance that enslaves them. As Mocarsto's power grew, he gained control over more of the land, consuming more resources to produce his hypnotic gruel. He expanded his dominion in all directions, conquering villages one by one, offering the defeated people a bitter choice of hypnofood or starvation.

"In the early days, many rebelled and fought bravely to slow the speed of his alarming encroachment. They camped at his borders to prevent his infection from spreading to the free minds of Sun-Rhea. Others of us sought to fight him with science, to find the means to end Mocarsto's tyranny over our people. Your mother and father were chief among us. Together we founded the Federation of Free Minds, a collective of individuals whose sole mission is to pursue truth and uncover and chronicle the yet unknown. The Federation supports various pursuits, and all here are free to follow their own inclinations. Our common purpose is to find a way to destroy him, Mocarsto, the great enemy of free minds everywhere. Our headquarters are here in this complex, overlooking the valley. It is known as "the Garden" because of your mother's beautiful flowers.

"The battle waged on for years until Mocarsto finally overcame the last of the rebels. Those few who still resisted retreated to our valley and joined us in the search for the mechanism of his defeat. The rest succumbed to Mocarsto's growing army, adding more fuel to the poison factories, the smoke from which darkens the eastern horizon. Mocarsto's lands have engulfed the eastern towns. An expanse of barren desert is all that separates his lands from ours.

"Our greatest efforts have only slowed his progress. Mocarsto has a profound hold on his conquered people, and his inner fortress is rumored to be impenetrable. The lands under his control are known as Cardew. Legend has it that the secret to his undoing lies with his origin in the Wildlands. As the legend goes, 'The Heart of Stone can only be broken upon the Rock of Memory.'"

Here Dr. Finnegan paused and looked thoughtfully out the window.

"What does that mean? 'The Heart of Stone can only be broken upon the Rock of Memory?'" asked Henry, wanting the doctor to continue his story.

"We aren't sure, Henry. That's what your mother was trying to find out. She was looking for the Memory Stone."

Dr. Finnegan sighed and continued, "As I mentioned, your mother could travel the path between Sun-Rhea and the Wildlands. She spent her girlhood in the Wildlands and loved it still, though responsibilities here kept her away for some time. Your mother knew well the story of Mocarsto's banishment from the Wildlands and the legend of his fall. Discouraged by our failure to defeat him, she was determined to return to her homeland to search for the mysterious rock and uncover its secrets.

"Somehow, we don't know how, the enemy must have learned of your mother's travels to the Wildlands and her search for the fabled Rock of Memory. Purportedly, the Memory Stone is the key to Mocarsto's undoing. The old stories say it will bring him to his end. Your mother believed she knew its location. We could not persuade her to postpone her search for the talisman. We could not move her from her mission, though we begged her to think of her own safety, and that of her unborn child.

"She was late in her pregnancy when she last traveled to the Wildlands. We never saw her again because she never came back. Naturally, we were worried, but we were utterly helpless. None of us could go to her; neither could we communicate. We didn't know why she would not, or could not, return to us, but we suspected

Mocarsto was to blame, or perhaps someone in the Wildlands still loyal to him. He must have known she had returned there to seek his ruin.

"Several weeks had passed when a strange, short, elderly woman tottered into your mother's garden. She was a sight I will never forget with her horn-rimmed glasses and disheveled gray hair poking out beneath her bonnet. She mumbled nervously to herself and looked about in every direction before she lay down her bundle beneath the shade of the giant blue irises. We watched curiously from this very window and ran out to see what she had deposited in the garden.

"By the time we got outside, she was a good distance away. She had left as quickly, and with as much agitation, as she had come. I called out to her to stop and speak with us, but she only murmured 'Not I. This is no place for me. But for her I came and will not again if I can help it. I must go. There's time yet to make the tea ....'"

"At least, that is what I heard her say. Her mumbling voice faded quickly with her hasty retreat. She left no doubt from whence she came because there, on the soft ground wrapped up in a blanket, lay an infant barely a few days old. It was you, Henry, and you looked so much like your mother we knew you the moment we saw you."

Dr. Finnegan paused again. He stared out of the large picture window into the garden, looking as if he were reliving the scene he had just described. His eyes glistened with love and threatening teardrops until he suddenly remembered his company and turned his gaze back toward Henry.

Amazed and uncomfortable, Henry searched for something to say to break the awkward silence. "What is her name?" he asked.

"Who's that?" said Dr. Finnegan, awakening from his reverie. "Your mother, you mean?"

"Yes." Henry agreed, although he was not quite comfortable calling her that. He disliked the moniker on anyone other than the mother he had known all of his life.

"Mirabel is her name."

Silence fell again as everyone weighed the magnitude of the conversation.

Henry felt conflicted by this new information. Mr. and Mrs. Harris loved Henry as if he was their own. They had not lied to him about his adoption. His parents told him how they found him as an infant, abandoned on their doorstep, like a scene from a Dickens novel. Nobody knew who his birth parents were, and Henry rarely wondered about them. He was part of a happy family, and their bond, though not of blood, was strong and genuine. To Henry, his parents were his parents and that was all there was to it. Now, Dr. Finnegan presented him with a knowledge he was not entirely sure he wanted.

"What about my father?" Henry asked. "Where is he?"

"Well, Henry," sighed Dr. Finnegan, "we don't know exactly. He was badly injured the night Mocarsto's army attacked the Garden, the night we sent you to Earth. After a long recovery, he simply ... vanished one day. Despite all efforts, we have gained no clue as to my brother's fate."

"Your brother?" asked Henry with surprise. "That means ..."

"Yes, Henry, I'm your uncle."

Chapter VII
Mirabel

"This is a lot to deal with right now," said Henry, anxiously pacing around the room. "You're telling me that I somehow traveled to another world where you found me years ago in that garden, and that my mom is not my mom and my dad is not my dad but my real mother and father are missing and my uncle is a scientist who is … you?!"

Dr. Scala wrung her hands. "We know that all this must come as a shock to you, Henry. We would never have sent you away if we didn't think it was for your own good. Sit down, please, and we'll continue the story. We still have time before we must send you back."

Henry looked carefully at the three doctors. They *looked* like nice enough people. He wondered again if he was dreaming. Dr. Finnegan's story challenged his perception of what he considered normal just the day before. His ordinary life seemed distant and foreign, and that thought frightened him. Henry decided the best thing to do was to hear the rest of Dr. Finnegan's story. He could figure out what it all meant later. He sat down on the couch and nodded for Dr. Finnegan to continue.

Henry sighed. "Okay. Tell me what happened after you found me in the flower garden."

"Well, after we found you in the garden, Henry, we were of mixed emotions. Of course, we were elated to have you with us. Besides, you were proof that your mother was alive and well, at least as recently as a few days prior. We couldn't imagine why she wasn't with you or why she would send that strange little woman to deliver her newborn son. We knew something must be amiss, but we were overjoyed to see you, nonetheless. As we lifted you up from the garden soil, we discovered a note tucked into the folds of your blanket. Written to your father, it's the only communication we have had from her these many years."

Dr. Finnegan handed Henry a folded piece of paper, worn soft from years of handling. Henry gently unfolded the paper and read the following:

Where I am the river flows through forget-me-nots, but I cannot remember the way out. He has put a spell on me that keeps me bound. I have found his echoes and he fears me now. Our son must flee both this world and the other for He knows him to be the child of Sun-Rhea, born in the Wildlands, the child of legend. He will not stop and we cannot protect our son, apart as we are, one without the other. You will know the time as well as I, for I do not know if I will be able to send again.

"We didn't appreciate the depth of Mocarsto's desire to find you until he attacked the Garden. We felt secure here. He and his minions never before dared to cross the no-man's land of the desert that separates our camps. Mocarsto consumes the free lands around him, tucked safely within his nucleus of power. For him to come in person was a desperate action, and he was poorly prepared. We outnumbered his small forces, and his power cannot yet reach into the hearts of free men. Our forces easily repelled him, but then he hardly expected to win the battle; he was merely looking for you. Mocarsto believed your mother imbued you with powerful magic meant to undo him. Your father feared he would stop at nothing less than your death.

"We knew then we had to send you away. The Garden was among the safest places in Sun-Rhea, and if we could not protect you here, we had little hope. Once Mocarsto had determined to find you, we knew he wouldn't stray from his obsession. It was your father's idea to bilocate you. He had achieved great success with his experiments in quantum physics, specifically with the phenomenon of matter existing on two planes simultaneously. We had never successfully bilocated an object as large as a human being before, even one as small as you were. The bilocation was your father's greatest success, and his greatest sorrow."

Dr. Finnegan sighed. "The evening has grown late," he said, looking at his wristwatch. "And this is a lot to absorb. Perhaps we should continue the conversation tomorrow?"

Henry nodded; he was happy to agree on this point. He wanted time to digest Dr. Finnegan's story. He craved the quiet of his bedroom and the comfort of familiar things, like the mother and father he had known all his life sleeping in the room across the hall.

He did have one last question, though, before he left his strange new friends. "Why didn't someone help her?" Henry asked. "If Mirabel couldn't leave, why didn't you go to her?"

"The logical minds of Sun-Rhea are rarely able to discern the path to the Wildlands, Henry," Dr. Finnegan explained. "Folklore tells of the rare few, not born in the Wildlands, who have found the path, but I have been unable to verify a single case. If these people do exist, they do not return to tell the tale. We've tried every experiment we could devise to locate the pathways, but with no success. But you were born there, Henry. The Wildlands and its secrets run warm in your blood. We're confident that you can find the path. After all these years, you, alone, can find her, and help her."

Chapter VIII
Proof

"Henry, it's time to wake up sweetheart."

His mother's voice preceded her up the stairwell. She poked her head around the doorjamb of his bedroom and smiled at her just-wakened son. "Up and at 'em, sleepy head. It's time to get ready for school."

Henry lay on his bed, staring sleepily off into space. He wasn't certain if he was awake, or rather, asleep and dreaming. Mrs. Harris noticed the expression on her son's face and sat down on the edge of his bed.

"Henry, are you feeling okay?" she asked with concern. Naturally, Henry's mother was worried about his health after the episode on the baseball field the previous day. Henry appeared unusually thoughtful to her this morning, and she wondered about the far-away look in his eye.

"I'm fine, Mom," Henry said shrugging up to lean against the headboard. "I'm just waking up, that's all. I guess I really was tired. I had a strange dream. I'll be down in a minute."

Mrs. Harris left him and went downstairs to cook breakfast. Henry sat thinking a while longer before getting dressed. He hoped to have more time to reflect on the evening's events before having to get up for another day of school. He didn't remember anything after he had left the scientists, so he figured he must have fallen asleep as soon as he got back to his bed. Dr. Finnegan's story echoed in his thoughts. The midnight encounter with the scientists had seemed vividly real, but now the images faded in the morning sun. Home again, in the warmth and comfort of his own bedroom, he felt calm. Life was back to normal. Talking to his mother and getting ready for school were reassuring parts of a typical day, not at all like traveling to a distant unknown planet while everyone else slept. He almost convinced himself it was no more than a dream after all.

When pulling back the covers, Henry noticed a small, dark object in the folds of his bed sheets. As he picked up the thing for closer examination, he suddenly recognized the little clock the scientists had given him. The events of the previous night flooded over him with a fresh wave of remembrance. The dream-like visions became vivid once more as he witnessed the tangible reality of the clock his hand. A new profundity weighted the words of his nighttime companions. Henry felt full of potential, as if he were standing at a fork in the road looking down two distinct paths. Each direction led to a different and distinct destination, linked together only through him and this one single point in time.

"Whaddaya know?" Henry said aloud, smiling at the gadget in his hand. "I guess it wasn't a dream after all."

Henry got dressed and shoved the little clock in his jeans pocket. He brushed his teeth, combed his hair, and headed downstairs to meet his mother for breakfast.

Chapter IX
Science Class

"Last stop: Colonial Heights Middle School!" said Mr. Waddleman cheerily as the school bus came to a stop along the painted curb. He opened the double doors with a slow click-hiss, releasing the passengers down the three black rubber-scented steps to a concrete courtyard, where children mingled in groups and streamed in pairs into the tan-colored brick school building. Mrs. Cross, Henry's regular bus-driver, must have called in sick today leaving Mr. Waddleman to take her place in the driver's seat. Henry noticed Mr. Waddleman glancing up at him in the rearview mirror.

He's probably worried about yesterday when I passed out, Henry thought to himself. As he got off the bus, he gave Mr. Waddleman what he hoped was a reassuring smile.

In the courtyard, Henry ran into Tommy and Kyle. The last time they saw Henry, Mr. Waddleman was carrying him off the field into Nurse Edna's office.

"What happened to you, Henry? Are you okay?" Tommy and Kyle both asked at once.

Henry wondered what he should say about his episode on the baseball field. With everything that had happened to him in the past sixteen hours, he hadn't thought about what to tell his friends. He didn't want to lie, but if he told the truth, surely they would think he had lost his mind. But he didn't want his friends to think he was weak or sickly, either. A fainting spell suddenly seemed undignified. He decided the best thing to do was to try to make a joke out of it, so maybe they would forget the whole thing.

"I guess I just got sleepy out there," Henry said. "No one had hit a ball to the outfield the entire practice, so I must have dozed off from boredom." Henry laughed as he tried to deflect attention away from himself, hoping his friends would follow the diversion.

"Yeah, until I got up to bat," boasted Tommy.

"Tell me about it," Kyle added. We need to step up our batting game if we're going to beat the Senators tomorrow. They're supposed to be pretty good this year."

Henry nodded relieved the conversation had moved on so easily. He and his friends talked about the upcoming baseball season as they headed to class. All three boys had Ms. Engle for Science first period, and they sat together in the back corner near the windows facing the baseball field and adjacent parking lot. The scent of cut grass and wildflowers wafted in on the spring air. The smell reminded Henry of a dream he had last night where he was in the most beautiful garden he had ever seen. But wait … it wasn't a dream, was it?

Henry began to doubt himself again. His nighttime experience seemed so real when it was happening—his conversation with the scientists, the beauty of the garden, even the smell of the cookies lingered in his sensory memory—but still he struggled to separate reality from dream. He fumbled in his pocket for the tiny clock, needing the reassurance of its physical reality. The tardy bell rang and Ms. Engle called the class to order.

"In today's class," Ms. Engle began, "we are going to continue our discussion about the most groundbreaking and influential experiments ever conducted in the world of physics. Recall, yesterday, we discussed Galileo's success at proving how a heavy object falls at the same rate as a light object. He demonstrated this phenomenon by dropping two different weights from the top of the Leaning Tower of Pisa and timed their descents. Sadly, Galileo faced much criticism and censure for his views even though they were simply accurate observations of the physical world around him. At that time, in the sixteenth century, the general belief was that heavier objects fell faster than lighter objects, because, after all,

Aristotle had said so. Back then, most people also thought the Earth was the center of the universe and that the world was flat.

"I say this to remind you all how important it is to keep an open mind when it comes to the world of physics. We must respect the observations of the physical world, even when these observations contradict our preconceived notions of reality. Today, we are going to discuss an exciting and influential experiment that has changed the way many people view the world. It's the known as the double-slit experiment, often referred to as the 'most beautiful experiment ever conducted.'

"Does everyone remember how we discussed the differences between particles and waves? Anyone?" After a moment of silence, she continued, "Very well, we'll review." Ms. Engle walked to the back of the class and pulled the cover off an object about the size and shape of a Ping-Pong table. "Gather round, everybody."

The children joined her in the back of the class around a low table with edges, filled halfway with water. A board with two vertical slits on either side of its center ran across the middle like the net on a tennis court. Ms. Engle stood at one end of the table and pushed the water with her hand toward the slit on the right side of the board. A rippled pattern radiated from the openings as the water passed through the slits.

"See, class," she began. "Here we see the properties of waves demonstrated. We see a regular pattern emanating from the slit in the board. Now watch what happens when the water comes out of both slits at the same time."

She used both hands to push the water through the two slits. "Now, what's happening, class?" Two wave patterns appeared on the other side of the wooden barrier and a new pattern emerged as these two waves crossed each other.

"Interference," said a small girl barely tall enough to see over the edge of the table down into the water below.

"That's correct, Susan!" said Ms. Engle. "The wave pattern changes where one path interferes with the other. Waves are made of peaks and troughs. The peak of one wave and the trough of another wave can cancel each other out, or two waves can match up to amplify the wave's resonance. Now, let's see how particles react."

Ms. Engle picked up another board with two larger slits in it and set it up horizontally between two prongs designed to hold it steady. A few inches away, on the back wall of the classroom, a white sheet of paper was taped to the wall behind the makeshift barrier. She then picked up two devices that looked similar to nail guns.

"These contraptions shoot tiny paint pellets. I'm going to shoot them at the board and see what patterns appear on the white paper on the other side."

"Cool!" said Kyle. "I want to shoot it." Most of the boys in class felt the same as Kyle and murmured excitedly with expectation.

"No. I'll take care of that part," said Ms. Engle to their disappointment. "Everybody stand back. The paint balls are small, but they can splatter."

She shot several tiny pellets out of the paint guns. With two hands, she shot both guns at the same time, aiming for the two slots on either end of the board. Several pellets hit the board and exploded in blue splats. Others made it through the slits to burst upon the white paper, forming blue splotchy patterns about the size and shape of the slits themselves.

"See, class, particles, unlike waves, do not interfere with each other. Each particle, or pellet, passes through the slit and hits the wall in much the same pattern as they went through."

Ms. Engle put down the paint guns and looked around at the twenty eager faces alight with a new thought. She had been teaching science for nearly a decade, and she still loved coming to work every morning. Every time the light kindled in a child's eyes with wonder and delight, she knew that this world, somehow, had become a better place.

"Okay, everybody, let's go back to our seats. We will watch a movie that details the experiment we just conducted. Now, what do you think would happen if we did this experiment with light, say from a laser? Do you think the pattern would look like waves with interference, or like particles?"

"Waves!" said some.

"Particles!" cried others.

"Let's find out," said Ms. Engle. She flicked on the projector and started a film that described Thomas Young's famous double-slit experiment. The film flickered and the narrator's voice spoke with that typical science-film narrator's tone that can make any subject boring.

"Let's turn the sound down and discuss the images ourselves," Ms. Engle suggested. The screen showed light from a laser shining through a slit in a barrier, which then passed through a second barrier with two equidistant slits, resembling the demonstrations Ms. Engle had shown them with the water and the paint. The two lights visibly intersected each other and became brighter where they crossed.

"The lesson here, class, is that the pattern captured from the light, when closely studied, reveals that light behaves like a wave. In other words, it interferes with itself."

"So, light is a wave then?" Henry asked.

"That was the conclusion Young reached from this experiment, and most people agreed with him for quite some time. But then, through the work of other scientists, most notably Albert Einstein, new experiments showed that light did, in fact, observably behave like a particle in certain situations."

"So, which one is it?" asked several students at once.

"The debate continued for some time indeed," continued Ms. Engle, "until the development many years later of quantum mechanics, which answers the question of whether light is a wave or a particle. The answer is that it's both, and neither, and when we observe things on a very small level, the assumptions we make in the larger physical world are no longer substantiated."

"Like what?" asked a redheaded boy in the front row.

"Well, for example, subatomic particles have been observed to be in more than one place at one time. Scientists have shown through a version of the double-slit experiment that when they shoot single photons through a single slit (so that there is nothing to interfere with it) interference patterns still show up. The only way this is possible is if the single particle actually passed through both slits at the same time so that it could interfere with itself. But the story gets even stranger. If any device is employed to measure whether the particle passes through the second slit, the interference pattern doesn't appear. The act of observing the dual locality forces it to pick a single locality. If we don't observe it, there's strong evidence to support that it was, in fact, in two places at one time."

A hush fell over the room as the children tried to comprehend such a strange idea.

"This is a challenging topic, students. We will delve deeper into it next week. I ask you not to bring untested assumptions with you into the science lab. The right answer should always fit the observable world. Remember the lesson Galileo taught us: refusing to believe that a heavy object falls at the same rate as a lighter object doesn't change the fact that a heavy object does indeed fall at the same rate as a lighter object."

Henry had only a moment to ponder her statement before the bell sounded for next period. Ms. Engle dismissed her class with this thought: "Trust me, children, things you never thought possible are happening around you all the time."

Chapter X
Mr. Televangi

After school, Henry walked the few blocks to his dad's novelty shop. *Someone Should Invent That!* was located off the town's main street, situated in an L-shaped mini-mall along with several other small businesses that flanked a communal parking lot. The Colonial Heights Boulevard cut a straight line through the center of town with most of the local stores and shopping centers crowded along either side. Beyond this strip of urbanity, sprawling neighborhoods stretched over hills and past creeks that flowed to the river below. Bicycles, grills, and tire swings adorned the yards of the working-class families who lived in the small, peaceful city.

Mr. Harris entertained a group of regular customers at his shop. These were mainly retired men who spent a good deal of time tinkering in their own workshops. They gathered at his store to discuss the newest and most outrageous gadgetry on the market. Among his other loyal customers were carpenters, mechanics, students, and busy mothers looking for any ingenious thing to save a minute in their hectic schedules. Curious people wandered in to browse while they waited for a pet grooming at an adjoining store, or an order to cook at the Chinese restaurant across the way.

Business was slow today, and the store was quiet when Henry walked in. An elderly woman near the large front window was talking to a small yapping dog whose head peeked out of her purse like a creature in a Whack-a-Mole game.

"Go ahead Ginger, tell Mommy how you feel," she coaxed the scrawny animal.

The dog obediently barked into a contraption the woman held in her hand. The machine processed the pitch and tone of the dog's voice and matched it to an internal database to translate her bark into English and display the results on a screen.

"This says she's hungry," the woman said to Henry's father.

"Sounds about right to me," said Mr. Harris.

"Well, I don't think I need to buy a thingamajig to tell me that my dog is hungry," she said, putting the gadget back on the table. She continued browsing as her little dog yapped, apparently in agreement with the translator's assessment.

Henry's attention turned to a stocky, balding man skulking around the back of the store. The man's complexion was olive, but his face was red as if he was in a state of overexertion. Henry noticed the man had been looking at him, and now, as if to allay any misunderstanding, the man broke into a broad grin full of large yellow teeth, which made him look even more menacing than before. A few dark hairs parted far on the right side of his head sprouted long greasy strands he had combed over his baldness. Henry found the man creepy, so he walked around the sales counter and behind a shelf full of merchandise to be out of his line of sight.

"Hey, Dad," Henry said to his father in greeting.

"Hey, buddy," replied his father. "How was school today?"

"Fine."

"Good. Oh, I want to show you something! I've been working on the hover-board and I almost have it figured out. Let me show you. It's in the back."

Mr. Harris disappeared behind a dusty brown curtain that served as a partition between the store and his cluttered workshop. The backroom was full of works-in-progress and old machine parts awaiting reincarnation into the next great invention. After a few banging and whirring noises, Mr. Harris flew through the curtain on an old skateboard from which he had removed the wheels. Henry was amazed to see that he was floating several inches off the ground. Mr. Harris balanced carefully on the hover-board and extended his arms in a gesture of success.

"Ta-dah!" he said suspended in midair.

"That's awesome!" said Henry. "Fly it around a little."

"Well, that's the problem," said his father. He carefully pulled back the curtain so as not to lose his balance. Behind it, Henry saw a cord running from the hover-board to an electric socket in the back room and a hose attached to something that looked like a vacuum.

"I can't find a power source light enough to attach to the board," his father sighed. "Right now I can only hover as far as the extension cord, and then it's tricky not to get tangled up in it."

"Can I try it, Dad?" asked Henry.

"Sure. Just be careful while you're getting used to it. It's kind of like riding a skateboard, but it's harder to balance because there's nothing solid beneath you."

Mr. Harris jumped off the hover-board. "Your turn," he said. He helped Henry gain his balance and stepped back to admire his invention.

"This is so cool, Dad! What happens if I go higher?"

Before his father could answer, Henry shifted his weight onto his back foot and the hover-board shot up at a sharp angle. He and the hover-board rose to a height of three feet off the ground before the vacuum cord pulled out of the electrical socket. The board sputtered and crashed to the floor, tossing Henry down with a thud.

"Well, I guess that answers your question," said his dad smiling down at him. "Are you alright?"

"Yeah, that was nothing," said Henry. "I want to try it again!"

"I'll tell you what. When these customers leave, I'll close up the shop and we'll find a nice safe place to test it. We should wear our helmets and skateboard pads, though, just in case."

The elderly woman had left the store, but the strange little man was still in the back doing some "hovering" of his own. Henry sensed that the man was more interested in what he and his father were doing than in the merchandise. He could understand someone being interested in the hover-board, but the man's demeanor was more indicative of a snoop than of an enthusiast.

Finally, the little man walked up to the counter and cleared his throat.

"Excuse me, sir," he said in a pinched and haughty voice. "That's a marvelous invention you have there, sir. Please, allow me to introduce myself. My name is Mr. Televangi and I have recently arrived in the area."

"I'm John Harris and this is my son Henry. What can I do for you Mr. Televangi?"

"Yes," the little man sniveled. "I was wondering if you happen to carry any of the latest spyware here at your store. I was unable to locate it amongst the shelves." Mr. Televangi spoke slowly and affectedly, drawing out certain words almost to the point of absurdity. His drawling speech had the effect of forcing Henry and his father to pay attention to him almost against their will.

Henry's father shook his head. "No, I don't deal with that sort of thing," he said. I don't support the invasion of people's privacy."

"Hmmm, I see," said Mr. Televangi, stroking his clean-shaven chin. "Very well, sir. Good day to you, and to your fine boy."

Mr. Televangi gave Henry another yellow-toothed smile. Then he turned on his heels and opened the front door causing the jingle bells to shake. Henry and his father watched him through the large front window as he ambled down the sidewalk. The queer little man put an old fedora hat onto his balding head as he whistled an unfamiliar tune.

Henry and his father watched the man until he disappeared from sight, then, turned to each other, similar expressions on their faces.

"That guy gave me the creeps," said Henry.

"Tell me about it," his father agreed.

Chapter XI
The Rabbit

A hard rain set in at dusk, cutting short Henry and his father's plans to do more testing on the hover-board. As Friday evening wore on, the rain showed no sign of letting up. No one wanted to go out in the rainstorm, so the Harris family settled in for a cozy evening at home. They made homemade pizzas and watched a movie, each person lounging lazily on his or her personal cushion of the sectional couch. As the credits began to roll, Henry got up, stretched, and decided to go to bed.

With him, he took a small leather-bound book of verses his mother had brought home from a project on which she was working, translating some old, rare texts into digital format for preservation. A bolt of lightning had struck a library and ignited a fire that burned some books and caused smoke damage to many more. The library officials decided to digitally-archive the old and rare editions to protect the stories and histories for future generations. This particular book was small and unremarkable. The cover was well-worn, but artfully made to withstand the stresses of time. Its table of contents listed no authors. The book was a small collection of short verses printed on yellowing pages with a few sketches featured alongside the narratives.

Henry went upstairs and snuggled deep into his bedcovers. He carefully turned the brittle, delicate pages of the small book. One picture in particular captured his attention. On the left-hand page was a sketch of a rabbit in a thicket next to a garden gate. The rabbit conveyed a certain attitude that Henry found intriguing. Peering out from the page with a half-smile on his pink lips, he looked as though he held a secret—one that made him powerful, yet serene. His

Mona Lisa smile seemed to say he would happily tell it to anyone who asked. On the opposite page was a poem that told this rabbit's story. Hoping they might reveal the secret behind the rabbit's smile, Henry read these lines before drifting off to sleep:

> There once was a rabbit,
>
> Who wanted a carrot,
>
> Well-hid behind the gate.
>
> There were perils and snares,
>
> His friends warned, "Take care,
>
> Or, you'll meet with a bloody fate.
>
> It's best if you stay
>
> With us here and play,
>
> That's just what you should do,
>
> For more rabbits than not
>
> End up in the pot
>
> For the farmer's stew."
>
> The rabbit's reply,
>
> With a gleam in his eye,
>
> Was "Not I, my friends, not I.
>
> I'm fast and I'm tough,
>
> I've studied enough,
>
> To keep myself from harm.
>
> I'm quiet and quick,
>
> I'll enter in slick
>
> And never give off the alarm."
>
> He wasn't a hothead,
>
> He planned and he plotted,
>
> He thought of how he would savor

Home grown in the sun,

A carrot hard won,

Though, the odds were not in his favor.

His friends cried, "Take heed,

For those who succeed

Up 'til now have been very few;

For more rabbits than not

End up in the pot

For the farmer's stew."

The rabbit's reply

With a gleam in his eye

Was "Not I, my friends, not I."

He waited for signs

That it was the right time

For the farmer to be sound asleep

The cat was distracted,

So quick-like he acted,

And did not make even a peep.

He snuck past the dog

Through a hollowed out log,

He managed to ward off the crow.

He crawled under the gate,

'Twas a well-planned escape

Made with the prize carrot in tow.

His friends gathered round him,

And all were astounded

At what he'd been able to do,

For more rabbits than not

End up in the pot

For the farmer's stew.

The rabbit's reply,

With a gleam in his eye,

Was "Not I, my friends, not I.

Chapter XII
Bilocation and Probability Density Curves

"Henry, are you with us?"

Henry's eyes fluttered as he opened them to the soft light. He had been dreaming, and part of him was dreaming still. His mind, free in a world of imagination, was slow to embrace the shift to reality. In his dream, Henry was in a garden with the rabbit from the story. This garden, however, was not an ordinary garden, but huge and beautiful like one he remembered having seen once before. The two were resting with their backs slouched against a giant sunflower stalk. The rabbit sat with one ankle crossed over the other knee, chewing lazily on a stalk of wheat. He wore torn, patched-up overalls and an old straw hat, low down over his eyes. He looked serene and secure with some secret knowledge, just as he had in the book.

Before Henry woke up, he remembered they had been talking about something—they had been talking about the rabbit's secret. Then someone had called his name and the rabbit looked up toward the voice. The rabbit glanced back at Henry and said in a country accent, "Henry, is it?" He hopped to his feet and looked at Henry with friendly curiosity. "Well, then, 'til next time Henry," he said, then scampered off toward the horizon.

Henry reluctantly emerged from his dream and opened his eyes to a now-familiar sight. The three scientists he met the other night, Dr. Finnegan, Dr. Scala, and Dr. Hector, were standing over him once again.

"Oh, hi," said Henry. "I guess this is really happening, huh?"

"It is Henry," said Dr. Scala, reassuringly. "The transition might be easier for you if you have a better understanding of what is happening. If you feel up to it, we thought tonight would be a good time to explain more of what happens when you travel between worlds. It's a complicated topic, and there's so much to tell you, but we need you to believe that all this is possible, or else .... or else it might not be ... possible."

Henry nodded, a little confused.

"Let's go into the other room, where we can be comfortable as we talk," said Dr. Finnegan.

The four of them returned to the room with the beautiful view of the garden, each taking the same seat as the night before. After a pause to let everyone settle in, Dr. Scala began her explanation:

"People in your world and ours have known for some time that it's possible for subatomic particles to be in two places at one time. In fact, it's more precise to say that these particles are often *several* places at one time. We cannot predict with certainty where we will actually observe these particles, but we can determine the probability of where we are likely to find them within a particular range. We call this a probability distribution curve. To say it another way, every particle has a range of possible locations it could be at any given time, depending upon its nature. We cannot know its exact location within that range prior to it showing up there. We can only determine the likelihood we will find it in any one location over the others.

"There are no natural laws that forbid this from happening on a larger scale, with larger objects, as well, although this is not a normally observed phenomenon. It was a long time before anyone was able to successfully bilocate an object as large as ... well, as large as you, Henry."

"And you say my father did this?" Henry asked.

"Yes," Dr. Scala continued. "Your father was able to bilocate your physical body when you were a baby. You were young enough not to have preconceived notions about such travel, or about anything for that matter, and this openness of mind is necessary for human bilocation. Older subjects are rarely successful because their brains expect a repetition of patterns from their pasts. This expectation actually creates a replication of the previous pattern, what we often call a 'self-fulfilling prophecy.' Although your body can physically exist in two places at one time, consciousness cannot. There is no scientific law that prohibits it, but the experience seems to be too much for the human mind to sustain.

"When we sent you to Earth, your consciousness went with you and your original, or 'first,' body remained here as sort of a placeholder. It was necessary to get you out of Sun-Rhea in order to protect you, but none of us intended for the separation to be permanent. We always planned to call you back once it was safe to do so. We had to make sure that you developed a mind wide open to possibilities, or else we would fail. If your mind grew closed, we would not be able to bring you back. Earth is a compatible environment to ours and its location falls within the applicable probability distribution curve, so it was the natural choice.

"Unfortunately, many of Earth's inhabitants are narrow-minded and frequently cling to unsupported or downright false notions of the real and the possible. We saw that you were placed in a loving home with people who would nurture a mind open to the wonders of scientific discovery and the secrets and magic that dwell in art and literature. Your Earth mother and father were fit to be guardians of our sacred trust, and we can see that they have done an excellent job of raising you."

Henry let out a long sigh. "I think the hardest part of all this is all of a sudden having two sets of parents. I knew I was adopted, but we never talked about it. It just wasn't important. I always thought of my mom and dad as my real parents."

"You aren't the only person who has preferred a happy delusion to an upsetting truth," said Dr. Scala. "No part of reality has been changed by this new information, Henry. The relationship between you and your Earth parents is what it was, is, and will be, regardless of how you categorize it. Labels do not change the substance."

"What do you mean 'labels do not change the substance'?" Henry asked.

"Let me give you an example," said Dr. Scala. "Say you have two test tubes: one has a red liquid in it and one has a blue liquid in it. Suppose I labeled the red liquid 'blue' and the blue liquid 'red.' Would a label marked 'blue' make the liquid inside red?"

"Of course not," answered Henry.

"No, of course not," she agreed. "But here's the trick. What happens if you cannot see through the test tubes and I present you with one labeled 'red'? What is the color of the liquid inside, now?"

Henry thought for a few second before he replied. "I guess it could be any color at all."

"That's absolutely correct, Henry. However, many people will assume the liquid is red simply because the label says so. Few people ever look to determine for themselves what color, if any, the liquid in the container is."

Dr. Hector, usually quiet, spoke up here. "Always remember this, Henry: when it's important, go find out for yourself."

"So, what's my other body doing right now?" asked Henry.

"It's right where you left it, sleeping in your bed," answered Dr. Finnegan. "You won't be tired when you return because your other body is resting, even though you've been awake here all this time. Your Earth body registers this like a dream, which leads us to an interesting point. Let's talk about your mother's contribution to the experiment.

"Although particles can be many different places at once, the observation of them at any one place locks them into that location."

"That sounds like what Ms. Engle taught in school today," Henry said.

The three scientists gave a meaningful look to each other and then looked back at Henry expectantly.

"Yeah, the double-slit experiment, or something like that," Henry continued. "Where a light particle is in two places at once but only if you don't measure it, because then it has to pick just one place to be. It was a pretty weird class."

"That is exactly what we are talking about," said Dr. Finnegan.

"And that's the tricky part," said Dr. Scala. "We want to be able to send you back and forth without noticeably disrupting your life on Earth. You cannot just vanish from your world every time you come here. In essence, you would still be 'there' but only until someone 'observed' you. That's to say you would be there are long as no one looked at you, but if they looked at you, you would cease to be there."

Henry was confused again and his face showed it.

"I know it's a difficult concept," Dr. Scala sighed. "We didn't know how to overcome this obstacle either. Mirabel was the one who solved the problem."

"How did she do that?" asked Henry.

"While in the Wildlands, she charmed you."

"Charmed me?"

"Yes, a charm is rooted in magic, but the science is psychological. The charm acts as a suggestion that you are there, and so in turn, people see you. This particular charm only works on people who have already seen you. It's based on the presumption that people expect you to occupy the same space from one moment to the next. All they need is a suggestion for their minds to manifest an expectation. However, if someone were to come along with no expectation, someone who had never seen you before and whose mind needed more than a suggestion to fill in the blanks ... well, we don't think that the charm would work then. We aren't sure what, if anything, they would see."

A buzzing in his pocket distracted Henry from Dr. Scala's words. He reached in and pulled out the tiny clock the scientists had given him last night.

"Thanks for reminding me," said Dr. Hector. "Did you set it to the correct Earth time?"

Henry nodded and handed the device to Dr. Hector, who recorded the time in a pocket notebook before handing it back. "Keep this with you at all times," advised the bald scientist, "to help you know when you are due home. You can set an alarm to give advanced warning."

"So how is it I can take objects along with me? How does that work?"

"It's really a matter of your own will," explained Dr. Scala. "Smaller objects require less energy, but there's no scientific reason why you cannot bring something as large as an elephant with you if you desired."

"Not an elephant itself, though," added Dr. Finnegan.

"True," agreed Dr. Hector. "You can only bring inanimate objects. A living consciousness creates too much disturbance, has too much independence, to bilocate by your will alone. You could begin practicing to bilocate larger items. Perhaps you could bring your clothes with you next time, to replace the body suit in which this body is clothed."

"How do I do that?" Henry asked.

"The same way you did with the clock," replied Dr. Hector. "Just expect your clothes to be there, and they will be there."

"Weird," said Henry, as he tried to digest this concept.

"Yeah, weird," agreed the scientists.

"Well, we should get started," said Dr. Finnegan. "We have a lot to do to prepare you for your journey."

"My journey?" asked Henry.

"Yes," said Dr. Finnegan. We need you to go the Wildlands and find Mirabel. Mocarsto is getting too strong and we need her skills to defeat him. His power is beyond what our science alone can do."

"Besides, we miss her," said Dr. Scala. "We couldn't get her back before. But you ... we ... think *you* can."

"It's getting late," interrupted Dr. Hector. "You should be getting home. It will be morning soon."

Chapter XIII
Take Two

Sunlight filled Henry's room, even though his curtains were still drawn. The late spring days were getting longer and the sun rose earlier each day. A couple of months ago Henry woke up to cold, gray mornings, begrudgingly leaving the warmth of his bed to get ready for school. Today, the world awoke before he did. The birds twittered outside his window as they welcomed the dawning day. Henry usually slept late on Saturdays, but this morning he felt wide-awake. He dressed himself and opened the door to the hall.

His parents were still asleep in their room, cattycorner to Henry's, across the landing at the top of the stairs. He could hear his dad snoring lightly through the bedroom door. Henry went downstairs to the kitchen and thought about breakfast. Morning sunlight burst around the edges and through the slits of the closed blinds. He loved having the house to himself when all was quiet, with the only sound a low hum of possibilities. The whole house seemed animated, as if it, too, was awake and eager to play games that would take Henry through its various rooms and doorways.

Henry walked outside and sat on the front porch steps. He squinted through the morning glare at his peaceful little neighborhood. The scent of budding flowers filled the air as early risers walked their dogs along the tree-lined streets. Mrs. Carter, who lived across the street, was busily working in her garden, and the three young Camden girls, two houses down, were gleefully screaming through an impromptu game of run-around-in-a-circle. Henry watched a spider crawl up the dew-dipped web it had spun between the porch railings the night before.

Out of the corner of his eye, Henry noticed a dark sedan driving slowly up his street. The speed limit was low in residential areas, especially where children play, but this car was moving unusually slow, as if the driver was uncertain of his destination. As the car passed him, Henry thought he recognized the man sitting in the driver's seat. He resembled the man who was in his father's shop the day before—Mr. Vangitelli. No, Mr. Televangi, Henry remembered now. The weird little man turned his head and caught Henry's eye. Mr. Televangi bared his large yellow teeth in a crooked smile. He lifted his hat from its perch atop his thin oily hair in a gesture of recognition and greeting. Henry watched the man slowly drive away down the street, but he didn't return his salutation. He couldn't bring himself to smile at that man.

"That guy gives me the creeps," Henry said aloud to no one in particular.

Later that afternoon Henry had a baseball game, so he and his parents made the short drive to the Colonial Heights Middle School. When they arrived, Kyle and Tommy were on the sidelines warming up with a game of catch. The day was a perfect example of early spring in Virginia, warm with a gentle breeze that blew refreshingly through the tiny holes in Henry's green and white baseball cap.

Henry had not been back to the baseball field since Thursday's practice when he had "passed out" and traveled for the first time to Sun-Rhea. So many strange things had happened in just two short days. Henry found himself looking forward to nightfall when he could return to his new friends and their tales of strange and exciting worlds. Still, he enjoyed a comfortable peace in the normalcy of a predictable Saturday afternoon spent with friends and family on the baseball field. Henry joined his friends as his mother and father found seats on the bleachers and greeted the other parents who had already arrived.

Mr. Kent, Henry's regular baseball coach, called the boys to gather for their usual pep talk before the game. There was no need for Mr. Waddleman to act as substitute coach today, but he was there, nevertheless. Henry noticed him and Ms. Engle sitting together on the top riser of the bleachers. They bent their heads together in a quiet discussion. Their casual glances in his direction gave Henry the feeling that they were talking about him. He hoped they were not too concerned about his "fainting" spell on the baseball field the other day. He understood why school officials would be concerned about a possible medical condition, and he hoped the scientists would take care not to bilocate him in public again, but with no repeat occurrences, Henry expected the whole thing to blow over soon enough. He had enough on his mind without having to think up a way to explain another blackout.

"Go, Colonials!" the boys shouted from their team circle before grabbing their gloves and taking position on the field. Standing out in right field, squinting through the bright sun, Henry had a rather unpleasant sense of déjà-vu—the familiarity of events made him feel nervous. He was standing in the same spot where, two days before, he watched Tommy hit the ball high out to right field. It was the last thing he knew before the worlds opened up to him, the last experience before his life took this unexpected detour.

"Crack!" went the bat, as a player in a red Senators' jersey hit a line drive to centerfield. Henry watched his teammate recover the ball and throw it into the infield. Kyle, at second base, caught the ball and turned toward the runner, who had rounded first but now thought better of it and dashed back to safety. The play ended, and Kyle threw the ball back to the pitcher as the next batter emerged from the cage.

Henry breathed a sigh of relief as his feeling of déjà-vu left him. Nothing out of the ordinary had happened after all. This was a normal game. As he waited for the next play, Henry saw something moving in his periphery. He turned to see two large animals walking slowly along the perimeter of the baseball field near the edge of a wooded area beyond the fence. Henry stared hard trying to make them out. One of them could be a dog, he thought, but it looked like a wild breed, more like a wolf than a pet. The other animal was a large spotted feline with a small head. It swished its long tail as it walked lazily along.

It's kind of small, but that's definitely a cheetah, Henry thought to himself, for he could see the telltale tear-streak lines that ran from the corners of its eyes down to its mouth. Henry knew this bit of information from a program he had watched with his dad the other day on the big cats of the animal kingdom.

Why in the world would a wolf and a cheetah be walking around down here? Henry wondered.

The sound of wood striking the baseball returned Henry's attention to the game. Another out and the team headed in to bat. When he looked around for the animals again, they were gone.

Chapter XIV
Jon and Jen

After the game, Mrs. Harris dropped Henry's dad off at his shop before heading to the grocery store. Henry declined both his parents' offers to join them and elected to walk home instead. He wanted a minute to be alone with his thoughts. As he walked, he scanned the horizon for any sign of the animals he had seen at the game. They appeared docile enough. Still, he wondered what he would do if he encountered a wild animal on the streets of his sleepy little neighborhood. In his mind, Henry mapped out all possible escape routes. On this side, he could climb up that big tree, or maybe he could make it over Mr. Johnson's fence and into his pool. He knew housecats didn't like to swim, but he wasn't sure about cheetahs. Water might not stop the wolf, though.

As he was wondering about wild animals and their proclivity for swimming, Henry heard something running up behind him. His heart quickened as he deftly moved out of the way of the approaching footsteps. He was ready to climb the drainpipe of Mr. Cutter's house and take refuge on the roof if need be. However, when he glanced behind him, all he saw were two children, a boy and a girl, both of them about a year younger than Henry. They were running, laughing, and pushing each other playfully. Henry stepped out of their way as they tumbled and rolled on the grass next to him. They rolled on their backs and splayed out on the grass, panting and giggling. Henry thought them odd, but he smiled politely as he walked around one's arms and the other's legs to pass by. He continued down the sidewalk and waited at the intersection for a lone car to pass before crossing the street.

"Henry, wait," said the girl, running to catch up with him.

Surprised, Henry turned around. He didn't recognize the children from the neighborhood. He waited for them to say something, but they just stood there, grinning at him as they caught their breath.

"Yeah?" said Henry.

"I'm Jen, and this is my twin brother Jon," said the girl in a loud whisper leaning in toward Henry. "We're supposed to keep an eye on you while you're down here."

"Keep an eye on me?" asked Henry. "What do you mean?"

"Don't mind my sister. She's overly dramatic," said the boy. "We've come from Sun-Rhea. To help, that's all."

"From Sun-Rhea?" Henry said. "Who sent you?"

"Dr. Finnegan," they both said in unison.

"Hmm," Henry replied. "You said you're here to help. Help with what?"

Jon and Jen exchanged a meaningful look and then turned back to face Henry.

Jen shrugged her shoulders. "You know, stuff."

"What my sister means is we're here to help with whatever you need. The scientists thought you could use some friends down here. We know that you can't travel to Sun-Rhea all the time without causing suspicion down here."

"And the old ones can't travel back at all," Jen said.

"Old ones?" asked Henry.

"Never mind," said Jon. "The point is that we can. We can send messages back and forth when you can't leave. We're here to make sure everything goes okay."

"And we are here to protect you," whispered Jen, looking side to side with a dramatic air of mystery and danger.

"You?" Henry asked looking down at the small girl skeptically. "No, offense, but from what exactly can *you* protect me?"

"Never mind," said Jon again, casually. "We'll be around if you need us. We have an important errand to run right now, but we'll see you soon."

As the pair walked away, Henry wondered why the scientists had sent such strange children. They didn't offer him much new information. In fact, Jon had avoided answering most of Henry's questions. Moreover, they didn't look capable of protecting anybody, including their own selves.

"That reminds me," said Henry, calling after the twins. "Be careful around here. I saw some wild animals on the loose earlier today."

The twins looked at each other and started giggling uncontrollably. Jon looked at his sister and asked, "Should we show him?"

Jen nodded her head eagerly. "Yes. We have time."

The twins looked slyly up and down the quiet streets to make sure there was nobody else around. What happened next was the most amazing thing Henry had ever seen. It was like watching special effects in a movie, but so much cooler because it was real life. He watched as Jon's features formed into that of a gray wolf, and Jen, likewise, morphed into a cheetah. The wolf growled and the cheetah purred before sprinting across the yard on the other side of the street. Henry watched in wonder as they playfully jumped on one another and rolled around in the grass. After a moment of frolicking, they ran back toward Henry and quickly and effortlessly transformed back into their human forms.

"How did you do that?!" Henry exclaimed.

"It's science," Jon replied, shrugging his shoulders. "Gene therapy, to be precise. We've been injected with animal DNA. They call it a viral vector. It's not really a virus, not like being sick, but the

61

DNA acts like one. In my case, when I want to transform, the wolf DNA takes over the human cells and replicates itself until I physically become a wolf. When I want to change back, the human DNA takes over."

"You can change at will?" Henry asked.

"Yeah," said Jen. "We are one of the earliest prototypes of animal morphing. We have been doing this since we were very young. Our DNA has been 'trained,' so to speak, so morphing, for us, is easy now."

"Wow!" said Henry. "Are there a lot of people like you in Sun-Rhea?"

"Not really," said Jon. "It's not easy to create an animorph and plus, it can be dangerous. A few years ago, there was a bad accident, which pretty much put an end to the whole thing. You see, children are usually the best subjects for these kinds of experiments, since our DNA is more 'trainable' than adults' DNA. But something went wrong with one child. Instead of morphing, he mutated. Naturally, some people were quite upset, and the Federation agreed to shut down the program. That was when Jen and I went to work with Dr. Finnegan and his friends. Since our DNA is so highly suggestible and our minds are used to altered perception, he thought we would be good candidates for their bilocation efforts. So, to make a long story short, here we are."

"But we should get going now, big brother," said Jen. "We are going to be late for our appointment."

"Okay, let's go," said Jon. "We'll catch you later, Henry."

Chapter XV
Warning

As soon as Henry got home, he looked up everything he could find about viral vectors and gene therapy on the internet. He didn't find anything that specifically addressed the ability to morph from one creature to another, but he did find evidence of the phenomenon on a smaller scale. Henry read how the practice of gene therapy uses new technology to treat certain diseases like cancer. Scientists try to replace sick or "bad" genes with good ones. Henry could see how this young science might one day evolve into the ability to animorph. The scientists of Sun-Rhea obviously belonged to an advanced society. Maybe they simply had been around longer, and therefore had more time to figure out stuff. Henry wondered what people living even a few centuries ago would have thought about modern commonplace realities like televisions and computers. Contained electricity must have been mind-blowing when Thomas Edison first invented the light bulb. Earthlings have since designed rockets that have transported humans to the moon. They have built robots and performed heart transplants, and even cloned a sheep. Even as recently as a few years ago, most folks would deem such a feat to be no more than science fiction.

Henry then searched for information on bilocation. Many references described bilocation as an ancient mystical phenomena pursued by Christian saints and Catholic monks. One entry in the Wikipedia sounded a lot like what Ms. Engle had taught in class the other day:

> The generally accepted theories of physics provide no mechanism by which bilocation of macroscopic objects could occur. Max Planck Researchers in Berlin show that for

electrons from nitrogen molecules, the wave-particle character exists simultaneously.

So, he thought to himself, *our modern science can't explain what happens to me when I travel from this world to Sun-Rhea, but just because we can't explain it, doesn't mean it can't happen. All it really means is that we haven't figured it out yet.*

Later that evening, Henry was practicing his balance on the hover-board in the backyard when he spied Jon and Jen heading toward him. He turned off the power source and unbuckled his helmet as the gleeful twosome approached. Now, as before, they radiated a silly happiness normally relegated to the very young. They weren't that much younger than Henry, maybe just a year or two, but he felt in himself a certain heavy wisdom in comparison to this carefree duo.

Perhaps, their animal genes made Jon and Jen seem so wild. They were undoubtedly independent for such young children, free to roam around and between worlds, free even to change their very selves at will. Henry marveled at the magnitude of that freedom, but such independence frightened him a little too. The scientists wanted him to go to the Wildlands and he had no idea what to expect. He was wary of that unknown and secret place even the scientists couldn't explore. And that meant he would have to go alone. At least Jon and Jen had each other. Henry felt a deep and sudden longing for the security he took for granted just a few days before. He missed the smallness of the universe when it was no larger than his own little world.

"Hey, Henry," said Jon, as the pair reached him.

"Hi, Henry," said Jen.

"Hi, guys," replied Henry. "What's up?"

"We do have something to tell you," Jon replied, furtively looking around like a spy. "We think we've found one of Mocarsto's agents down here."

"He's a very evil man," Jen whispered in her dramatic style. "You should do your best to stay away from him!"

Jon rolled his eyes at his sister's theatricality.

"He must be looking for you," Jon continued. "We don't know how, but the scientists think Mocarsto knows you've returned to Sun-Rhea. He's getting stronger all the time. He has spies all over the place, but it's not as easy for us to spy on him. They say no one ever comes back from the dark fortress of Cardew."

"Now, who's being dramatic?" asked Jen.

Jon ignored her. "We know this man is one of Mocarsto's most trusted officials. They say he is so evil that Mocarsto doesn't even have to make him eat the hypnofood. He serves him of his own free will."

"Who is he?" asked Henry. "I can't stay away from him if I don't know who he is."

"He is very ugly, for one," said Jen. "He goes by the name of Mr. Televangi."

"Televangi!" Henry exclaimed. "I've met him!"

"Where?" asked Jen.

"When?" Jon inquired.

"He came by my dad's shop yesterday, and then I saw him driving by the house this morning."

"He must have already figured out who you are," said Jon. "You must be very careful around this man. We don't know why he's here. He may only intend to report on your whereabouts, but ..."

"We do know that he's capable of anything," interrupted Jen.

Jon nodded solemnly. He didn't call his sister overdramatic this time, and this omission sent chills down Henry's spine.

"We should get back and report this," said Jon, turning to leave. "Maybe we will see you later tonight."

"Goodbye, Henry," said Jen.

Henry watched them walk out of the yard and down the pebbled driveway. The twins weren't as jolly as they were when they first arrived. They left a heaviness in the air that made Henry feel cold and suddenly vulnerable. The orange sun, dipping below the tree-lined horizon, cast long shadows on the ground. The eastern sky turned deep blue as the first stars twinkled in the dark and cloudless sky.

The stars will be out tonight, Henry thought.

Chapter XVI
Allegory of the Cave

Henry lay on his back on the top of his porch roof, his hands behind his head, staring up at the night sky and enjoying the clear spring evening. A gentle breeze rustled the green leaves in the trees. Next to him, his dad roasted marshmallows over a portable fire pit of his own design. The low fire was surrounded by metallic petals, which automatically closed over the flame if the candle were jostled to extinguish the flame before it could catch anything else on fire. Mrs. Harris squashed the melted marshmallows and chocolate squares between two graham crackers.

"The s'mores are ready," she said. "Henry, would you like one?"

"Sure, Mom," he replied.

"Me, too," added Mr. Harris.

They sat together and ate their desserts as their shadows danced against the side of the house. The flickering shadows mesmerized Henry as he wondered at the unpredictability of the shapes along the wall. Sometimes they grew suddenly tall and sometimes they danced wildly, depending upon the movement of the fire and the strength and direction of the wind. The scene reminded him of Peter Pan's shadow, separated from the boy as it caught in the closing of the nursery window, so that Wendy Darling had to sew it back onto Pan's stockinged foot.

His parents, too, had been silently watching this dance of darkness and light. "This reminds me of a story," said his mother.

Henry and his father took her cue and prepared to listen to whatever weird or wonderful tale she had in store for them tonight.

"This is called 'The Allegory of the Cave' and it's one of Plato's most resonant analogies," she began.

"Now, imagine there are prisoners inside a cave who are chained and cannot move, nor can they turn their heads. Also, imagine they've been imprisoned all their lives so they know no other experience. Straight ahead, they see the wall of the cave. Behind them is a fire along a raised walkway whereupon various puppets play. The puppets cast shadows along the cave wall and the prisoners watch the show. Behind the cave is a well-traveled road, and upon this road people are walking, talking, and generally making noise. The prisoners, then, associate the noises with the shadows they see on the cave wall. They only see the shadow of the puppets, but they attribute a relationship to the arbitrary and unrelated sounds outside the cave. Together, the prisoners make sense out of the shadows and the outside sounds. In this communal reality, they easily agree upon their meaning and relationship.

"Now, suppose one prisoner breaks free of his chains. And suppose, after some time learning how to use his newly freed limbs, he leaves the cave and ascends to the road beyond. The sunlight immediately blinds him and forces him to find solace in the shadows on the ground. Over time, he slowly works his way out of his deluded mind. Before long, he's able to bear the intensity of sunlight and begins to fashion his understanding of the world like that of the people on the well-traveled road.

"Once enlightened, the free man does not want to return to the cave to free his fellow prisoners, but he feels compelled to do so. However, the prisoners aren't eager to be freed, for they're in accord with the reality they've come to accept. These partial views and confused relationships define their reality and have done so all of their lives. Back in the cave, the free man's eyes begin to readjust to the familiar darkness. For a time, he slips back to his old habit of viewing the world in only two dimensions. His newly trained eyes have difficulty seeing in the darkness, and he stumbles. The other prisoners conclude that his experience in the outer world has ruined him. His explanations of the shadows on the wall don't make sense to his former peers and they no longer accept his interpretations of them. They conclude that his brush with the sunlight had not brought illumination, but rather made him blind."

"That's true," said Henry's father. "Some people will cling to their old ideas, no matter how strong the evidence is to the contrary. And they label true visionaries "witches" and "cranks" and denounce anyone who threatens the power balance of the status quo."

"Yes," Mrs. Harris agreed. "This is all true. History is full of examples of this line of thinking. For instance, the Inquisition and the Catholic Church forced Galileo to repudiate his well-founded claim that the sun is the center of the universe. Something we all now accept as fact was once a heresy punishable by death."

"People are often uncomfortable when something deeply challenges the perceptions upon which they have built their expectations," his mother continued. "For the prisoners in the cave, it was simply easier to deny the brighter, deeper reality of three dimensions than to challenge the flat shadow world they had come to accept as true."

"So how can the people on the road be sure that what they see is 'real' and not shadows and echoes from an even higher plane?"

"That is exactly the right question, Henry," she replied, smiling.

Chapter XVII
Into the Wildlands

Henry knew where he was the moment he opened his eyes. The whirring machines and gray light was now familiar to him. His excitement about seeing the scientists again had made it hard for him to fall asleep; in fact, he didn't remember drifting off. Perhaps, he thought, his waking consciousness had traveled to Sun-Rhea like on that first day on the baseball field.

Henry had many questions to ask his new friends. He wanted to learn about Mr. Televangi, and if he was as dangerous as the twins had said. He was eager to hear more about his birth parents and about the one they call Mocarsto. Henry had witnessed many strange things over the past three days. He wanted to understand how any of it was possible, and what he was supposed to do about it.

The three scientists were waiting for him as before. After a few words of greeting, they adjourned to the room with the comfortable couch and the large glass window overlooking the garden. Henry thought the scientists appeared grave and tired, which increased his anxiety. He sensed a weight in the air and experienced a sudden stab of jealousy for the people back on Earth asleep in their beds—people who knew nothing about Sun-Rhea, or bilocation, or twins who can morph into animals. For a brief moment, he wished he were one of them again—warm and comfortable, unconscious and dreaming, entirely, blissfully unaware of this new and different world.

"Henry," Dr. Finnegan began, wearing a solemn look on his face. "We want you to begin your search for the Wildlands tonight. I know you have had little time to prepare, but time is a luxury we lack. We now fear Mocarsto has been able to locate you on Earth. The twins have verified that one of his vile agents has arrived there. They say you have met him. Is this true?"

"Yes. His name is Mr. Televangi. I met him at my dad's shop the other day."

"We're not certain how he found you. None but a few members of the Federation knew what transpired the night Mocarsto attacked the Garden. We suspect he may somehow know about your bilocation back to Sun-Rhea. Perhaps your return has triggered something, somehow. He has potent resources, unknown to our kind. We do know that if Mocarsto is still looking for you after all these years, he must still fear you. He must believe, as we do, that you are the one who can free Mirabel and reveal the secret of his weakness."

"How am I going to do that?" Henry asked.

"We don't know, exactly," sighed Dr. Scala. "You'll have to figure it out as you go."

"The Wildlands are a mystery to us, Henry," said Dr. Hector. "There's not much we can tell you. We're relying on you to find the way."

"But how do I get there?"

"Well," said Dr. Hector, "you find the path and follow it."

This answer only confused Henry more. He looked quizzically from one face to the other, searching for a clue to decode their cryptic speech.

"Perhaps we should just show you," said Dr. Finnegan as he stood up. "Here, we brought you some clothes to change into so that you will be more comfortable on your journey."

Henry looked down and noticed he was still in his pajamas, and not the blue body suit he usually wore when in Sun-Rhea. "Hey!" he exclaimed. "I brought my clothes with me this time!"

"Yes," Dr. Finnegan replied with a small smile. "Good work, indeed, but unless you wish to battle evil in your jammies, I suggest you wear these. Once you are ready, meet us outside in the Garden."

Henry was grateful for the blue jeans, t-shirt, and sneakers Dr. Finnegan left for him. He hadn't thought to dress the part, and in fact, he didn't wish to battle evil in his pajamas. Once dressed, he met the scientists in the Garden where he found them underneath a clump of giant sunflowers, all three squinting off toward the sunny horizon. The afternoon was clear and bright once again, and Henry wondered if the weather was always perfect in Sun-Rhea.

"In that direction is one known entryway into the Wildlands," said Dr. Finnegan pointing to his left. "There is where your mother would go through, and from where the little old lady came when she brought you to us as a baby."

Henry's gaze followed Dr. Finnegan's outstretched arm past the garden and over a low hill into the receding sunlight.

"Past that hill is a small wooded area that leads down to the villages in the valley. Look for the path there. Mirabel could find it easily, but alas, whenever we tried to retrace her steps, we would walk straight through to the other side of the wood." Dr. Finnegan sighed at the remembered failure. "Be sure to take note of your surroundings once you get to the Wildlands so that you will know how to get back. We should set your clock alarm to ensure you return in time to get home by morning. Six hours should give us plenty of time."

"What should I do when I get there?" asked Henry. "Supposing, I *can* get there."

"You can get there," Dr. Scala reassured him. "You must. Mirabel is depending on you."

"You must believe that you can get there or else you will not be able to get there," said Dr. Hector, shaking his round head in perplexity at the riddle.

"Find her," said Dr. Finnegan. "Find Mirabel and bring her out again."

Henry nodded and walked slowly toward the low hill past the edge of the garden. Below his feet, the grass sloped down into a shaded copse of bushes and trees. Ivy and vines twined around an old trellis that marked an entry through the thick foliage. Henry turned to look back at the scientists. They all three waved, reminding Henry of a family on the shore watching a boat leave the harbor. Henry looked back toward the shady thicket, took a deep breath, and walked down the gentle slope toward the mouth of the wood and under the arbor's arch.

Under the fragrant canopy of pine trees and ivy, the air was easily ten degrees cooler. Sunlight pierced through the pine needles, spearing the silent coolness with dusty shafts of yellow light. Henry found himself in a dark and silent place, encircled beneath foliage and separated from the world outside. His eyes took a moment to adjust from the bright light of the afternoon sun.

A trail through the underbrush wound through the wide-spaced trees. Henry followed the trail for some minutes through the deepening wood, wondering how he would know when he arrived in the Wildlands. He chuckled to himself as he imagined a sign like when you enter a new state on the highway: "Now Entering the Wildlands." Somehow, Henry doubted this would be the case, and he wished he had asked the scientists more questions when he had the chance. Not that they could have told him much, Henry mused. That was the reason they needed him, after all: to go where they could not. As Henry walked on, the trail became fainter, consumed by the deepening underbrush. Trees, large and small, sprang up from the ground in a haphazard fashion, their tall branches choking off the light from above. Henry traveled deeper into the darkening wood.

Henry spotted a clearing up ahead and wondered if he had walked through to the other side like the scientists had done. He worried about failing them. He had been walking for a while, though, and should have cleared the woods behind the garden before now. Moreover, he sensed a difference from the well-manicured garden and structured trees of Sun-Rhea. The air was thick and wet with a swampy smell that permeated Henry's skin. *There must be water nearby*, he thought.

He emerged from the woods onto a mossy plain with patches of bare dirt and clumpy grass. Behind and beyond him, the forest spread out in the distance as far as his eyes could see. Ahead, on his left, ran a grass-tufted dirt bank about three feet high with a rabbit hole dug in the center. Henry took particular notice of it because it reminded him of Rabbit's house in *Winnie the Pooh* when Pooh eats too much and gets stuck in Rabbit's front door. A few paces further, Henry came to a fallen log grown over with moss and wildflowers. Large dragonflies darted through the air, buzzing close to his head and then quickly retreating, as if playing a game meant to annoy him. He almost thought he heard one giggle.

Henry arrived at an earthen ledge overlooking a great expanse of unsullied nature. Several stones, set into the dusty clay, served as a makeshift stairway leading down to an immense field of reedy grasses. To his right lay a lake, its edges crowded with cattails and moss-covered lily pads. A giant willow tree bent its low branches far out over the water.

Henry could see no buildings or structures, only wild, untended nature. To his left, a flat stretch of overgrown ground spread toward the horizon lined with distant trees. Ahead, rolling hills undulated toward the blue sky, dotted with white plush clouds. Henry followed the stone staircase down to the lake. He found a seat on a low branch of the willow tree, bent at nearly a right angle like half of a goal post. He looked out over the muddy blue water rippling with the activity of insects and fish. A rushing breeze rustled the field grasses and blew the long streaming leaves of the willow tree. He was completely alone in this place.

"Well, now what?" he asked aloud.

"Aye, and what to do then?" came a voice from behind him, which startled Henry so that he felt his heart quicken.

Chapter XVIII
Eulalie

There, on a limb near Henry's head, sat a miniature, winged girl. She wore a dress of bright gold cloth nearly the same color as her rich blond hair. A set of double wings, also tinged with gold, sprang from her shoulder blades. The creature flew in buzzy circles around Henry's head, dashing and darting through the tree limbs. Watching her frenetic dance, Henry realized with amazement that she was one of the creatures he had earlier mistaken for a dragonfly. The girl landed on a branch directly opposite Henry's face and the two looked at each other for a long moment. Finally, Henry broke the silence.

"Hi," he said tentatively.

"Hello," the girl responded in a bright clear voice much louder than her size would suggest.

"Y-y-you can talk?" stammered Henry.

"Aye, can you?" she asked.

"Yes."

"Good then, that should work out all right."

"My name is Henry ... Henry Harris."

"'Tis a pleasure to make your acquaintance, Henry. My name is Eulalie."

"Eulalie ... What are you, a fairy?"

"Aye, haven't you ever seen a fairy before, silly?"

"No, I haven't. At least, not in person. I mean, only in books and stuff."

"Books!" she exclaimed. "Books about fairies? That's a silly thing indeed."

Eulalie leaned in closer and looked quizzically at Henry. "You're not from around here, are you? Where do you come from?"

"Earth," Henry responded.

"An Earth boy!" she exclaimed clapping her hands together. "What a long time since we have had an Earth boy in these parts. Why, I thought the gateway all but closed. Sometimes the very young girls wander through, but an Earth boy is indeed a rare visitor. Tell me now, how did you come here?"

"Through the woods. I mean, I came from Sun-Rhea. The scientists sent me here to find my mother and bring her back to them. They say she is in danger."

"How very exciting!" Eulalie said, rubbing her hands and her wings together at the same time. "An adventure. I haven't had one of those for some time now. Tell me your story please, and I shall listen." She plunked herself down on the tree branch and leant in for the story.

"Okay," Henry agreed. He felt an instant liking for the wee girl and began talking easily. He told her everything that he could remember about traveling to Sun-Rhea, and the stories the scientists had told him about Mocarsto and Mirabel and the Wildlands. Eulalie listened intently, nodding her head as Henry's tale unfolded. When he got to the part about the little old woman who had left him in the garden, Eulalie interrupted.

"That sounds like the Tea cup Lady!" she said excitedly.

"The Tea cup Lady?" Henry asked. "Who is that?"

"Come on then, I'll show you."

Eulalie buzzed her wings and flew off over the field. Henry scrambled to follow her, walking quickly through the tall grass to keep pace as Eulalie flitted and flew in circles around him. She led

Henry over the far hill that hid the horizon from view. Beyond the crest, the land flattened out and the grasslands thinned to a vast dusty expanse rimmed with tall thin trees. Several small holes pocked the dry ground. *Probably the work of a gopher or prairie dog,* thought Henry.

After several minutes of walking, they came upon a carved wooden door built into the hillside at a slant, like the entrance to an old-fashioned cellar. The wood and the surrounding dirt were so close in color that Henry could barely make out the doorway. *You would have to know what you were looking for to be able to find this,* Henry thought.

"She lives down there," said Eulalie. "Pull the ring to raise the door."

"Shouldn't we knock first?" Henry asked.

"Heavens no!" exclaimed Eulalie. "You'd rattle her teacups."

Henry shrugged and pulled the smooth metal ring, which attached to a chain pierced through the wood. The door creaked heavily. Below them, a narrow staircase cut into the ground. The sun's rays poured through the animal holes, little spotlights illuminating the dust swirling in the cool, dry air. Henry could see a long way down the passage to the bottom of the stairs, but could make out nothing beyond them. Eulalie buzzed in through the door and started down the corridor. "Come on, then!"

Henry carefully followed her down the earthen steps until they reached bottom. To his left, a huge underground cavern opened before him. The dirt ceiling was at least two stories high and the single room was as large as a small house. Shelves upon shelves were carved into the dry, dusty ground. Sunrays beamed through the holes overhead, creating a beautiful effect like sunshine streaming through the clouds. Hundreds of teacups and matching saucers lined the many shelves, which ran on all sides of the room and nearly to the top of the ceiling. The teacups were delicate and exquisitely beautiful, the more so considering their improbable location.

"Let me guess," said Henry. "She's called the Tea cup Lady because she collects teacups?"

"That's entirely possible," shrugged Eulalie.

"Isn't it kind of odd to collect this many teacups?" Henry asked.

Eulalie paused a moment to think. She folded her arms and placed a tiny finger upon her tiny chin. "I never have thought about it before, but aye. Aye, 'tis odd. Marvelously odd!"

"Marvelously odd?" Henry wondered. "Then you think it's a good thing to be odd?"

Eulalie thought hard about this question, too. "Well, 'tis better than being even after all," she said with great satisfaction, as if that summed up the question for her perfectly.

Henry and Eulalie noticed some movement in a shadowy corner of the great underground room. A remarkably short, elderly woman approached them and said in a small ringing voice, "Hello, yes, may I help you?" Then, peering closer: "Eulalie, is that you!?"

"Aye, 'tis me, and I've brought an Earth boy with me. He has come to rescue his mother, and we think perhaps you may know her."

"An Earth boy!" the woman exclaimed. "Now I hardly think so. I've not been to Earth in a hundred years." As she spoke, she shuffled closer to Henry and raised her horned-rimmed glasses to examine his face. She gasped suddenly and quickly stepped back again, obviously surprised by the recognition.

"It must be you after all," she said. "You look so much like her." The Tea cup Lady appeared to be greatly agitated as she fidgeted with her apron. "Come, let us have some tea. I was just making some when you came."

Eulalie gave Henry a searching look and hitched up one eyebrow quizzically. She was excited that the Tea cup Lady had recognized Henry, for she thought this to be a good indication that something interesting was about to transpire. She was glad to have happened upon the boy. She was growing bored of the fields and her friends and secretly had been wishing for some grand adventure to come her way. So far, Henry's story had all the elements of a good fireside tale: a damsel in distress, an unfolding secret, the promise of a perilous quest. Eulalie longed to be a character in some thrilling escapade, preferably with a starring role.

Chapter XIX
The Tea cup Lady

The Tea cup Lady responded with considerably less enthusiasm to Henry's unexpected arrival in the Wildlands than had Eulalie. The old woman looked upon him with a resigned sadness. His coming marked the end of an era for her—a rather peaceful era. She knew Henry's presence here would enrage Mocarsto, perhaps even enough to spur his return to the Wildlands. Thera's banishment spell had proven effective, but the Tea cup Lady knew there was stronger magic than hers. A man such as Mocarsto could find a way back, if he wanted to badly enough.

The Tea cup Lady greatly feared the day Mocarsto returned to the Wildlands, not so much for herself as for Mirabel, and for Thera. True, he had trapped Mirabel these many years, but where she was, time was meaningless. Besides, she was safe. Mocarsto would come for Mirabel first to reclaim what she took from him. But Mirabel was only a technicality, a pest to exterminate. His thirst for vengeance would be sated only when he had dominated Thera. He would punish her for his exile. She would suffer his blind fury for refusing his love. He would not rest until he commanded her, one way or another. The Tea cup Lady loved Thera more than anyone or anything, and she would do anything in her power to protect her.

The Tea cup Lady led her guests to a small wooden table set for tea. A delicate porcelain tea set adorned with pink and gold flowers sat atop an ancient, ornate lace tablecloth. The display was complete with matching cream and sugar bowls, and tempting tiers of cookies, biscuits, and tarts. Henry noticed the tiny pot-bellied stove in the corner of the room and wondered how she had prepared all these wonderful delicacies. He also wondered if she was expecting more company, as there was enough food to feed several people and he didn't think Eulalie would eat much, considering her size.

The tempting pastries made Henry's stomach growl, and he sat down to tea with an appetite. He had never been to an actual tea party before, and he felt unmannerly among the antique elegance of her table. The Tea cup Lady poured tea and invited her guests to help themselves to the array of sweets, which Henry and Eulalie both did with enthusiasm. Soon all three were feeling jolly and at ease. Eulalie and the Tea cup Lady chatted happily about the weather and inquired about mutual acquaintances, of whom Henry could have no knowledge.

"Goodness!" the Tea cup Lady said. "Where are my manners? I know the young man is not interested in our drivel, Eulalie. I'm sure that you have brought him to me for more than just tea and pleasantries! And I must tell you, Henry, I do know what those reasons are." She paused and took a long slow sip of tea. "I know your mother, Henry, and I know where you can find her. She is still where I last saw her last, many years ago, when she entrusted me with her precious child to take out of harm's way, out of here and into Sun-Rhea. I didn't want to make the journey. I don't like to leave the Wildlands very much anymore. I'm old and I prefer my home to any other place in the universe. But Thera insisted, and her, I cannot refuse."

"Thera?" asked Henry. "The one who tricked Mocarsto out of the Wildlands?"

"Yes, Henry," she replied. "That is a story unto itself. And I suppose now would be as good a time as any to tell it."

Eulalie clapped her hands. She liked nothing so much as a good story. She had heard the story of Mocarsto and Thera, of course. Nearly everyone in the Wildlands knew the story of the powerful Mocarsto and the beautiful Thera. However, few things are written down in the Wildlands and word-of-mouth stories vary as much as the people who tell them. She knew the Tea cup Lady would tell the truest version, for she had been there herself all those many years ago.

Chapter XX
Thera and Mocarsto

"Thera is a most beautiful woman," began the Tea cup Lady. "It was her intense beauty that first attracted Mocarsto in his youth. He was a strong and willful young man, yet ill prepared for a woman with a will as strong as his own. Theirs was a stormy relationship. Thera has always been fierce and free and would never allow a man to rule her. But Mocarsto was a jealous man. His jealousy turned to rage when Thera refused to be his bride. She would not relinquish her freedom to a man so willing to dominate her. In his stubbornness, Mocarsto would not meet her terms. He wanted nothing less than to lay ultimate claim to the woman he loved. Both of them were powerful, and their arguments legendary. Thera's magic was strong even then, among the strongest in the Wildlands. Mocarsto's lack of imagination has always curtailed his powers, but no one could match him for sheer force. No one had ever refused him—not successfully—until Thera. She was the one thing he could not control and it ate at him until it consumed his very heart.

"One night, after an especially terrible fight, Thera determined that she would free herself from his tyrannical hold. The next day she went to Mocarsto and promised to be his bride if he would complete but one task: He must venture forth into the land of reason and retrieve the elusive Caurus. He must ask no questions of her, but obey this one command. Once he captured the Caurus, then, and only then, could he return and claim his bride. Mocarsto boldly accepted the challenge, assured of success and thinking only of his reward. Thera helped him prepare for his journey. She supplied him with nets and weapons for his deadly encounter with the deadly beast. Before he left, we brewed a tea from special leaves in honor of the occasion and sent him out of the Wildlands.

"The path led him to Sun-Rhea where he began his quest for the fabled Caurus. Soon enough he discovered Thera's trick. The Caurus is no beast. In the ancient language of Sun-Rhea, Caurus is the name for the northwest wind. Though she told no lie, Thera had sold her metaphors for truth and played upon his assumptions. When Mocarsto realized the depth of Thera's treachery, his rage was unbounded. He cursed her a thousand times and swore to return to the Wildlands despite his oath. He was determined to make Thera pay dearly for her deceit. Of course, we had anticipated this reaction. Mocarsto always lacked imagination, and the subtler context of Thera's riddle was lost upon him. For surely, if he had discerned its true answer, she would have kept her word and married him.

"When he tried to return here, he found the path had been lost to him. Mocarsto had lived his entire life in the Wildlands and the path would be clear to him under normal circumstances, however, the drugged tea had served to cloud his memory of the passage and obscured the gateway from his sight. He could sense it, even now, if he would open his mind to less tangible realities, but his stubbornness perpetuates his exile. We weren't surprised to hear that he was successful in the land of reason. He is much like them, although his anger and disappointment have poisoned him, made him into something worse than he once was. He must not ever find his way back. He's now devoted to destruction, a final destruction, and his heart thirsts for vengeance against us all. We must withstand him at all costs. He can never return."

She paused to refresh her cup of tea.

"What about Mirabel?" Henry asked. "How can he keep her trapped here in the Wildlands if he can't even come here?"

"There are those here who are sympathetic to Mocarsto and would protect him still. The Wildlands are not like Sun-Rhea, Henry. You will find all sorts here. Perhaps we are simply less organized, but the inhabitants of the Wildlands are less inclined to force a consensus on every little thing. Your Earth is much like Sun-Rhea;

its people have a strange need to define, to label, to capture, to force homogeneity upon the most trivial matters. Alas, Earth is less interesting to me than it once was."

"You look pretty organized to me," Henry said, looking up at the hundreds of neatly arranged teacups.

The Tea cup Lady smiled. "Order is not out of the natural order, dear. Nothing thrives under utter chaos or total control, and life is best met in the balance."

"But I digress," she continued. "If you have found your way here after all, your mind must not yet be narrow. There must be more of your mother in you than just your looks. You must go to her now, Henry. It is time. You must find your mother and release her from Mocarsto's spell. You will find her in the Land of Echoes, where she resides in the Sky in the Lake. Eulalie can take you there. She knows the way. It must be so, come what may ...."

The Tea cup Lady trailed off into silence, and for some moments, nobody spoke. She suffered some moments of guilt for leaving the girl trapped for so long. She had rationalized her decision throughout the long years. She knew not how to free her after all. Besides, she was afraid of that place; she was afraid of him. She had kept the secret of Mirabel's location, even from Thera, for she knew Thera would have risked herself to save Mirabel, and the Tea cup Lady could not abide losing her. She had kept her promise and delivered the child to the land of his father. Looking at the boy, she could hardly believe how many years had passed. The boy standing before her in the flesh renewed her culpability, and she heartily regretted her weakness.

While the Tea cup Lady reflected on her personal shame, Eulalie's eyes were alight. She was ignorant of the Tea cup Lady's darker motives, and instead focused on the elements of passion and intrigue in her story. She felt an electric excitement at the threat of danger. She relished the sweet thrill of approaching adventure. She was certain to be part of the story's next chapter, for indeed, she did know the way to the Land of Echoes.

Chapter XXI
Crossroads

Henry's pocket buzzed rudely. The alarm on the tiny clock the scientists had given him was alerting him that it was time to go home.

"I should be getting back," he said. "This buzzer means it's time to return to my Earth body. First, I have to find my way back to Sun-Rhea so the scientists can send me home."

Eulalie and the Tea cup Lady both tittered at Henry's last statement.

"Silly!" said Eulalie. "You can reach Earth directly from the Wildlands. Didn't you know that?"

"It's true," remarked the Tea cup Lady. "I wonder why your scientists didn't know that."

"Really?" asked Henry. "I don't think the scientists know much about the Wildlands. They never have been able to find the path."

"No, no, they would not," said the Tea cup Lady, shaking her head. "Not with their measurements and calculations."

"But they're expecting me back in Sun-Rhea," Henry said. "Besides, what would happen if I went back directly to Earth? They say my body is still there in my bed. It's both there and here—bilocated, they said. What would happen if both of my bodies were at the same place at the same time? Besides, if both bodies were back on Earth, how could the scientists call me back to Sun-Rhea? And then how would I get back here to the Wildlands to help out Mirabel?" Henry's voice crept up in pitch and his palms turned sweaty as he verbalized the conundrum.

"Henry," Eulalie said gently. "You're on a bit of a ramble."

"Goodness!" exclaimed the Tea cup Lady. "Those scientists of yours certainly pick the hard way to go about things. With all their knowledge, do they still not understand the connection between all our worlds? Well, I suppose you had best go back the way you came this time, but there is little time to lose. When you come back again, I advise you to cut out the middleman, so to speak, and return directly here."

"But I don't know the way from Earth," Henry replied. "I only just now found the path from Sun-Rhea."

The Tea cup Lady sighed and thought for a moment. "The gateway to the Wildlands is not so much a definite location," she said. "It's more a function of your comprehension. Truly, gateways are all over the universe. It's a matter of which ones you can find, and which ones you are able to traverse. The path is a realm unto itself that's only detectable by a special perception. It holds a magic that your language cannot define. Few of your kind ever do find us, at least, not anymore."

Henry looked puzzled and worried. He tried to understand what the Tea cup Lady was telling him, but her meaning was lost in abstraction. He was hoping for more specific directions such as, "turn left at the giant elm and walk twenty paces."

Eulalie sensed his anxiety. "Don't worry, Henry," she said, encouragingly. "You'll find us again because you already have."

"Yes," the Tea cup Lady agreed. "The first time is the hardest. You had best be going now. Come back as soon as you can. Eulalie will look out for your return."

"Yes, come on Henry. I'll show you the way back."

Henry said goodbye to the Tea cup Lady and he and Eulalie followed the dirt staircase back up to ground level. Respectful of the teacups, Henry carefully closed the diagonal door so that gravity wouldn't slam it shut. The sun had begun to set and a gentle breeze blew through the tall, sparse grasses. The sky had turned beautiful shades of pink, blue, and gold. The scene so resembled a painting, it seemed unreal. Henry pondered the relationship between reality and representation as he followed Eulalie back to the pond where he had first met her, which, strangely, felt much longer ago than a few hours. They climbed the rock steps back to the fallen, mossy log where Eulalie's kin, the mislabeled dragonflies, sat and watched the strange visitor.

"You can find your way from here?" Eulalie asked.

Henry nodded. He remembered the way. The new friends said goodbye and Eulalie promised to meet Henry the next day on the path in from Earth. Henry walked toward the woods from whence he came and again noticed the rabbit hole in the side of the dirt bank.

This is where I came in, he thought to himself. *I recognize that rabbit hole.* He espied a long-eared rabbit sitting atop the bank chewing on a piece of dried grass, and felt another wave of déjà vu.

Henry easily found the way back to Sun-Rhea. He followed the path through the woods and emerged from the shady copse where he had entered. As he returned to the garden, the scientists rushed out to greet him, elated that Henry had found the path to the Wildlands, and that he returned safely, but there was no time for a full report.

"According to our calculations, you haven't much time until day breaks on your section of the Earth," Dr. Finnegan said. "We should send you back presently. Jon and Jen will meet you for a detailed report, and then they can report to us."

Henry nodded. The scientists turned and walked back into the building and Henry followed with quickened pace.

"Eulalie told me that I could enter the Wildlands straight from Earth," said Henry hurriedly, "and that I don't have to go through Sun-Rhea at all. She wants me to come straight there tomorrow. She says she knows where Mirabel is and everything."

"Hmmm," said Dr. Finnegan. "We weren't aware of that possibility. Who is Eulalie?"

"She's a fairy. She took me to the Tea cup Lady, who is the one who brought me out of the Wildlands in the first place."

At this point in the conversation, they had reached the inner room with the padded table.

"Um, Dr. Finnegan," murmured Dr. Hector. "That's interesting news indeed; however, it's late. We should get Henry back before his parents become suspicious."

"He's right, Henry," said Dr. Finnegan. "We will have to hear your story later. I don't see a problem with you traveling directly to the Wildlands, if this is in fact possible. Jon and Jen will be available to you on Earth, so we can communicate through them if need be."

"Okay," Henry said, as he lay down on the slab and prepared to make the strange journey home.

Dr. Scala spoke slowly as if the thought was forming in her head as she was saying it. "Henry, if you do go directly to the Wildlands from Earth, do not return to Sun-Rhea."

"Why not?" asked Henry.

"Because then both of your bilocated selves would be in the same place, and quite frankly, I'm not certain of the repercussions of such a thing."

"Interesting thought, Dr. Scala," added Dr. Finnegan. "Could your two selves exist on the same plane at the same time? Could a person witness both simultaneously? We'll have to think through the possibilities of—"

"Doctors," interrupted Dr. Hector with a sense of urgency. "We need to send him now or we might compromise the experiment."

"Yes, yes, very well," answered Dr. Finnegan. "Goodbye Henry. We'll be waiting."

Chapter XXII
Home

"Hen-reee!"

Henry opened his eyes in response to his mother's voice. Mrs. Harris arrived at the top of the stairs with a laundry basket perched on one hip. She knocked lightly on his bedroom door, which stood slightly ajar. Without waiting for an answer, she pushed the door open on its hinges and poked her head around the doorjamb. She smiled when she saw that he was finally awake.

"There you are!" she said. "I thought you were going to sleep all morning."

"I guess I'm just feeling tired today," mumbled Henry drowsily.

"Your father and I were thinking about driving down to Williamsburg today. Your dad wants to go to the skate park and I was planning to do some shopping at the outlets. Do you want to come?"

Henry did want to go. He loved going to the skate park with his dad. However, he was anxious to get back to the Wildlands and see what he could find out about Mirabel. He didn't want to pass up this opportunity to have several hours to himself with no parents or teachers around to miss him.

"I don't know, Mom," Henry began. "I haven't finished my homework yet and I'm feeling kind of tired anyway. Maybe I should just stay home and read my science chapters."

Henry was telling the truth about his homework. He had gotten behind in his reading these past couple of days. He was not too worried about science class, though. He had learned more about science in the past few days than he normally did at school. Besides,

Ms. Engle was teaching the exact same topic the scientists had described as bilocation. He had experienced it first-hand. Maybe tonight he could go back to Sun-Rhea and ask the scientists to help him study. Henry suddenly thought it curious that Ms. Engle happened to be teaching this particular subject at the exact same time it become a personal reality. He wondered if it was merely coincidence. A memory flashed through Henry's mind of Ms. Engle and Mr. Waddleman whispering together on the top of the bleachers at the baseball game.

"Okay, that sounds very responsible of you," his mother replied warily. "We'll be gone most of the day. We'll bring back dinner on our way home." She gave Henry a thoughtful look. "I hope you're not getting sick, honey."

"No, I'm fine, mom," said Henry. "I'm probably just growing again."

This answer seemed to satisfy his mother and she went off about her business. Henry worked on his homework until his parents left. Williamsburg was an hour's drive each way and they would probably stay until dinnertime. It was eleven a.m. now, so he figured he had about six hours until they got home. He carefully set his tiny watch alarm to remind him to get home before they did.

Henry walked outside and pondered where he should look for the path to the Wildlands. He had no idea where to start. The path from Sun-Rhea was through the woods, but in his neighborhood, there weren't more than a few trees clumped together in one place. Henry imagined it must be out of the way somewhere. He tried to think of a secluded place where one might discover a hidden path. The river was not far from Henry's house and trails meandered through the foliage where people had cut paths to the water to swim and fish. Maybe that would be a good place to look, he thought. But the weather was warm, and people were sure to be there. Then, he remembered a creek that ran behind a cul-de-sac a couple of blocks away. Henry and Kyle had gone there before to catch frogs and climb trees one dull afternoon last summer. For some reason, this struck Henry as the perfect spot to try. He packed some snacks into his pants pockets and headed out to find the path to the Wildlands.

A block from his house, Henry heard someone calling his name. He turned around to see Jon and Jen headed toward him. He walked back to meet them half way.

"Hey, Henry," said Jon.

"Hi, Henry," added Jen.

"Hello guys," Henry answered. "I forgot the scientists said they would send you around today. I was just on my way to look for the path to the Wildlands. My parents are gone for the afternoon so I figured I should take advantage of this time to myself."

"Right," answered Jon. "The scientists did send us. Naturally, they are curious about your adventures last night. They have never been able to see the Wildlands for themselves. With all their knowledge, the place simply eludes them."

"Perhaps it's all that knowledge that keeps them out," suggested Jen.

"What do you mean?" asked Henry.

"Nothing really," said the girl carelessly. "Just that there doesn't seem anything 'wild' at all about the scientists. They are all so organized and deliberate, which is fine and all, but after I spend any length of time with them, all I want to do is morph and run free as a cheetah as fast as I can. Sometimes, all that logic is confusing."

"Anyway," continued Jon. "We won't keep you from your plan. The scientists would like you to give a full report this evening. They will call you when you sleep. They told us to remind you not to come through the Wildlands. They are concerned about your two selves being in one place at the same time."

"I'm not sure I understand that part either," said Henry. "What are they afraid might happen?"

"We don't know," answered Jen. "Maybe you can ask them tonight."

"Good luck on your trip," said Jon.

"Do you guys want to come with me?" asked Henry. "I'm not exactly sure what I'm supposed to do."

"No," Jon and Jen answered at the same time.

"We can't travel to the Wildlands, either," explained Jon. "We tried."

Jen sighed, "We've spent too much time with the scientists after all, I suppose."

"We'll walk down with you, though," offered Jon.

The three young people walked down to the end of the dead-end road. A few feet below the paved cul-de-sac, a creek ran merrily through its shallow bed. Birds chirped in the tree branches above and frogs hopped along the muddy bank. Several trees clumped together in a group and Henry thought it a good place to start looking for a secret entrance to a magical world. There weren't enough trees to call it a forest, but it was dense enough that he couldn't see through to the other side. He thought he would find the path to the Wildlands only if he was able to lose his bearings. He wanted to lose sight of any landmarks that tied his perception to this place, to free his mind of expectations. He left Jon and Jen at the edge of the creek and walked toward the thickest grouping of trees.

He had taken several steps into the woods when he heard the wheels of a car crunching the small rocks on the road's shoulder. Jon and Jen looked over their shoulders to see a car slowly driving along the edge of the road in order to turn around in the circle at the road's end. *Someone must not have realized that this is a dead end,* thought Henry casually. He positioned himself behind the trunk of a large tree to wait for the car to drive out of sight. As the car swung around, Henry recognized its driver. "Mr. Televangi," Henry whispered to himself.

That instant, a cheetah and a wolf sprang onto the road and hurtled toward the car, which spun its wheels in the soft gravel, causing small stones and dust to fly. Mr. Televangi sped off down the road with the twins close behind. Henry ducked back behind the tree and hid his face from the rocky dust cloud. When the dust settled, Henry lifted his head and looked around.

"Well, there you are! I knew I would find you!" exclaimed a familiar voice.

"Eulalie!" said Henry.

"Aye, and who were you expecting, then?" she teased.

Chapter XXIII
And Back Again

Henry looked around him. He could no longer see the road. Instead, he found himself surrounded by a deep forest, more of a jungle, really. Brilliant green vines hung down from giant mossy trees. Insects and amphibians chirped and croaked underneath the thick, verdant brush at his feet. The entire place was teeming with life and vibrant color. Eulalie looked especially pretty as the gold of her dress and sunny hair offset the crisp green hues of the tropical forest.

"So I made it?" Henry asked with mild surprise. He hoped Jon and Jen were okay, but he supposed they were able to take care of themselves. He didn't think Mr. Televangi would be a much of a match for them in their animal forms.

"Aye, you made it," affirmed Eulalie. "And you picked a good spot, too. We aren't far from the Land of Echoes."

"I suppose we should get going then," said Henry. "I have about six hours before I need to get back. Do you think that is enough time?"

"Oh, don't worry about time. Time does not exist where we are going. At least, there is no future. The Land of Echoes is full of the past. 'Tis the land of ghosts and shadows, where memories go when we stop remembering them."

"Ghosts?" asked Henry, who was beginning to regret he hadn't gone skateboarding with his father.

"'Tis nothing to be frightened about. These ghosts are only echoes, traces of previous experiences. They are remnants, shadows, nothing more. They aren't real in the sense that you and I are real. 'Tis like watching a memory walk in front of you."

"Like an old home movie or something?" Henry asked.

"What's a 'home movie'?"

"It's a recording of a past time that you can watch over and over again," said Henry.

"Something like that," agreed Eulalie, cheerfully. "We shouldn't stay there too long, though. The longer you stay, the harder it is to leave. They say you can get stuck in a pattern, right along with the ghosts, until you no longer realize the future has stopped coming. Ghosts are stubborn; they don't like change. 'Tis the whole reason they're ghosts."

Henry thought about her last statement as he followed Eulalie out of the jungle. A well-traveled path led them out into the open where the bright blue sky expanded on the horizon. Henry saw tents and wagon-like vehicles surrounding a large campsite. He instinctively shrunk back behind a thick tangle of vines.

"What are you doing, silly?" asked Eulalie. "There's no need to fear the gypsy folk as long as you're in the company of a fairy."

"These are gypsies?" asked Henry as he cautiously followed Eulalie out of the thicket. "We have them on Earth, too. At least, I have read about them in books before. I've never seen a real live gypsy."

"Of course there are gypsies on Earth. Don't you know that Earth and the Wildlands were once deeply connected?" Observing Henry's blank expression, she explained:

"A long time ago, the creatures of Earth and the Wildlands roamed freely between the two worlds. As time went by, humans became more organized, more structured, more restricted, more … governed. As their desire for power and order grew stronger, our worlds became less compatible and began to break apart. Fewer and fewer people remembered the path, and eventually the children of the new generations stopped looking for it. Then came the men who desired a complete break with the Wildlands. They sealed up all known pathways. They renounced magic and turned their backs on nature in the name of control and domination. The glory of the beautiful and dark mysteries of the universe had become for them an anguish of unknowing. They sought to define everything through a single authority and dedicated their cold, gray lives to erasing any trace of our ways in human hearts.

"Our worlds are now farther apart than ever. Most of the paths from Earth are paved over now. Even the stories of the Wildlands are rarely told among your people anymore. Sometimes the children wander through, but they rarely stay for long. The Tea cup Lady says your kind no longer believes in our world. The breach was too wide and too long ago. She doesn't like to go to Earth anymore. She says you no longer even believe in fairies."

"I do believe in fairies! I do believe in fairies," exclaimed Henry, clapping his hands excitedly. He didn't expect Eulalie to appreciate the allusion to Tinker Bell, but he could not resist teasing her a little.

"Why do you applaud me?" asked Eulalie.

"It's from a book called *Peter Pan*. When Captain Hook poisons Tinker Bell and she's about to die, Peter gets the children to clap their hands and chant that they believe in fairies to make her well again."

"You and your books," Eulalie sighed. "Did it work?"

"Yes."

"Hmmmm."

Suddenly, they heard a rumble along the ground. The sound grew louder as several men on horseback galloped past them toward the camp. They were so close that Henry could feel the hot breath of the horses as they rushed by. The men were large and strong with long, coarse beards and sunburned faces. Frightened, Henry ran and hid himself behind a tent.

"Come on, Henry!" sang Eulalie. "I've told you there's nothing to be frightened about."

"Oh, now I wouldn't say that," said a deep, rich, yet feminine voice from somewhere very near the two travelers.

Chapter XXIV
The Tarot Card Reader

Henry turned in the direction of the voice to find a gypsy woman sitting at a card table inside a nearby tent. Through the open tent flaps, he could see she was playing with a deck of cards. She looked otherworldly to Henry as she grinned at him with her bright red lips while caressing the cards with long, painted fingernails. A long scarf entwined around her dark hair, and layers of thin bracelets lined her dark arms. A tight bodice, fitted over layers of flowing material, completed her exotic ensemble. She looked so intently at Henry that he began to feel uncomfortable.

Eulalie buzzed her way into the open tent. "None of your nonsense!" she said to the gypsy woman.

"Dear me! Admonished by a fairy," snapped the woman through her thickly painted lips. "Don't fluster yourself darling, but I have a story for Henry." She didn't look at either of them as she spoke. She focused her attention on the cards on the table in front of her. She held the deck in one hand and drew the top card with the other. She smiled with secret knowledge and gestured with her eyes for Henry to come inside and sit opposite her.

Eulalie buzzed out of the tent in a huff and came to a rest atop Henry's shoulders. Henry wondered if the two knew each other, and why they spoke so rudely to one another. He sensed there was a history between them.

"Go on," whispered Eulalie. "Let's hear what she has to say."

Henry walked through the open flap of the tent and sat down in the chair the woman had indicated. Henry looked at the cards on the table in wonder.

"These," she said, "are called Tarot cards. Have you never seen them before?"

"No," answered Henry.

"Well, then, allow me to explain. These cards reveal to me the future. When I saw you two hiding in the wood, I knew you would have an interesting story. And as it turns out, I see it's very interesting indeed." With this comment, she made a sweeping gesture across the cards with her painted, tapered fingers. The cards lay face up on the table displaying strange and beautiful pictures. Henry had never seen anything like them before. Once, he saw a woman dressed up as a fortune-teller at a street fair several years ago, but she had used a crystal ball as a prop. Even as a child, Henry knew her game was only a matter of make-believe. For some reason, this time, he didn't think this woman was a fake.

"How did you know my name?" Henry asked. He looked first at the woman and then at Eulalie on his shoulder.

"Don't look at me! I didn't tell her," said Eulalie, a little indignantly.

"I read it in the cards, dear," answered the woman. "And there is much more that I see. Would you like to hear?"

Henry shrugged his shoulders and tilted his head in a response that meant yes.

"Very well. I will tell you three things that I see in the cards."

"One," she said as she held up a finger. "The past is your future. Two,"—as her middle finger rose to form a V with the other—"it will rain on Sunday."

Eulalie snorted at this last one. "Come one Henry," said Eulalie. "Let's not waste any more time with this drivel. We should be on our way to the Land of Echoes."

"Ah, you're going to the Land of Echoes. I see that I've gotten one right already," purred the woman.

Eulalie gave the gypsy woman a pert "hummph!" and flew out of the tent.

"Thank you," Henry said sheepishly, as he turned to follow Eulalie.

"Wait!" said the woman in a loud whisper. "I will tell you one more thing before you go." She motioned for Henry to step closer to her as the many bangles on her wrists jangled with the gesture. Henry reluctantly obeyed and leaned in towards her. "You will live to tell the story of your own death."

"What does that mean?" Henry asked her with a high voice that registered his uneasiness brought on by her last prediction.

The woman only shrugged and said, "I can tell you no more." She turned back to her cards dismissively.

Henry left the tent without looking back and quickly caught up with Eulalie. He waited until the gypsy camp was out of sight before he spoke again.

"Why don't you like the gypsy lady, Eulalie?" he asked.

"Oh, she's alright," answered Eulalie. "But you cannot believe she knows your future. Do you, Henry?"

"Oh, I don't know." Henry thought for a moment. "I would think that a fairy, of all creatures, would believe in magic," he said, somewhat perplexed.

"Magic! Oh, no. She has no magic. Art, aye, but no magic. Magic cannot exist with a predetermined future. There's no ... wiggle room."

"But then how did she know all those things about us?"

"'Tis not so difficult, really. We give off little clues all the time as to what we are about. Practiced minds perceive and interpret these hints. She divines personality traits, which fuel one's choices, and along with observable external factors, lead to predictable outcomes. I'm not saying she's not good."

"She sounds like Sherlock Holmes, when you describe it like that."

"Who?" Eulalie asked. "Oh, let me guess. He must be from one of your books."

"Yes, Sir Arthur Conan Doyle wrote about him. Sherlock Holmes is a famous detective who can figure out crimes and criminals from the smallest clues that nobody else notices until he points them out."

"Ah, so he is from books! I was right then! I must be a psychic as well!"

"But you didn't predict the future there," objected Henry. "You only made a guess because I had talked about books before. You just recognized a pattern. Besides, it was a logical guess."

"The gypsy woman does more or less the same thing," said Eulalie. "We all of us experience a kind of momentum, that carries us from one moment to another. Chances are we will stay on the path we are currently on, until something makes us want to get off. The Tarot Card Reader looks a little further down the road we are on, that's all."

"Like inertia," Henry mused. "I remember from science class." Henry repeated the lesson that described Sir Isaac Newton's First Law of Motion: "An object in motion tends to stay in motion; an object at rest tends to stay at rest."

"That sounds reasonable enough," said Eulalie.

"Yeah, but we *can* change course. We have free will to change direction," said Henry.

"Aye, of course," agreed Eulalie. "But we do not do so randomly. We have good reasons to stay the predictable course, just as you were wise to keep to the forest path because of the snakes and spiders that thrive in the underbrush."

"True," said Henry as he glanced round his feet, having become suddenly nervous about slithering things. "I wouldn't choose a dangerous path fraught with hidden dangers unless I had no better choice. But just because experience has taught us to make better choices, it doesn't mean the outcome of all choices can be known before we make them."

"Precisely!" said Eulalie, happy that Henry was finally coming round to her point of view.

"I still don't understand how she knew all that stuff, though," puzzled Henry. His circular conversation with Eulalie had left him confused. "How could she have known my name?"

Eulalie shrugged. She had grown bored with the argument. "I don't know. I guess perhaps she has a bit o' magic after all."

They had traveled some distance during the course of this conversation. The sky was growing dark and the air began to cool.

"Is it almost night time?" Henry inquired of his guide. He had wondered how long the days were in the Wildlands. Henry had observed it wasn't the same time here as on Earth. Now he wondered if the two worlds even revolved around the same sun.

"'Tis almost always dusk in the Land of Echoes. Specters live best in the twilight."

"We are here, then?" Henry asked, a little nervously. All around him, the scene had turned somber. Patches of withering grass and ancient-looking, gray-barked trees lay scattered throughout the landscape. The remains of a low, broken stone wall crumbled upon the ashen ground, and a fallen wrought-iron gate leaned unsteadily against it. The sun had almost set, which cast the scene in tones of gray. Henry could barely discern objects from their shadows. The air was still and hushed as a chill ran up Henry's spine and the hair on the back of his neck stood on end. The place reminded him of an old cemetery no longer cared for, its inmates no longer visited.

"Aye," answered Eulalie. "We are here. Up ahead there, through that gate. We have reached our destination."

"Mirabel is in there?" said Henry with gravity, more to himself than to Eulalie. His feet felt heavy, as if he himself were turning into a cold, gray statue. Henry peered into the deepening gloom, but objects refused to solidify against the darkness. Drifting, thick clouds muted the moon's light, though it was nearly full. "How will we see where we are going?" he asked.

"No problem," chirped Eulalie agreeably. A warm hum ignited a soft, bright, golden light. Henry turned to see Eulalie's wings alight with electric golden threads like filaments in a light bulb. Henry thought her beautiful, and her radiance cut a tunnel of light through the thickening haze.

"Come on, then," she said, buzzing her way ahead, steadily, into the Land of Echoes.

Chapter XXV
The Land of Echoes

Henry followed Eulalie's light into the deepening gloom. He turned sideways to squeeze through the cold bars of the wrought-iron gate. The place was perfectly silent. No animals skittered, no crickets sang, no bullfrogs called. Even the small, spindly trees looked dead, their low branches leafless and dry like brittle bones restless in the night breeze, bending the slim trunks even closer to the parched ground.

They walked on as mist rolled in on the quickening wind. The damp, smoky air swirled and danced on the breeze. Up ahead, a man emerged from the fog and distractedly lumbered toward the pair. Henry's heart leapt into his throat when the cold presence brushed against his shoulder. The man walked thickly, slowly, but with purpose. He seemed unaware of his surroundings, yet he emanated a sense of urgency. He appeared grayish, like the rest of this place, as though he was made of the mist from which he emerged.

"'Tis okay, Henry," whispered Eulalie comfortingly, but quietly. "He doesn't know we're here. He won't notice us if we stay out of his way. Ghosts are very self-absorbed."

They watched the man disappear into a fog bank before continuing cautiously onward. The mist was growing thick, and despite Eulalie's light, the friends could barely see a few feet ahead. Someone cried out in the darkness. Another ghost appeared in the distance, a woman this time. She stood with her back to the pair, murmuring to herself. Her head was bent, her shoulders stooped, and her back heaved with choked sobs.

"What's wrong with her?" Henry whispered. "Can't we do something to make her feel better? Can't we get her out of this place?"

"Nay," said Eulalie. "There's nothing we can do for her. She's not crying over us. Besides, she is free to leave this place any time she wants."

"Then why doesn't she?"

"Because she doesn't want to let it go."

"Let what go?"

"Whatever it is that keeps her here."

The woman sobbed as if her heart was breaking. Henry couldn't resist the desire to help her. He approached her timidly and said, "Ma'am? Are you alright?"

Upon hearing Henry's voice, the ghost stopped and perked up her head to listen. She turned around and faced him wearing an intense expression that sent chills up Henry's spine. She looked quite mad, and Henry was sorry now that he had spoken to her.

"Is it you?" she asked, taking a step toward him. "Is it my own darling boy? I've been waiting for you for so long. Oh, why did you leave your poor, poor mother?" She walked quickly toward Henry with her arms outstretched for an embrace. Henry braced himself for the contact, but she passed directly through him, leaving Henry cold and uncomfortable. Ghost or no ghost, he distinctly felt that there was something wrong with her, something sick and unwholesome. The woman looked down at her empty arms, closed around nothing, and sighed pitifully. "No, it's not you after all. You are always leaving me, and now you are gone again. I must find you. I will find you. You are mine, my boy." She wandered off into the mist muttering to herself and wringing her hands.

"Come on," said Eulalie with a shudder. "This place gives me the shivers. Let's get out of the mist and go find your mother."

Henry was happy to move on. They walked quickly, searching for a break in the fog. The wind picked up again and a great gust cleared the air, freeing the moon's light from its cloud cover. The sun had fully set and the sky twinkled with a multitude of stars. The breeze had died to a whisper and the night sky was now clear, so Eulalie turned off her wings. She and Henry stood in the full, shining rays of the moon and looked around as far as its light allowed. A few yards away, a brook babbled over gray stones. Upon its banks beautiful blue flowers shone in the moonlight.

Henry noticed a shadow flicker out of the corner of his eye, then, a sudden movement in the other direction caught his attention. He sincerely hoped these weren't more ghosts—he had seen enough already. A shadow creature dashed behind the trunk of a large, rotting tree. A moment later, a head poked out from its hiding place and called playfully, "Catch me! Catch me! If you can ..."

A young boy with dark hair bolted from behind the tree and ran across the field. Another boy, small and fair, sprang from the shadows and ran after him. He tackled the dark-haired child and they fell on the brown grass, rolling and laughing.

"Are they ghosts, too?" Henry asked Eulalie.

"Nay, these boys look like echoes to me," she said. "Powerful memories also live here. They are playing out an important scene to someone, somehow, someone who is linked to this place, someone who can't—or won't—forget."

The boys laughed and played at hiding, chasing, and wrestling until they disappeared into the shadows.

"That looks like a good memory," Henry commented. "They seem so carefree."

"Hmmm," said Eulalie distractedly as she flew on ahead.

"What did the Tea cup Lady mean when she said Mirabel lived in the Sky in the Lake?" asked Henry.

"I supposed she meant that lake right there," said Eulalie pointing ahead. "That is why I have brought you here."

Eulalie came to rest on Henry's shoulder as the two stood before an expansive lake. The water was so still it looked like glossy black stone inlaid with twinkling diamonds. The yellow moon reflected in the lake's center with the last trace of cloud trailing behind it. Not a ripple troubled the jet-black water. Nothing dispelled the illusion that the sky lay right there at their feet.

"That's amazing!" said Henry. "It looks like we could just walk right into the sky, right there at our feet."

"Well, better get on with it," said Eulalie.

Chapter XXVI
The Sky in the Lake

"What do you mean?" asked Henry. "We can't just walk into the water? Mirabel can't possibly live in there ... can she?" Henry peered into the dark shimmering water. "I'm not sure I understand."

"'Tis a good thing I'm here, then," said Eulalie. "Follow me."

Eulalie flew off Henry's shoulder and hovered over the water, a few feet from shore. Henry reluctantly stepped down onto the wet banks lined with cattails and reeds and waded into the dark water. When he reached Eulalie, he was already waist deep.

"At least the water is warm," said Henry. "I hope you know what you're doing."

"Have a little faith," she answered with a wink. "Follow me, this way," she said and dove into the black water.

Henry peered into the darkness of the lake, but he could not see Eulalie. Her wings were unlit and he could not detect any motion underneath the glassy surface. He waited a moment to see if she would come back up for air, but after several seconds she had not returned.

"Oh, well," he thought. "I know how to swim, after all." Henry took a deep breath and dove forward into the dark, warm pool of water.

Suddenly, Henry felt as though the world was turning upside down. The sensation reminded him of the previous summer, at the beach, when a big wave caught him unawares and crashed down on top of him. The force of the water knocked him under the surface and rolled him around on the sandy bottom until he didn't know which way was up. Now, like then, Henry struggled to find his feet and lunge upward for air. His feet felt bottom and he stood up hard. He heard a sound like water rushing through a grate. He was on the underside of the lake's surface, but somehow he could breathe, like in a dream. He was not underwater so much as inside the reflection, inverted like a sleeping bat in a cave.

Still disoriented, Henry looked about him to get his bearings. He saw Eulalie a few feet away wringing water out of her dress. She appeared dreamlike to Henry, sort of wavy and weird, like she, too, was made out of water. Henry was dripping wet as well. He heard the sploosh, sploosh of the water as it dripped from his hair and clothes and plopped into the water under his feet. Henry took a few steps, stirring the shallow puddle that somehow supported him.

"Where are we?" he asked Eulalie.

"Oh, there you are!" said Eulalie, looking up at Henry. "I thought you'd chickened out."

Henry chose to ignore Eulalie's last comment. "Really, what happened? Where are we?" he asked again.

The moon and stars were bright and fantastically close, but the lake itself seemed to have disappeared. Their voices echoed gently as if they were standing in a large, empty room.

Eulalie looked around her and said casually, "We're in the Sky in the Lake. Isn't that where you wanted to go?"

"But where did the water go?"

"'Tis beneath us."

Henry looked down at his feet. A thin sheet of water covered the black floor. He bent down for a closer look and realized it wasn't quite a floor after all. Through the shimmering ripples of the water's surface, he could see the moon and the stars shining somewhere beneath him.

"What are we standing on?" he asked.

"We're on the other side of the lake, silly. We are in the reflection."

"We are *in* the reflection?" asked Henry.

Eulalie sighed. "Don't you know that when you see a reflection on a lake, it's always upside down?"

"Yeah."

"So, we've gone topsy-turvy. We are in the mirror image."

"But people can't walk on water!' said Henry, still confused on this point.

"Oh, dear," sighed Eulalie. "You humans *have* forgotten everything!"

"Come on," she said. "Mirabel shouldn't be too hard to find. There's not a lot down here, especially at night. I don't know how big the lake is, though. It's hard to tell when it's this dark."

Eulalie lit her wings and led the way through the black expanse. There was little to see and hear down here, only the glistening stars, the huge moon, and the slosh of the water stirred by Henry's sneakers.

"I think I see something up ahead," said Eulalie. "This way."

Henry followed Eulalie's lead, and as they neared the shimmering image, Henry perceived a small rowboat drifting gently on the still surface. "I think there's somebody in there," he said. "Is it her? Is it … my mother?"

"I don't know who else would be down here at this time of night," answered Eulalie matter-of-factly.

There, in the middle seat of the rowboat, sat a woman with long, flowing brown hair. She wore a far-away expression on her face as she absently dipped her hand into the water alongside the boat. She seemed lost in reverie and didn't notice Henry and Eulalie's approach.

Eulalie nudged Henry forward with a push on his shoulder. Henry took a few tentative steps toward the watery woman.

"Excuse me, ma'am?" he said timidly. "Is your name Mirabel?"

Upon hearing his voice, the woman looked up suddenly and turned her head toward the sound. "Henry, is it you?" she asked.

"Y-y-y-yes," stammered Henry, suddenly nervous. "And this is my friend, Eulalie."

Eulalie made a slight curtsey and said, "Pleased to meet you."

"We have come to help you," Henry continued. "The scientists from Sun-Rhea sent me. They want me to get you out of here. We need your help to fight Mocarsto."

Mirabel sighed. "He is the one who trapped me here. I've been waiting all these years. Is it really you, Henry? Has it been so long already?"

Henry didn't know what to say, so he just nodded his head.

"Come closer, let me look at you," said Mirabel.

Henry obeyed and took another step toward the beautiful woman in the rowboat.

"Yes, it *is* you," she said with certainty as a smile lit up her face. She looked like an entirely different person when she smiled. Henry felt a deep and instant liking for her. She was a marvelously beautiful woman and Henry stood for a moment in awe of her.

"Henry," Mirabel whispered, as her mischievous eyes filled with dancing light. "Do me a favor, won't you?"

"Sure," answered Henry. "Anything. What can I do?"

"Get me out of here!" said Mirabel, laughing.

Chapter XXVII
The Rock of Memory

"And how do we do that, if you don't mind my asking?" said Eulalie.

"You must find the Rock of Memory," said Mirabel. "The Rock of Memory is the only thing that can end the spell and break the barrier of my prison. It lies not far from here—in the valley where the forget-me-nots grow."

"Those blue flowers?" Henry inquired. "We saw some on the way in."

"Yes," said Mirabel. "There, you will find it. He guards it, though. He won't let you have it willingly. You'll have to trick it from him."

"Who guards it?" said Henry.

"Mocarsto," Mirabel answered, and she spoke his name with a hiss as though the word tasted foul on her tongue.

"Mocarsto!" exclaimed Henry. "He is here?"

"Only his child self," Mirabel explained. "He is an echo of his past. When we banished Mocarsto from the Wildlands, he was desperate to return. Rage as he might, he could not find a pathway back; Thera saw to that. But not even Thera could block the man from his own past. Mocarsto found a way into the Land of Echoes through his child self, for only his child self can enter the Wildlands. Only as a memory can he survive here."

"It can't be too difficult to get a rock from a child," said Eulalie, optimistically.

"Be careful," warned Mirabel. "He is beyond his years. I, too, was fooled by his guise of innocence. Child or no, he is not to be trusted.

The evil lives in him already. All that he is now lies in the child as well, however dormant. Remember that."

"The Rock of Memory?" Henry said. "Isn't that the thing that's supposed to be Mocarsto's downfall? What you came here to look for? How does it work? What does it do?"

"I don't know exactly," she answered. "It is powerful and the child guards it jealously. He used it to trap me here, in the reflection, separate from the outer world. We need it to break its own spell. The rock generates barriers in temporal reality. Through it, this place exists. He needs the rock to stay here as an echo, to keep apart from the man. As bad as he is, the child is not as bad as the man. He rather dislikes him, I think. If the rock is destroyed, the temporal spell will be broken. The child and the man will reunite, and the boy will fight against that fate."

"Go," said Mirabel. "Release me. I want to look at you in the full light of day. One cannot see clearly here, in the reflection. If you stay too long, the distortion will appear normal. I do not wish for that to happen to you. Free me, and then we can talk. I'll be waiting." Mirabel turned her gaze back to the water and resumed dipping her hand into its darkness. The faraway expression returned and Henry knew that the conversation had ended.

He looked at Eulalie and asked, "How do we get back to the other side?"

"Same way we came. We dive," she answered. "Topside, here we come!" Eulalie folded her wings against her body and executed a perfect swan dive into the water near Henry's feet, barely making any splash at all. Henry was decidedly confused about how this was happening. If he was standing on the under surface of the water, then how could he dive through it? How could it be both solid and liquid at the same time? He figured he had seen stranger things this day alone, so he gave a little shrug, took a deep breath, and dove into the water after Eulalie. He felt the dark chill of the water envelop him. He swam for some seconds before bursting through to the air above. He couldn't touch bottom here; they surfaced in a deeper part of the lake than where they went in.

"Pssst! Over here!" called Eulalie. Henry followed her voice toward a rowboat tied to a pier. Eulalie was sitting on the backmost seat, shaking the water from her long hair. Henry swam over and climbed aboard it, catching his breath. He looked down into the dark lake and at the reflection of the boat atop the rippling water. There, in the water, sitting on the middle seat between Henry and Eulalie, was Mirabel, staring gently off into the distance. When he looked up at the boat itself, the middle seat was empty.

"That is pretty weird," said Henry.

Eulalie looked down and noticed the third party in their rowboat under the water. "She looks so sad," Eulalie commented. "Oh, Henry, we must help her!"

"Yeah," Henry agreed. "Let's go find that rock and get her out of there."

They scrambled up onto the pier and made their way back to the valley where the bright blue flowers shone in the silvery moonlight. They followed the white noise of rushing water to a stream splashing down from a stony height of ten feet, forming a frothy pool below. Running brooks gurgled through rocks as the water chased itself downhill.

"I wonder why these flowers are called 'forget-me-nots'?" Henry asked.

"Oh, I know," replied Eulalie. "I heard the story once when I was a wee girl. Let me see if I can remember."

She alit upon rocks outcropped among the rich blue flowers. Henry sat down in the grass next to her. He agreed it was time for a rest.

"A long time ago, in the age of knights," she began, "Sir Tristan and his lady love were gathering wildflowers in the meadow. He was, of course, clad in shining armor, the weight of which toppled

118

him headlong into the river. His lady called for help, but by the time his squire reached them, his heavy armor had sunk him to the bottom. As the story goes, before he went under, he called to his love, "Forget-me-not, my lady!" And so she kept his memory by tending the flowers whose beauty had lured him to his doom."

"That's ironic," said Henry. "The armor he wore to protect himself actually caused his death."

"Funny," Eulalie agreed.

"So, what do you know about this rock?" Henry asked. "What does it do? How will we find it?"

"Aye, the Rock of Memory," said Eulalie. "I have heard the legend. The Rock of Memory fuels this place. Through it, memories embody themselves here. Powerful guilt and deep longing materialize as ghosts and haunts. Lost dreams whisper in the breeze. The Rock is a powerful talisman that strengthens these traces into pseudo-physical realities. It must grant the boy Mocarsto a separate life from the man. Here, he never has to grow up; he never has to leave; he never has to face the pain of moving on, of trying, of losing.

"As to how we find it," she continued. "The Rock must be kept from the elements, protected from the wear of time. It will not be near the water, because the water erodes the rock, like time chips away at our memories. He will keep it somewhere safe and dry." Eulalie picked herself up off the ground and lit her wings. "Off there, in the distance, I think I see a cave. Let's go check there."

It seemed as good a place to look as any, so Henry stood up and brushed the leaves off his pants before he and Eulalie sauntered off in the direction of the cave.

Chapter XXVIII
The Crystal Cave

As the two neared the cave, Henry enjoyed the soothing sound of the waterfall splashing down among the rocks. The air was moist and humid, and the scene reminded him of a grassy lawn wet with morning dew. The moon and stars cast enough light for the pair to navigate the landscape. Several yards away, the lake glistened silently with reflected moonlight. Henry felt sad when he thought about Mirabel trapped in her lonely place. He was beginning to grow weary of his stay in the Land of Echoes.

"Let's find this rock and get out of here!" Henry whispered to Eulalie. He wasn't sure why he whispered, but a hushed voice seemed appropriate to the scene.

"Let's try in here," Eulalie suggested as she lit her wings and cautiously approached the mouth of the cave. Henry had to duck his head to clear the entry. The cave's width and height were similar to that of a large family room; however, its length disappeared into a lightless gloom. The air in the cave was stale and stuffy with no sign of ventilation. The atmosphere was thick and heavy with its own stillness. No vegetation was evident, just dirt-colored rock walls and barren ground.

"Well, this definitely looks like the land where time stopped," said Henry. "This would be a perfect place to hide some weird old rock."

"Aye," Eulalie agreed. "There's not so much as a trickle of a breeze in here. 'Tis altogether oppressive." Eulalie flew on ahead and soon reached the rock wall at the back of the cave. "Look," she called out to Henry. "I see a passageway through here. I think it opens up down around that bend. I'm going to check it out."

"Wait for me!" said Henry, rushing after the disappearing glow of Eulalie's golden light. As he turned the corner, he almost ran into Eulalie, who had stopped suddenly. She was hovering spellbound, as she stared into the space in front of her.

"Look Henry!" she sighed. "Isn't it lovely? I didn't know this place was here."

Henry followed her gaze to the walls of the cave made of a crystalline rock, like quartz. The light from Eulalie's wings bounced off the angular edges with sharp, reflecting beams of white light, and through the glassy planes creating prisms of rainbow colors. Eulalie's wings were the sole source of light in the cave, so the effect, though beautiful, was dim and darkly colored, like gasoline on brackish water. Eulalie was captivated by her own light as it danced and reflected along the carnival angles of the quartz rock face. As she flew in circles and twirls, the shadows of the crystal stalactites elongated and shrank in rhythm with her frantic dance.

Henry ventured forward. He was growing tired, and even the beauty of this spectacle seemed little more than a diversion from the task at hand. He thought of Mirabel, alone and wistful, waiting in the Sky in the Lake, and he considered Eulalie's current fascination with shiny things unseemly under the circumstances. The flicker of light from Eulalie's flapping wings created a strobe-like effect that made Henry unsure of his surroundings. Up ahead, he saw something on top of what looked like a pedestal. He walked over for a closer look and discovered an oblong, ragged rock of the same crystalline material as the cavern walls. It was about the size of a football and sat atop an opaque slab of rock that resembled a birdbath in height and shape.

Henry walked over and picked up the rock, which was surprisingly heavy for its size. As he wondered at its weight, he noticed Eulalie had stopped her dance. A single shadow stretched itself over the top of the cave to loom over them both. In the passageway, at the opening of the crystal cave, stood a small boy—

the same dark-haired boy Henry had noticed earlier playing in the open field.

"Mocarsto," said Henry.

"Mocarsto," hissed Eulalie.

The boy calmly walked into the cave. As he approached Eulalie and her lighted wings, his shadow shrunk back from the cavern roof and fragmented around him in twisted angles. Her light, reflecting from the quartz walls, cast shadows on all sides of the boy. He stood in the midst of the fractured shadows in the thickest part of his own darkness. "You know me?" the boy asked with a wicked smile.

"We know you," said Eulalie. "So spare us your tricks. We are no fools come to play your games."

The child smiled innocently, but his eyes glowed with thoughtful mischief. Henry could sense in the boy the same desire for destruction he had seen in playground bullies. The boy looked upon Henry holding the rock, and his expression changed abruptly. The smile vanished from his face. His unexpected visitors no longer amused him.

"What are you doing with that rock?" he asked Henry menacingly.

From the child's reaction, Henry was certain the hunk he was holding was The Rock of Memory. He had to get the rock past the boy in order to free Mirabel. He cradled the stone close to his body and walked briskly toward the entrance of the cave.

"Not so fast," the boy warned. "You're not taking that out of here."

"Well, who's going to stop us?" taunted Eulalie.

The boy looked frantic for a moment. He was younger and smaller than Henry and could not physically stop him. Besides which, they'd caught him off his guard. The rock had lain there for many years undisturbed. The boy didn't know why anyone would want to take it from its rightful place. No one ever left the Land of

Echoes. No one ever wanted to. They lived on only through The Rock of Memory. It was the source of their power and longevity. The Rock allowed them to continue eternally in their respective ruts, free from the insistent pull of time and inevitable change and the pain of uncertain futures. Without the rock's power, this place would be lost. The wandering souls would once again be cast upon the temporal plane. The passage of time would consume them and they would fall to shadow and nothingness, fading out of all memory and into the great void.

There was a woman once, the boy remembered. She had wanted to take him away from here. She said the man needed him—that he had left the boy behind and that had made him incomplete. But the boy liked it that way. The boy didn't want the man to remember him. He didn't want to know what the man knew. He didn't want to be dominated or silenced by his rage. The boy was king here, and he was happy reliving the same day over again. It was a good day, and he wouldn't let the man take it as he had taken everything else the child had ever loved. The woman wouldn't understand this. She wanted to leave. She wanted to take him with her, but he wouldn't go. Then she had seen the rock. She knew its power. He had no other choice. He wouldn't let her take it. He couldn't let her leave. He trapped her in the Sky in the Lake and left her to her own echoes. He had saved her from the outside world, protected her in a watery dream. And it had been so simple—all it took was a little lie.

The boy Mocarsto knew he must act fast. Henry had The Rock of Memory in his hands and obviously was intent on taking it out of the cave. The boy reached in his pocket and pulled out a handful of pebbles, which he hurled violently at Eulalie. One big rock pegged her wing and spun her around. She landed with a thud on the cavern floor. The light in both of her wings died and the cave went dark. Eulalie cried out in pain and surprise. Henry ran toward the sound, but slid on some loose pebbles. He tucked the memory stone into his body like a football and braced his fall with his upper arm. The ground was cold and hard when he hit, but he wasn't badly hurt. He still had a solid grip on the rock. He could see nothing but darkness. He had never been anywhere so dark before in all of his life. All he could hear was his own breathing and the beating of his heart.

"Eulalie!" Henry cried. "Are you alright?"

"Yes, I think so Henry," she answered. "But my wings are hurt. I cannot fly and I cannot light them."

"Where are you?" Henry asked. "I am coming to get you."

"I'm over here toward the center of the cave. But be careful!" she exclaimed. "Don't step on me!"

"I'll be careful, Eulalie. I won't hurt you. Where is Mocarsto? Is he gone?"

"Yes, I think so. He ran after his missile hit its mark, the coward."

Henry was glad that she was well enough to show her usual spunk.

"Just keep talking," said Henry. "I can follow your voice."

Still nervous about being trod upon by Henry's relatively large feet, Eulalie sang an old song she learned as a girl:

When first we met, you were yet small in youth and gentle ways.

We'd idle in the garden bright on clear and sunny days.

Grown to such height, you fail to see your once and faithful friend.

The span, too great to navigate, and you, too proud to bend.

Don't tread on me though you've moved on and up to grander views.

I humbly ask a simple task, be wary of your shoes.

"Don't worry, Eulalie," Henry said. "I got the message. I promise not to step on you. I can hear you right in front of me. I'm going to bend down and put out my hand until I feel you, okay?" Henry placed the memory stone directly next to his right foot and bent down gently to find Eulalie. He slowly reached his hand until he felt Eulalie's warm, soft breath on his fingers. He lightly touched the hair on top of her head.

"I can put you in my shirt pocket, if that's okay with you," Henry said. "I think you'll fit. It's probably the safest place for you while we find our out way out of here."

"Your shirt pocket! Hummph!" snorted Eulalie, indignant at the suggestion. "Aye, but you're right," she ceded after a pause. "If I were to fall off your shoulder, I don't think I could fly."

Henry gingerly picked up Eulalie and placed her in his shirt pocket. He fumbled around until he felt The Rock of Memory and hugged it close to his other side.

"I'm surprised Mocarsto left without trying to take this from me," Henry said.

Just then, a flickering gray light glowed through a recess in the crystal cavern wall.

"Look, Eulalie!" said Henry. "That must be the way out!" Henry walked toward the lighted area of the cave.

"Nay, wait Henry!" Eulalie cried. "That's not the way we came in."

"But how can you tell?" Henry asked. "We are all turned around. Besides, the sun must be coming up by now. That must be its light coming in through the mouth of the cave."

"I don't trust it," Eulalie warned. "This cave will play tricks with lights and shadows. Besides, we don't know where the boy has gone. This could be a trap."

"I'm going to check it out!" Henry said. He took a few steps toward the enclave from where the light was emanating. Eulalie grew tense inside Henry's pocket. The feeling of powerlessness disheartened her as she rode, bruised and contained, inside a boy's shirt.

"Henry, stop!" Eulalie yelled urgently.

Henry stopped. "What are you yelling at me for?" he asked.

"I really don't think we should go that way."

"But look," Henry said, as he pointed toward the glow. "Don't you see the light? Let's get out of here already!"

"No, Henry. I think that's a false light. That's not the way we came in, and the air is so stale in here that there can't be another opening."

"Let's just have a quick look," said Henry impatiently.

Eulalie was mad now. She hated being carried against her will. She pinched Henry hard through the cotton of his shirt.

"Ouch!" Henry cried. "You pinched me!" But he had stopped walking. Eulalie had his attention, at least for the moment.

"Wait!" she said. "Be quiet and listen. Do you hear that?"

Exasperated, Henry stood perfectly still and listened to the silence. Then he did hear something—a soft, pinging, wet noise. It was rain—the unmistakable sound of rain pouring down outside.

"Oh, Henry!" said Eulalie. "'Tis raining. I can smell it! Can't you smell it? 'Tis behind us! The way in, and the way out, is behind us!"

Just then, a loud clap of thunder startled them both. A single bolt of lightning flashed behind them, and reflected and refracted through the prismatic walls, clearly illuminating the entire cavern room. In the momentary brightness, Henry and Eulalie saw a terrifying scene. Directly in front of them, no more than two inches from the toes of Henry's shoes, a gaping hole yawned without bottom in sight. The lightning flash reached into the black void, but its light could not penetrate the depths of the abyss to reveal its unknowable end.

Hiding partially behind a large crystal rock beyond the chasm stood the boy Mocarsto. He held a flashlight in one hand, which he shone through a chunk of orange quartz to simulate the sunrise. He intended to lure Henry and Eulalie into the darkness of the unforgiving pit.

Henry and Eulalie quickly surmised Mocarsto's dark plan as Mocarsto cursed nature's interruption of his evil scheme.

"Run!" exclaimed Eulalie, as Henry was already turning on his heels. He ran blindly to the opposite side of the cave, as lightning granted brief spurts of visibility. He ran down the earthen corridor and outside into the pouring rain. He didn't stop or look behind him, but he heard a childish wail emanate from the mouth of the cave. He knew Mocarsto had followed them that far. Henry ran as fast as he could while Eulalie hugged herself, for protection, into a ball at the bottom of Henry's pocket. Henry ran, lugging the heavy rock, past the waterfall, through the field full of forget-me-nots and onto the bank of the lake. He turned in a circle as he swung the Rock of Memory and threw it with all his might high and far out over the water. The crystal stone arced and followed gravity's pull toward the water's surface. When the rock hit the water, a loud crash split the air as the lake's surface smashed into large glassy bits like chunks of ice. Henry raised his arms to protect his face from the watery splinters. When he raised his head, the water was calm and the sun was shining full bright. Walking toward the shore, waist deep in the water, came a beautiful, and water-soaked, woman.

Chapter XXIX
Time's Up

Henry's pocket started to vibrate. The tiny alarm clock was buzzing again.

I guess this thing is waterproof, Henry thought to himself, pulling the device out of his soaking wet clothes newly drenched from the rainstorm.

Eulalie, too, was dripping wet. Henry's shirt pocket had done little to protect her from the elements. Mirabel had joined them on the shore. She turned to Henry and as if waking from a dream, she looked at him with love and wonder.

"Oh, Henry!" she sighed. "How I have longed to see you again. There is so much to tell you. Have I been gone all these years? You have grown into such a handsome boy."

Henry blushed despite himself. Mirabel was exquisitely beautiful. *I must take after my father,* thought Henry modestly, but the family resemblance was unmistakable.

"I really want to talk with you, too," Henry said, "but this alarm clock is telling me I need to get back home before my parents miss me. Besides, Eulalie has been hurt. We should get her back home so her people can take care of her."

Mirabel winced only slightly at the mention of his other parents. In fact, her response was so subtle that Henry failed to notice. Eulalie, however, recognized the sadness underneath Mirabel's smile, an undercurrent that clouded her joy at her release and reunion with her long lost son. Eulalie stood in Henry's shirt pocket, her arms folded over the pocket seam. Mirabel turned her attention to the wet golden head of the battered fairy. She held out her hand for Eulalie to climb out.

"Come here, my dear," she said. "I know how to fix a fairy's wings."

Eulalie eagerly obeyed and climbed out into Mirabel's waiting hands. Mirabel gently placed Eulalie on a mossy rock while she looked in the folds of her dress, still heavy with the water of the lake.

"I know I have some healing dust here someplace," said Mirabel. "I never travel without it." She pulled out a small vial and uncorked the top.

"See!" she said. "It's still as good as new!"

Mirabel sprinkled the glittery sand into her palm and rubbed her hands together until they grew warm. She cupped her hands around Eulalie's broken wings. After a moment, she drew back, and Eulalie gently flapped her wings, slowly at first and then vigorously as she felt the strength return. Next, she lit them and a thin circuit of luminescence traveled through her delicate veins like golden thread. Her wings were as good as new.

"Oh, wonderful!" Eulalie exclaimed, flying in circles around them both. She gave Mirabel a quick kiss on the cheek. "Thank you!" said Eulalie. "A fairy is nothing without her wings!"

"It's the least I could do," said Mirabel. "You two rescued me, after all."

Eulalie proudly beamed at Henry, flapping her beautiful wings. "Just look at that!" she said. "Now, that's what I call magic!"

Mirabel smiled indulgently. "I suppose Henry's right, though," she said. "We should all be getting back. I won't be sorry to leave this place. I'll be glad to see Sun-Rhea again."

"Sun-Rhea. Yes. I can come visit you tonight at Sun-Rhea!" exclaimed Henry. "Tell the scientists to bilocate me tonight."

"Bilocate?" asked Mirabel with a short intake of air. "Then your father was successful! Oh, how is he, how is your father?"

"I don't really know," answered Henry, a little uncomfortably. "Until a couple a days ago, I didn't even know you, or he, or any of this existed. You should probably let the scientists fill you in on the details."

Mirabel took one last look at the lake that had been her prison for so long. She was sad for the lost years she had sacrificed to its false depths.

"Yes," she said wistfully, "let's go home."

The three of them made haste back to the place where Henry had entered the Wildlands from Earth. Conversation would have to wait until they had more time to spare. Henry was nervous about staying away too long. He had never been gone this long before, and he hoped his parents hadn't decided to come home early.

"I'll continue on with Mirabel to make sure she gets home safe," offered Eulalie.

"Come and see us tonight!" said Mirabel, beaming her beautiful smile at her beloved and long-absent son.

"I will," said Henry. "I promise."

Henry walked a few minutes through the woods before reaching the clearing near the cul-de-sac. All was still and quiet. From the sun's position in the sky, Henry figured the time to be near five o'clock. He headed home directly, hoping to arrive before his parents returned. Henry observed the rubber marks on the road left by Mr. Televangi's speeding car, but he saw no other sign of a struggle. He thought about Jon and Jen and hoped they were okay.

Henry walked into his thankfully quiet house and immediately went to the bathroom for a hot shower. He was still damp from the lake and the rainstorm in the Wildlands. By the time his parents arrived a half hour later, he was studying quietly on the couch. He was truly happy to see them, and glad to be home. He ate his dinner with true appetite and enjoyed hearing his parents talk about their day. Henry stayed up later than usual that night, eager for a break from his otherworldly excitement. He sensed a renewed appreciation for things he once considered ordinary. He knew he would return to Sun-Rhea tonight, to see Mirabel, and to learn more about the strange new worlds, in which he now, somehow, belonged. For the time being, however, he was happy to pull his comforter over his head and fall asleep dreaming about baseball.

Chapter XXX
Intruder

CRASH! BANG! Woo-woo-woo-woo!

A loud noise woke Henry from a sound sleep. His eyes flew open to a darkened room. His first thought was that he was in Sun-Rhea with the scientists, but as he regained his senses, he realized he was still home in his own bed. An alarm was sounding loudly throughout the house. Henry heard some scuffling noises outside of his window. He got out of bed and pulled back the curtains. From his second story window, Henry spied a short, fat man running through the yard and into the shadows, the moonlight glistening off his bald head.

Mr. Televangi! thought Henry. *What is he doing here?*

Two large animals chased after the man and nipped at his heels as he gracelessly scaled the wooden fence and disappeared into the darkness on the other side. Henry recognized the wolf and the cheetah as they leapt over a low rail on the fence in pursuit of the fat man. His mother burst into Henry's room.

"Honey, are you okay?" she asked.

Henry nodded, turning away from the window. "What's going on, Mom?"

His father came up the stairs to join them, holding some sort of gadget in his hand.

"Dad, what happened?" asked Henry.

"It looks like somebody was trying to break into the house," his father answered. "He was trying to come in through the downstairs window when he tripped my homemade burglar alarm. I'm glad to know it works! The alarm must have scared him off because by the time I got downstairs with the net-shooter he was gone. Darn. I really wanted to try this thing out."

"How terrifying!" replied Henry's mother shuttering. "What if he tries to come back and finish the job?"

"That's unlikely dear," said his father, reassuringly. "Now that he knows we have an alarm, I doubt he would come back. He's probably just some common thief looking for quick cash. I'm sure it was a random, isolated event."

Henry wasn't sure he agreed with his father's last comment, but he didn't want to frighten his mother any more than she already was. Through the window, he saw the bright yellow gleam of two sets of animal eyes shining up at him from the edges of the yard.

"It's okay, Mom," he said. "I don't think he'll be back tonight."

Henry's father had to quick-fix the window and rearm the alarm before anyone felt comfortable enough to return to bed. Henry was eager to go back to sleep. He had had a very long day and he was tired. Besides, he was a little worried that the scientists would send for him while he was still awake. He didn't want to pass out again. After all that had happened tonight, his parents would definitely freak out if he fainted in front of them.

Maybe Jon and Jen were able to get a message to Sun-Rhea, Henry thought. The clock on his bedroom wall read half past midnight. He was glad to know that Jon and Jen were outside standing guard. It scared him to think Mr. Televangi was actually trying to enter his house when everyone was asleep.

What was he planning to do, anyway? he thought as he fell into an exhausted sleep.

Chapter XXXI
The Annwyn

Once more, Henry opened his eyes to the gray-lit room filled with humming machines. This time, however, he found himself alone. Henry hopped off the cushioned slab and peered through the observation window. The light in the hallway was on, but the corridor was empty in both directions. Curious, he started toward the great room that overlooked the garden. The door was closed, but unlocked.

"Hello?" Henry called out as he pulled the door open and cautiously entered the room. By appearances, Henry had interrupted a tea party. Dr. Hector, Dr. Scala, and Mirabel sipped tea from dainty china cups, while Eulalie and Dr. Finnegan were enjoying little powdered cookies. They each smiled at Henry as he stepped into the room.

"Oh, hello, Henry!" beamed Dr. Finnegan. "How wonderful to see you!"

"Weren't you expecting me?" Henry asked, a little confused that nobody had met him upon his arrival.

"We were hopeful that you would come," answered Dr. Scala. "Jon and Jen told us about the trouble you had this evening, so we thought it best to wait and see if you could make it here on your own."

"Yes, and you did it, my boy!" said Dr. Hector. "You found your way back all by yourself. That's marvelous, really marvelous!"

"By myself?" Henry asked. "What do you mean?"

"Well, Henry," said Dr. Finnegan. "You have been to Sun-Rhea a few times now, enough times to lay down the pathways in your brain. We were curious to see if your mind could remember the way. Besides, with all the excitement at your home this evening, we didn't want to call you here at an inopportune time. We decided to wait and see if you would come to us on your own."

Henry sat down on the couch next to Mirabel and Eulalie.

"Hello Henry," said a smiling Eulalie. White powdered sugar stuck to her tiny lips. "You should try one of these cookies. They are scrumptious. They're even better than the ones the Tea cup Lady makes."

Mirabel wore a gold and white flowing robe that complimented her long, wavy, soft-brown hair. She still wore the faraway expression Henry had first seen when he met her on the underside of the lake. Mirabel, more than anyone else Henry had met on his strange journeys, seemed downright otherworldly. She looked different now with her shiny hair and dry clothes. His first impression of her lingered and he imagined he would always think of her as an element of water.

"Now, don't worry about Mr. Televangi," Dr. Finnegan continued. "Jon and Jen will find out what he is up to. And in the meantime, they will keep watch over your house to make sure he doesn't disrupt your family again."

Mirabel stirred as if awakened from a daydream. "Oh, Henry," she smiled. "It's wonderful to be back in Sun-Rhea again. The garden is still so beautiful. How I have missed this living, growing world." She paused and reached into the folds of her white dress and pulled out an object that looked like a small snow globe. "Here," she said, gently pressing the orb into Henry's hand. "Take this with you when you go."

Henry examined the present Mirabel had made him. Through the glass, a rainbow kaleidoscope of pulsating color swirled and danced liquidly. "What is it?" he asked.

"This ball holds millions of tiny microorganisms, known as Annwyn," she answered. "They display different kinds of phosphorescence depending upon the environment, or their mood. Look, I think they like you."

A sandy cloud of bright cerulean blue swirled from the bottom of the orb and danced like a slow tornado inside the glass. The blue cyclone melted into liquid yellow and warm orange as the orb warmed in his hands.

"You say they are alive in there?" Henry asked.

"Yes," said Mirabel. The Annwyn are tiny creatures; a single one is too small to see with the naked eye, but when they move together, see what beautiful pictures they make. It's an entire world in the palm of your hand."

"I like it. Thank you," said Henry, "but if they are alive, I can't take them with me when I bilocate, can I? Like the scientists said, I can only bring inanimate objects, like the clock." Henry looked from Mirabel to the scientists for an answer, but it was Mirabel who spoke:

"The Annwyn are alive," she explained, "but they can travel these worlds and many others through their own power. How can I explain this?" She paused for a moment as she sought a description her young, Earth-raised son would be able to understand. "The Annwyn are a singing world; they produce a sort of resonance in harmony with their surroundings. They amplify certain conditions. They find a wavelength, a frequency, and build upon it. They can navigate the worlds by feeding this energy until the doorway is opened wide enough to traverse it. They will have no trouble keeping up with you on your travels."

Mirabel pressed the Annwyn into Henry's hand. "Keep them with you," she urged. "The longer they stay with you, the better they tune into your own personal frequency. Then, they will be able to find you in any of the known worlds."

"Keep them safe," she warned. "Let no one know you have them. The Annwyn can be powerful in evil hands." Mirabel smiled and held Henry's face in her hands. "You will want their company. The colors will cheer you up. It is a bleak place where you are going."

Henry looked up into her eyes, blue and liquid like water, and then back to the three scientists sitting together on the oatmeal-colored couch.

"Where am I going now?" he asked.

Part II

Chapter XXXII
Back to School

Henry sat in the back row of Ms. Engle's science class and stared out the window at the vacant baseball field. He wasn't worried about the quiz Ms. Engle was handing out. He remembered everything the scientists taught him about wave-particle duality and probability density curves. Things were much easier to learn, he thought, when they happened to you personally. Henry mused on the Tarot Card Reader and the similarities between her art of prediction and the mathematics of probabilities.

He remembered a book he once read about the game of poker, written by a successful gambler, a rare enough persona. The author described how he applied his mathematical knowledge of probabilities as he counted cards and weighed the odds of realizing certain card combinations. He also used his understanding of human nature to discover "tells" in his opponents. A "tell," Henry remembered, is an involuntary mannerism that inadvertently gives away some information about the cards a person is holding. The gambler called it "tipping one's hand." Henry again recalled the ominous words of the Tarot Card Reader and wondered at Eulalie's strange mix of skepticism and wonder. He contemplated the blurry lines between magic and science, reason and art.

Henry's sharpened pencil was poised over his paper, ready to write in the first answer, when Ms. Engle called him to the front of the room. Somewhat surprised, Henry laid down his pencil and walked to her desk positioned next to the large green chalkboard.

"Henry," she whispered to him. "You are excused from the quiz today. Mr. Waddleman needs to see you in the principal's office right away." She smiled knowingly as she handed him a hall pass.

I wonder what's going on now, he thought as he headed toward Mr. Waddleman's office. He felt strange to be alone in the quiet halls, without the usual bustle of prattling students. Sunlight streaming through a high window made a crosshatch pattern against the horizontal locker slots. Henry watched the dust swirling in the distinct rays and stood for a moment, mesmerized, before he continued to his destination.

Henry entered the glassed-in administrative lobby, but no one was there. He knocked quietly on Mr. Waddleman's door, which stood slightly ajar.

"Come in, come in!" said Mr. Waddleman excitedly. "Please, Henry, come in. Close the door behind you, won't you? And please, have a seat."

Henry wondered why he would need to close the door, especially with no one around, but he knew Mr. Waddleman to be a kind and friendly, if a somewhat bumbling, man, so he did as he was asked. Henry sat in the chair opposite Mr. Waddleman's large desk, cluttered with papers, manila folders, and framed pictures of smiling people among botanical scenery.

Mr. Waddleman noticed Henry staring at a particular photograph. He picked up the framed portrait and said, "These are some old friends of mine. Friends I haven't seen in a very long time."

"They look familiar," Henry said. "Where was that picture taken? It looks like somewhere I've been before."

"It is," said Mr. Waddleman. "This is your mother's garden in Sun-Rhea. In fact, this is a picture of your mother and father, Henry."

Henry almost fell out of his chair; he was stunned that Mr. Waddleman knew about Sun-Rhea. Mr. Waddleman handed Henry the picture so that he could take a closer look. Yes, it was definitely Mirabel. She was smiling brightly and was even prettier than the last time he saw her. She stood beneath the immense sunflowers that grew in her garden. Next to her was a man Henry didn't recognize. The man had a kind and gentle face. He was smiling too, but more mechanically than Mirabel; there was worry behind his eyes.

"This man is my father?" Henry asked, looking up into Mr. Waddleman's sweaty, chubby face. "You knew him?"

"Yes. That's a likeness of your father, and yes, I knew him. Ms. Engle and I were founding members of the Federation of Free Minds, along with your mother and father. We were all close friends. When your father successfully bilocated you to Earth, and after he … was incapacitated, Ms. Engle and I volunteered to leave Sun-Rhea to keep watch over you here. Unfortunately, it's a one-way ticket for us. We cannot travel between worlds as easily as you and the twins. We are too old, too … set in our ways. Though we are always advancing in our understanding of the universes, our knowledge of bilocation is still very young. You were the first human ever to be successfully bilocated. It's part of what makes you special."

"You and Ms. Engle are from Sun-Rhea?" Henry asked. "How did you get here?"

"The old-fashioned way, I suppose," Mr. Waddleman answered. "At least old-fashioned where we come from. Ms. Engle and I traveled from Sun-Rhea to Earth physically through what is commonly known as a wormhole."

"A wormhole," Henry repeated. "That sounds familiar."

"It's a simple concept really," continued Mr. Waddleman. "Just think of space and time as two dimensions, or two axes on a graph. Here, let me demonstrate." Mr. Waddleman picked up a flat piece of printer paper from his desk. "Imagine the width of the paper is the space continuum, and that time runs lengthwise, like this." Mr. Waddleman motioned along the long edge of the paper. "Say Sun-Rhea is located along one edge of the paper and Earth is at the other. Now look what happens if I fold the paper over." Mr.

Waddleman folded the paper over, without making a crease, so that one edge of the paper was directly over top of the other edge. "Now, if we build a bridge to hop from the top edge to the bottom edge instead of walking the entire length of the paper, we save ourselves a lot of time and distance in the traveling. Do you see?"

"I guess so," answered Henry. "But how do you make a wormhole?"

"Well, that's a little more difficult to explain," said Mr. Waddleman. "Wormholes are inherently unstable and collapse upon themselves almost immediately upon opening. A significant amount of energy is required to keep the passageway open long enough for travelers to pass through. Once this tunnel collapses, there is no way back, at least from this end. It's nearly impossible to get the energy resources necessary to open and sustain the wormhole on Earth. We can get here, but we can't get back. It's effectively a one-way ticket."

"Can't you go back to Sun-Rhea through the Wildlands? There's a path to the Wildlands not far from here."

"Is there really?" asked Mr. Waddleman, scratching his balding head. "I've never heard of that. However, I'm afraid that wouldn't be any good to us, either. Surely, the scientists have told you that we're unable to enter the Wildlands."

"If the Wildlands connect both to Earth and Sun-Rhea, maybe that is a wormhole, too," said Henry.

"Technically, no," said Mr. Waddleman. "The Wildlands are not on the same physical or temporal planes as our two worlds." Henry looked confused, so Mr. Waddleman referred to his visual guide. "They're not on this sheet of paper at all."

"Hmm, let's see." Mr. Waddleman tried to think of a way to help Henry understand the confusing interrelationships between the three worlds. "We've had difficulty quantifying the existence of the Wildlands because few of our ranks have ever made the trip. We know it exists, nevertheless, because some have been able to cross the barrier."

"Like me?" asked Henry.

"Like you," answered Mr. Waddleman, "and your mother before you. The Wildlands aren't so much a physical location one can point to on a map, or in our example, on our sheet of paper. They exist in another dimension altogether and therefore might be bridged from anywhere. But this is highly theoretical on my part, Henry, as I myself have never visited the magical realms."

"But it's possible, right?" asked Henry.

"Nearly anything is possible," said Mr. Waddleman. "Limitations are primarily in us, ourselves, in our ability to perceive and articulate the abundant profundities of life. We humans have only begun to scratch the surface of the immensity of possibilities that can be known!"

Here Mr. Waddleman paused, aware that his excitement was causing him to raise his voice. "Pardon me, my boy," he said. "These things do fascinate me, but let's move on to the issue at hand. I've called you out of class today, Henry, to allow you some uninterrupted time for your next mission."

"My next mission?" Henry asked.

"Yes, yes, your mission to Cardew. The scientists have discussed all this with you, haven't they?"

"Well, some," Henry answered. "They said that Mocarsto controls everything and he makes the people eat something called "hypnofood" to make them mindless servants. Mirabel said the place was dreary."

"I'm sure it must be. Can you imagine a place with no choice, no free will, no adventure, no … no possibilities?"

Henry did try to imagine it—a world without decisions or the stress of making the right one, or the guilt of making a wrong one.

"Anyhow," continued Mr. Waddleman, "we have no time to lose. Mocarsto might very well know by now that Mirabel has escaped her prison in the Wildlands. He will come looking for her, and for you, no doubt. Mr. Televangi already knows where you live. Waiting any longer serves no good purpose. We have the strength of Mirabel again, and of her son. It's time to meet our enemy and defeat him."

"Defeat him!" exclaimed Henry. "But what can I do?"

"Destroy him! Release his hold upon the people of Cardew!" said Mr. Waddleman getting excited again.

"But how do you expect me to do that?" asked Henry.

"I'm not sure, exactly," shrugged Mr. Waddleman, a gleam in his eye, "but the possibilities are endless."

Chapter XXXIII
Transitions

"Here we are," said Mr. Waddleman, opening the door to the nurse's office. "This will be the perfect place." He ushered Henry inside and motioned toward a nearby cot. Its white, starched sheet looked itchy and uninviting under the fluorescent lights. "Make yourself comfortable."

Henry sat on the edge of the cot, while Mr. Waddleman perched awkwardly on an olive-painted metal chair opposite him. The chair creaked slightly under his generous weight. "We understand that you've been able to bilocate yourself to Sun-Rhea at will. This is truly, wonderful news, and we want you to try it again. You have a long journey ahead of you, and you will be safe here. You have all day if you need it."

"What about Nurse Edna?" Henry asked.

"No need to worry about Nurse Edna," replied Mr. Waddleman. "She just happens to be away at a nursing conference this week. Ms. Engle is qualified to assist in case anyone needs medical attention. You should be entirely undisturbed. Of course, Ms. Engle and I will stop by to check on you from time to time."

"Won't people wonder where I am? My friends saw me go to your office. They'll be curious when I don't go back to class," said Henry.

"Hmmmm"—Mr. Waddleman tapped his chin as he thought— "Well, if anyone asks, we will simply tell them that you have been chosen for a special project ... that you are being evaluated ... tested for an advanced learning program. There, that is true enough. Now, no worries, Henry. Ms. Engle and I will take care of everything on this end. You have more important things on which to focus."

"What do you want me to do?"

"Make yourself comfortable and try to translate into Sun-Rhea. The scientists will show you the way from there. Good luck. I won't be far away." Mr. Waddleman closed the door softly. Henry heard his footsteps pattering down the silent halls.

Henry sat on the stiff cot for a few moments before turning off the buzzing overhead lights. The nearly two-inch gap at the bottom of the door provided enough light to make out his surroundings. Henry stretched his legs out long on the cot and leaned his back against the wall. He searched his pockets for his tiny alarm clock and synchronized it with the wall clock. Then he pulled out Mirabel's present: the globe teeming with life and color. Whatever creatures lived inside the smooth glass were creating a beautiful show of swirling colors that cooed like a lullaby. Henry tried to remember what he had done the first time when the scientists told him he had bilocated without their help. He couldn't think of anything he had done in particular. It was no more than a thought. The swirling melting dance of colors was mesmerizing, and Henry felt himself dropping off to sleep.

Henry knew he had slept, because he had dreamed. It was a vivid dream, tinged with magic, where everything felt enigmatic, but meaningful. He remembered the rabbit was in it—the one he had dreamt about before, after reading the story in the book his mother had brought home. Mirabel was in it too, just for a moment, standing inside the swirling life of the globe she had given him, before the colors turned to gray and the glass orb smashed to pieces on the ground, leaving Mirabel lifeless atop its ruined shards. Then, Henry stood alone on a windy, barren plain looking toward the gray horizon. The landscape was cold and sterile, save for the rabbit, who jumped in zigzags toward the setting sun. The rabbit paused as he made his way through the blowing tumbleweeds, looking once over his shoulder toward Henry. Before he bounced off into the darkening gloom, Henry heard him say, "Not I, no not I."

When Henry awoke, he found himself once again in the familiar room with the scientists. Each one of them looked worried and relieved and the same time.

"There was never any doubt you could do it!" said Dr. Finnegan cheerfully, referring to Henry's ability to bilocate at will.

Henry thought the relieved look on his face indicated there might have been *some* doubt. At any rate, Henry was glad the trip had been so easy. Being able to bilocate, at will, might come in handy one day. Still, he was concerned about the worried looks on the scientists' faces. Dr. Finnegan was obviously preoccupied, Dr. Scala was downright nervous, and Dr. Hector's baldhead was beginning to sweat.

"What's up?" asked Henry. "Why is everyone so tense?"

"What? Oh, oh, it's nothing really," stammered Dr. Finnegan. It seemed to Henry that he had difficulty looking at him, as if he was reluctant to tear himself away from his thoughts.

"We are only concerned for your safety," interjected Dr. Scala. Her eyes looked red and tired as if she had not slept in a long time. "This isn't an easy journey we are asking you to make."

"No, it will not be easy," agreed Dr. Finnegan. "And you must know that we aren't forcing you to go. It's your choice, Henry. We would never ask you to go unless ..." Here, Dr. Finnegan broke off from speaking. Dr. Scala came up behind him to finish his sentence for him.

"We don't wish to put you into harm's way, Henry," said Dr. Scala. "But we know of no other who can succeed. You are the one of legend, the child of Sun-Rhea, born in the Wildlands. You have both magic and reason within your grasp. You alone among us can travel the pathways between the worlds. You alone can survive the perils of Cardew and resist the potent effect of Mocarsto's hypnofood. There is a great evil looming over our world, Henry. We need you to help us stop it."

147

"Are you willing to go forth into Cardew?" Dr. Finnegan asked. "Are you willing to do what no one but you can do?"

Henry noticed that Mirabel had entered the room. She stood near the doorway smiling at her son. She looked so peaceful and happy, so beautiful. Her long flowing hair was brushed to one side so Eulalie could perch herself atop her shoulder. Henry looked at the two women for a moment before he answered Dr. Finnegan's question.

"Can Eulalie go with me?" he asked.

"Just try and stop me," said Eulalie, as she flew from Mirabel's shoulder onto his.

Chapter XXXIV
The Road to Cardew

"We will go with you as far as the borders of Sun-Rhea," said Dr. Finnegan as he polished his misty glasses with the front of his white lab coat. "The distance between us and our enemy is shrinking. Only a few miles of uninhabited land remain between Cardew and the Federation of Free Minds. You will not have far to travel to reach your destination."

"We can take the hover bubble," said Dr. Hector, trying to sound cheery. "It's a nice day. We can even open the sunroof."

"What's a hover bubble?" asked Henry curiously. With a flash, he realized he hadn't noticed any cars, or even roads, on his previous visits to Sun-Rhea.

"I suppose Earth is still in its primitive stages," mused Dr. Finnegan. "Your civilization hasn't even discovered hover technology yet?"

"No, not exactly," Henry responded. "We have cars that run on gasoline and travel on paved roads over the ground. But my dad has built a hover-board. He's still working out the kinks, but it's really neat! He even let me ride it!"

Henry saw Dr. Scala glance at Dr. Finnegan in a meaningful way. Her expressive countenance made him wonder at her thoughts. She turned back toward Henry and smiled. "Well, if you know how to ride a hover-board, perhaps you should take one with you on the road to Cardew. It will shorten your trip considerably."

"Cool!" said Henry. He was beginning to get excited about this trip after all.

Henry and Eulalie followed Mirabel and the scientists down a long corridor past many doorways. After some minutes, they exited on the side of the building opposite the Garden. A stepped valley stretched out below and beyond into the distant horizon. To his left and up a rocky slope, a glass-domed observatory stood with large-lensed telescopes pointing upward toward the strange sky.

"Wow," Henry said under his breath. "What is that?"

"This is our finest observatory," replied Dr. Finnegan. He motioned out over the vast horizon to the valley below dotted with cottages, animals and other signs of happy life. "As you can see, we chose to build our laboratories on high ground, both for protection and for the lovely view. The observatory requires unobstructed observation of the skies, and the scientific community naturally banded together geographically to share resources and insights. This location also provides a natural defense from enemy attacks. The Federation of Free Minds is concentrated here on top a high mesa that looks over the valley where the last free citizens of Sun-Rhea live. Behind us, on the other side, are farmlands bordered by untamed wilderness that expires at the seashore."

Dr. Finnegan pointed out over the hazy valley where people and animals moved across the landscape like so many ants. "Some miles beyond this valley, known as Ermintrude Dell, are the borders of the Federation's lands. Beyond that, the land grows barren and dry, a desert place where plants and animals do not thrive. On the other side of this 'no-man's land' lies Cardew and the encroaching evil of Mocarsto."

"We should be going," interrupted Dr. Hector. "The passing of time is a thing beyond our control, and we have little of it to spare."

Henry double-checked his alarm clock and packed away the small provisions of food and water the scientists had given him. They also equipped him with a hover-board that looked remarkably similar to his father's prototype. This one was more slender, however, and did not require an external power source. Henry wanted to ask if he could take the board home with him, but he decided to wait for a more appropriate time. The hover bubble itself was little more than a large version of the hover-board. Dr. Hector removed a rounded plank, fashioned like a tabletop, out of a slot in the external wall. He rolled it to a flat spot of ground and laid it down on the grass. At the push of a button, soft seats inflated from its flat surface.

"All aboard everyone," smiled Dr. Hector, appreciating Henry's face full of wonderment.

Henry, the scientists, Mirabel, and Eulalie climbed aboard the hover bubble. Another push of a button and a clear plastic cover rose to enclose them. Dr. Hector engaged the power source and they elevated several inches off the ground, which, indeed, gave the sensation of being in a giant bubble. They flew through the Ermintrude Dell toward the borders of the Federation's lands. The scenery below fascinated Henry. He flew over people a hundred yards below his feet; they reminded him of fair-goers as seen from the top of a Ferris wheel.

Henry had once ridden a roller coaster at an amusement park that shared an uncanny resemblance to his experience in the hover bubble. The powerful machine had whirled him through a replica of a German countryside, imitating a wolf's eye view on a midnight rampage. Now, he wondered at the quaintness of the cottages and yards in Ermintrude Dell. He would have thought an advanced society would be living in floating apartment buildings, or something similarly futuristic. Instead, the land here looked rural and spacious, and evoked memories of his grandparents' farm in Virginia.

The hover bubble traveled quickly and the party soon arrived at their destination. Signs of life grew sparse as they approached the borderlands. The hover bubble alit on a grassless piece of dusty dirt. In all directions, there was little to see but dry, cracked ground. Lizards and salamanders slithered through the fissures, surfacing to sun themselves on the dirty, brown rocks nestled between scant, tawny grasses.

"Here we are," announced Dr. Finnegan as the plastic bubble top slid back to allow Henry and the others to exit the hover bubble. "I wish we could give you more guidance, but we know little of what awaits you, except that you must always keep your guard. Mocarsto dominates the will of those who cannot escape him, so be careful to whom you speak. You must not betray yourself. Blend in with the crowd and find out what you can about his operations, and if possible, the location of his fortress. You don't have much time, so just gather as much information as you can. This is a reconnaissance mission only. Keep yourself from notice. If Mocarsto were to see you, he might discern who you are. The twins believe they have discovered Mr. Televangi's means of communication with Mocarsto. To be safe, they've sent word, pretending to be Televangi, saying that you're under his observation on Earth. That ruse may not hold for long, so be careful."

"We know practically nothing about where you are going," continued Dr. Finnegan, "as no one has ever returned from Cardew. You are special, though, charmed through your mother and through your very birth to resist the temptations of his powerful spell. We will wait here for you. Return as soon as the alarm clock gives you notice, for you must have time to get home before your Earth parents miss you. Your job is too important to jeopardize the mission by drawing attention to yourself at home. You have five hours. We will be here when you get back."

Henry took a few practice turns on the hover-board before he felt adept enough to control it over a distance. Luckily, the desert sands provided a soft landing, and before long, Henry was proficient enough to traverse the withered landscape into Cardew. Eulalie was excited to have a flying partner. She had never been to Sun-Rhea before, and she was not altogether sure she liked the place. The scientists were nice, but their perpetual logic and order were alien to the fairy, accustomed to the unbridled freedom and magic of the Wildlands.

Mirabel, who had been silent during the trip to the border, approached Henry and presented him with one final gift.

"What is it?" Henry asked as she pressed the small object into his hand.

"It's a lucky rabbit's foot," she replied. "It comes from a rabbit who made his own luck, but he was injured in the fight against the one you go to meet. You have magic and reason behind you, Henry. And now, you have luck. It's all I have left to give you, except for my love, my son." She bent down and kissed Henry sweetly on his forehead, causing Henry to blush. Henry bid farewell to his friends and mounted the hover-board, with Eulalie buzzing excitedly beside him.

"One more thing," Dr. Finnegan said. "Remember, no matter what, do not eat the food."

Chapter XXXV
Miles to Go

The friends found the trip to Cardew altogether too short. Henry and Eulalie enjoyed challenging each other with flying tricks and races across the desolate wasteland. The frolicking pair had so much fun that they soon forgot about their dark destination. Henry was a natural on the hover-board. Once he got used to the sensitivity of motion on a frictionless ride, he found it no more difficult than skateboarding. In fact, he could go faster and jump higher than he could on a skateboard, and landing was a breeze. He would definitely encourage his father to keep working on his version. *It would be so cool to have one of these at home!* Henry thought as he sailed effortlessly through the air. Eulalie flitted and flipped her way happily beside him, wildly free again and alive with speed and wind.

Then, like a cloud over sunshine, the ominous smokestacks of Cardew rose over the horizon. Gray smoke billowed out of gray pipes onto a cold steel backdrop of squared factories and angled buildings. Here were the drab but futuristic apartment buildings Henry had looked for in Sun-Rhea. They were modern, and they appeared efficient, but they had no color or character, only clean straight lines, lines so sharp they looked as if they could cut.

Henry slowed on the hover-board as he turned his attention toward the imposing skyline of Cardew. The front edge of the board struck a rock and stopped abruptly, while Henry's body continued onward, carried by momentum. He sailed through the air for a full two seconds before he hit the soft ground, tumbled several times, and came to rest against a low embankment.

"Henry!" screamed Eulalie. "Are you okay?"

Henry had kicked up a lot of sandy dust during his kerfuffle and he came up coughing, with grit in his eyes. "I'm alright, *cough*," he answered. "I'm okay, Eulalie."

"Ain't you gonna ask how I am?" asked a curt, irritated voice emanating from somewhere within the dust cloud.

"Who said that?" said Eulalie, squinting through the swirling dust.

"I'll be asking the questions now, if'n you don't mind," said the unidentified voice, thick with accent like a man from the old South.

The dust settled to reveal a large, long-eared rabbit. He looked strangely like the picture Henry had seen in his mother's book, complete with the torn overalls. The impact had blown his straw hat off his head and on to the embankment into which Henry had crashed.

"The rabbit!" said Henry is amazement. "I know you. I had a dream about you once. Are you real? Can you really talk?"

"Can I really talk?" squawked the rabbit, brushing dirt off his fur. "I'm talkin', ain't I?" he answered gruffly. "Hey, there sugarplum," he said to Eulalie, who bristled slightly at the uninvited endearment. "Who's this jeen-yus you brought here? Why'd you bring 'um for that matter? This ain't no place for fairies no how."

"My name is Eulalie, not sugarplum," the fairy answered curtly. "And this is Henry. He comes from Earth. And frankly, what we are doing here is none of your business."

"Very well, very well," grinned the rabbit. "No need to get your knickers in a twist. Name's Miles. Didn't mean to be rude, but you did come bustin' up on my front door and I don't recollect sendin' out any invitations."

"I'm sorry," Henry apologized. "I'm not very good at landing yet."

"Did you fly in here, Earth boy? Where's your ship then?"

"Here it is," said Eulalie, locating the hover-board underneath a sheath of sand.

"Well, look a' here now," said Miles. "What'll they think of next?"

"Excuse us, sir," said Henry. "But we're on our way to Cardew. That's it, up ahead?"

"Of course it is," said Miles. "Nothin' else around for miles, but why would you want to go there? Used to be a time when people were tryin' to get out, but not anymore. They don't even need them gates. You can walk right in, pretty as you please. Now, gettin' out's another story."

"Have you been there?" asked Henry.

"Sure, I've been there. Used to live there. Time was, it was a right nice place, but not anymore. I guess you could say I'm the one that got away."

Just then, Henry noticed that the rabbit was missing its left front paw. Henry gasped in amazement. He felt in his pocket for Mirabel's fuzzy parting gift. It was still there. He thought for a moment to ask Miles if it were his, but he decided that would be in very poor taste. Instead, he said, "If you don't mind my asking, what happened to your paw?"

The rabbit looked down at his crippled paw and was quiet for a moment. "If yer really plannin' on goin' in there, then no, I don't suppose I mind you askin'. But that don't mean I've a mind to answer. Where I come from, a fella without scars is called a coward."

"Now, if you don't mind *me* asking," continued the rabbit. "Why in the blue sky would you two want to go to Cardew fer?"

"The sky's not exactly blue anymore," said Eulalie, looking up at the ominous smoke billowing out of the giant factories.

"Well," said Henry in answer to the rabbit's question, "we are going in to stop Mocarsto from spreading his evil." As he spoke these words, he began to realize how ill prepared he was for such a grand mission. Once they got to Cardew, what were a boy and a fairy going to do in a strange and hostile land? He looked at his tiny partner with new gravity. "But I don't have any idea how."

"That's it boy," said Miles smirking a little, good-naturedly. "There's nothin' like a plan."

"Come on," said Eulalie, starting toward the smoky horizon. "We'll just have a look about. We don't have to save the world in one day. We don't even know what we're dealing with yet."

"A reconnaissance mission?" said Miles perking up his long ears. "Don't mean to offend, but you two will blend into Cardew like a pickle in the licorice. A golden fairy and a flyin' boy!"

"Why, what is it like in there?" asked Henry. "Is it as bad as the scientists say?"

"Well, I don't know anythin' about any scientists, but it's pretty bad," Miles answered. "They're all drugged-like, sedated, on account of the food."

"Hypnofood!" said Henry, remembering Dr. Finnegan's story.

"That's right," said Miles. "They're like zombies. Mocarsto assures 'em a world free from cares in return for their unquestionin' and unfalterin' devotion. They sacrifice their own wills to serve his."

"But I don't understand," said Henry. "What's in it for them?"

"A world of no surprises," said Miles. "No sickness, no worries, no bills, no sufferin'...."

"And no joy," said Eulalie.

"Now you're gettin' it," said Miles. "They work for Mocarsto in them factories, producin' the very thing that ties 'em to his yoke. The hypnofood weakens their minds; it makes 'em fools for his hogwash. Mocarsto is clever, though. His hoopla and puffery is ever'where. He never leaves 'em with a minute to doubt. They're so mixed up they trade their very self for a peaceful night's sleep and thank him for it in the mornin'. He's got 'em turned so sideways, it hurts your neck to look at 'em."

"But what does Mocarsto want?" asked Henry. "What does he want from these people?"

"No one really knows but him, I reckon," said Miles. "Looks to me like he's growin' an army. His minions are multiplyin', and it don't look as though he plans to stop anytime soon. And if'n he does manage to stamp out all free will on the face of the planet, well, I'd hate to be around to see that."

"And what about you?" inquired Eulalie. "How did you manage to remain unensnared?"

Miles shrugged his shoulders dismissively as Henry thought he caught a familiar gleam in his eye. "I'll give you one piece of good advice, though," Miles said seriously. "Don't eat the food."

Chapter XXXVI
Donegal

Without further ado, Henry and Eulalie started for Cardew. The city didn't match Henry's preconceived image of a fortress for the enslaved. As Miles had said, no walls or fences surrounded the city; rather, it sprung up out of the desert lands like a wild, errant weed. Henry had left the hover-board behind with Miles for safekeeping and made his way toward the tall buildings, shrouded by a cloud of smoke belched forth from the factories. Within minutes, he was walking along the city's clean streets lined with steel buildings, as Eulalie rode in his shirt pocket to keep out of view, poking her head out occasionally to look about her. Mirabel had been right: Cardew was a drab and dreary place. The rolling smoke clouds blotted out the warming rays of the sun and cast the scene in muted tones of shadowy gray. Still, the quiet streets were tidy and orderly.

"I wonder where all the people are," said Eulalie.

"I wonder why they don't they just walk out of here," Henry mused. There's nothing to stop them."

"There's nothing at all," agreed the small voice in his pocket. "There is no life here. Did you notice? There are no plants or flowers. Even the sun doesn't shine. Everything's the same color, too, or rather, lack of it. I don't like this place."

"I don't know," said Henry. "It doesn't seem all that bad. I mean, it's a little dreary, sure, but it doesn't seem exactly *evil*."

The two turned a corner and traveled another street packed with storefronts and eateries. The buildings were constructed of steel, some shining and new, some weatherworn and oxidized, all conveying a utilitarian purpose without adornment. A large smoking factory loomed ahead.

"Shhhh!" said Eulalie, ducking her head inside Henry's pocket. "Some people are coming!"

A throng of men and women poured forth from the factory doors and traveled en masse down the sidewalk toward Henry. The steady stream of people parted like water to flow past him. They didn't appear to notice him, even as they made way for him, but marched onward with cold, vacant eyes. Each of them wore gray coveralls with blue patches, and heavy black boots that clicked the sidewalk in eerie unison. Eulalie poked her head out of Henry's pocket for a better look. She was no longer worried someone might see her; they seemed entirely oblivious to their surroundings. As they plodded on, like blinded horse, one of them stopped and turned around—a man toward the end of the pack. He looked at Henry with a confused, almost wistful expression, as if he were trying to remember a receding dream, or hear far away music lifted on the wind.

Eulalie quickly ducked her head inside Henry's pocket, but the man gave no indication he had noticed her. Instead, he looked directly at Henry, calmly and plaintively. The man crinkled his brow and asked, almost with pain, "Do I know you?"

"I don't know," Henry answered, timidly. "You look kind of familiar to me, too."

"Well, you're here now," said the man, turning back to follow the others. He took a few steps and then turned back around. "You are coming, aren't you?"

Henry nodded and took three quick steps to catch up to him. Together they walked in silence behind the crowd, walking off into the dimming light from the sun straining behind the darkening clouds.

Henry and Eulalie followed the group through the city streets. A few of them turned at one corner, and several more at the next, until gradually the crowd thinned to only a few people who dispersed in different directions at the outskirts of town. The sun had nearly set. Henry followed the man into the shadows, away from the newly lighted streetlamps that lined the last of the paved streets. The man did not speak. The only sound came from the gravel crunching under his heavy boots.

Soon, they came upon a lone, ramshackle cabin built haphazardly in the midst of nothing. Unlike the city structures, the one room shack was made of natural wood, its knotted boards nailed together to provide a crude shelter from the elements. The small house slumped on its slanted walls, looking pitiful in the gathering dusk, just beyond the illumination of the city lights. Behind the hut, lumpy shadows closed in around deepening darkness. A strung hammock lolled between two old clothesline poles, its metal chain clanking like melancholy clockwork in the evening breeze.

The man sat heavily on a cinderblock step at the edge of the slatted porch and pulled off his work boots. He appeared relaxed as he stared dreamily into a night sky alive with the first twinklings of distant suns. He seemed unaware of Henry and Eulalie's presence only a few feet from him. Henry wanted to speak, but he hesitated. He was unsure what to say to this strangely thoughtful citizen of Cardew.

"Perhaps we should go," Henry whispered to Eulalie.

"What's that?" the man said, turning toward Henry. "Oh, where are my manners? Please stay. I will get you a seat. It's such a nice evening for a visit. Please, don't go. I'll be right back."

The man ducked into the cabin and returned with a twenty-gallon plastic bucket and a worn throw pillow. He arranged the makeshift seat and gave it a satisfied pat. "Here, you go," he said to Henry with a welcoming wave. "I know it's not much, but it's good enough, I suppose."

"Thanks," said Henry, sitting down on the bucket. They sat together in silence for some seconds before Henry decided to speak. "My name is Henry," he began by way of introduction, "and this is my friend Eulalie." Eulalie poked her yellow head out of Henry's pocket. "Pleased to make your acquaintance," she said.

"Oh, my goodness!" the man said raising one eyebrow. "I didn't realize there was a fairy in your pocket. Excuse me, ma'am." The man bowed his head slightly to Eulalie in greeting. "Please allow me to introduce myself. My name is Donegal." After a pause and an inquisitive stare like a child at a puzzle he continued, "You two must not be from around here."

"No, sir, we're, uh, we're just visiting," replied Henry.

"Hmm, don't get many visitors around here anymore," said the man. "But you are certainly welcome. I'm glad for the company. Most folks keep to themselves around here. It's easier that way, I suppose."

"Don't you have friends?" asked Eulalie as she looked around the desolate yard. "Or neighbors?"

"I like it away from the hustle and bustle of the city. Most people live in town, to be closer to work. I guess it's hard to teach an old dog new tricks. I've never been much of a mover and a shaker. I'm more of an observer, a spectator."

Henry had little difficulty believing this about Donegal. His movements were slow and methodical. His very aura seemed soaked in anesthesia.

"What about your family?" Henry said. "Do you have any family?"

Donegal looked full into Henry's face with a searching expression, as if he were trying to remember something he once knew.

"I had a family once," he began. "A wife and a son. But I lost them somewhere ... somehow ...." the man trailed off. "That was a very long time ago." He took another deep look at Henry. "Are you sure I don't know you from someplace?"

"I can't imagine from where," answered Henry thoughtfully. There was something familiar about the man, but Henry couldn't place him in his memory. "Tell me about Cardew," he continued. "Why do you stay here all alone?"

"Oh, here's not so bad," replied Donegal. "You get used to things pretty quickly. Everything's predictable and orderly. There's always enough to eat, and no one ever gets sick. All we have to do is go to work and stay out of trouble."

"What do you mean, 'stay out of trouble'?" asked Eulalie.

"You know, if you don't draw attention to yourself, then they will leave you alone."

"Who's 'they'?" Henry wondered.

Donegal looked around suspiciously and leaned in towards them. "Do you two want to see something? A secret?"

Henry and Eulalie looked at each other and nodded yes.

"Come on, around back," said Donegal. He left the rickety porch and led his guests into the shadows behind the shack. Old scrap metal and rusting junk littered the yard. A dilapidated refrigerator with the door torn off sat full of cogs and wheels from dead machines. Corroded blades from a large tiller lay on the ground. Old abandoned tires and tarnished wire amassed in a rotting, rusting pile. Donegal led them around to the other side of the scrap heap to show his new friends his treasured secret. Among the junk, cleverly hidden from view, a neat little garden struggled for life.

"Root vegetables, mainly," explained Donegal. "These are potatoes and carrots; over here are beets and turnips, and on the far end are onions and radishes. Root vegetables seem to thrive here. Plus, they are difficult to spy since they grow mainly underground. Outside food is strictly forbidden, and I want to follow the rules." Donegal let out a big sigh. "I don't know why, but I can't seem to let go of this garden. This little patch of tubers makes me feel ... peaceful, somehow."

Henry looked at the sparse sprigs of green growing up between cracks in the rotted, rusting trash and thought of his mother's radiant flowers in the Garden. Donegal's garden was certainly not beautiful, but here, in the midst of this depressing landscape of cast-off rubbish and eternal gray, the struggling patch did possess a certain charm, some promise of life hidden beneath the dirt.

"Oh, bother," said Donegal, digging into the soil of his secret garden.

"What is it?" asked Henry and Eulalie together.

"That blasted rabbit's been in my garden again."

Chapter XXXVII
A Cautionary Tale

"What's it like in Cardew, anyway?" said Henry as Donegal worked to repair his violated plot of meager vegetables. "I mean, what do you do all day?"

"Same as other folks, I guess," said Donegal. "We work and eat and sleep and live ordinary lives."

"What do you do for fun?" asked Eulalie with a mischievous glint in her eye. She was eager for tales of adventure and amusement. She decidedly didn't care for Donegal's dismal trash pit of a backyard.

"Well, there's television to help pass the time," Donegal sighed. "And on Saturdays we go to Affirmation."

"What is Affirmation?" asked Henry.

"Oh, you know, when we all get together and remind ourselves how this is the best of all possible worlds and how lucky we are for Mocarsto's wisdom so that he may protect us against the tumult of confusion and unhealthy urges." Donegal rattled the sentence like a litany.

Eulalie and Henry cut sidewise glances at each other in response to Donegal's monologue. Henry had liked Donegal almost immediately. He was drawn to the man for some reason, but listening to him prattle on like a programmed robot was creepy.

"Affirmation used to be led by that nice little man ... now, what was his name?" Donegal wondered aloud. "Oh, I know, it's Televangi—Mr. Televangi. He hasn't been there these past few weeks. There's a new fellow now. I wonder what's happened to him."

Mr. Televangi! thought Henry as he and Eulalie exchanged a knowing look.

Looking down at Donegal's paltry garden, Henry's stomach started to rumble with hunger. He figured it must be past his regular lunchtime, even though it was well into the evening hours in Cardew. It was difficult to keep track of time when he traveled through so many worlds, all in separate time zones, or "temporal planes," as Mr. Waddleman had put it. Donegal heard Henry's stomach growling and apologized to his guests. "Please, let me make you some food. I have several cans still left from rations day. I don't eat as much the others do. Sometimes I forget. And after all, I have my garden to supplement."

"No thanks," said Henry. "We are fine, really. We don't want to impose on your hospitality any longer. We should be going."

"Going?" asked Donegal. "Where would you be going at this hour? Besides, there is the curfew. You cannot be out on the streets after nightfall. That would be disorderly conduct. They don't like it when you break the rules."

"Who is this 'they' you keep referring to?" asked Eulalie.

"Oh, I forget you don't know. I mean the Patrols, the men with the tasers, those whose job it is to protect us from outsiders and reprimand the wayward. If they catch you breaking the rules, they will take you away. Some say they take you to see Mocarsto himself, the great father, who teaches his errant children the wisdom of his rule."

"What does he do to them?" asked Henry, wide-eyed.

"No one knows for sure, but when they come back, they never break the rules again. I knew a young boy once, who liked to paint pictures on the old brick walls. He was stubborn. Mocarsto had banned all false images, but still the boy would sneak out at night to paint on the run-down buildings. I was his friend, so I counseled him to stop his nighttime excursions. He said he could not resist the pictures in his mind. He said he had to get them out of his head, or else they would explode in there, taking his brain with them. He suffered with it," Donegal said with sorrow.

"The boy was taken to the Black Fort," he continued, "and he never suffered again. Mocarsto was right to free us from the pain of our own minds."

"How can that be so?" asked Eulalie. "Suffering is a part of all life. In fact, it's a necessary part. Death itself makes life meaningful."

"You praise death! You sound like someone who has never known it!" Donegal said with some warmth. Henry was surprised by the sudden display of emotion in the hitherto taciturn man. "Televangi is right; life and love are man's destroyers. Love is a false idol sacrificed on death's insatiable altar. There is only one worthwhile desire: to be free from desire, free from pain, free from will. Only then will death cease."

Donegal stopped, arrested by the awareness of his rising temper. He hung his head and quietly shook it. "I, I don't remember what I was saying. I'm going inside now. I need to eat something, maybe watch some television ..."

Donegal trailed off as he slumped back toward his piteous shack. The man looked as broken as the hovel he lived in.

"I wonder what happened to him," said Henry, taken aback by Donegal's sudden outburst.

"I don't know," said Eulalie. "But I'm guessing it was bad."

"Well, what do we do now?" asked Henry.

"Let's get out of here, for one thing," answered Eulalie. "We will find Miles and see if he knows of a safe place to rest while you check in at home."

Chapter XXXVIII
Hunted

Henry woke up in the infirmary at school. He checked the wall clock, barely visible in the darkened room. *Good*, he thought. *It's 2:30. I still have half an hour before baseball practice.*

Henry decided to find Mr. Waddleman to tell him he was back and well. He found him in his office, along with Ms. Engle, Jon and Jen, who were all were happy to see Henry had come home safely from his first excursion to Cardew. Henry related as many details as he could remember about his adventure. Jon and Jen were to make a full report to the scientists later that evening. Henry told them about the steel and the factories, Donegal and the Patrols. He told them about Miles and the rabbit's burrow in the stretch of land somewhere between Cardew and the Federation, where his body and Eulalie rested.

Henry grabbed an apple out of his unopened lunch sack and raced off to change for baseball practice. He desired normalcy after the whirlwind of events these past few days. He changed out of his jeans and t-shirt, and placed the alarm clock and Mirabel's miniature world of Annwyn on top of his clothes in his gym locker. Then he headed out to play ball with his friends.

Kyle and Tommy were surprised to see Henry. He hadn't been in class since first period when Ms. Engle had sent him to the assistant principal's office. They wondered about Henry when he wasn't around at lunchtime and assumed some sort of family affair called him home. Henry somewhat clumsily explained that he was called out of class for a special science project. It was not exactly a lie, but Henry felt uneasy about keeping such a giant secret from his friends and family. He eagerly took his position in the outfield to avoid his teammates' questioning looks.

Henry played hard and enjoyed himself. He felt release in exercise and a sense of achievement from a familiar pastime at which he was skilled. Henry could anticipate where the ball would fall as it arced in response to the angle of the pitch and the response of the batter. He could gauge to whom and how quickly he needed to throw the ball into the infield based upon a split-second assessment of the runner's speed and the distance to home plate. The game moved in slow motion as Henry keenly focused on all the elements that informed his instantaneous decisions. He felt his perceptions heighten, as if he were seeing common everyday happenings on a deeper, more intricate level.

Henry recalled the time his father explained the geometry behind the game of pool. His father taught him to envision the trajectory of the pool ball on its way to the pocket. He explained the ball's reaction to the angle and force of the strike against the bank wall. As Henry learned to think through the action and reaction of the balls as they made contact with the cue, the bank wall, and each other, his pool game improved. Henry recited Newton's third law of motion: "For every action, there is an equal and opposite reaction." This same logic applied to baseball and many other things, too.

Henry lingered after practice to talk to Tommy and Kyle about what he had missed in school. They told him there was going to be a quiz on Wednesday about calculating areas, perimeters and circumferences. Luckily, Henry was good in math, but he would need to brush up on the subject. The boys also related that they had witnessed a fight in the cafeteria during lunch. Mr. Kent had to break it up. Other than that, it had been an uneventful day at Colonial Heights Middle School.

Henry left his friends, grabbed his gym bag from his locker, and started for home. As he was leaving the schoolyard, he ran into Jon and Jen.

"Hey Henry," said Jen cheerfully. "Glad we found you. Do you mind if we walk you home? We want to make sure we have all the information we need to report back to the scientists."

"Sure," Henry agreed. "But there's not much more to tell. I only talked to the one person."

"Yeah," said Jon. "Tell us more about him. The scientists made it sound like Cardew was full of drooling zombies. Your guy doesn't sound that bad. We thought this hypnofood made people totally zonked."

"Well, he was a little," replied Henry. "Only, he did mention that he didn't always eat the hypnofood. He has a little secret garden in the back of his house. Maybe that's the reason he's more lucid than the others. He was the only one that spoke to us. I think he was the only one who noticed us."

"Hmmm," said Jon. "That could be useful information. Tell us anything you can remember. Sometimes the tiniest details are the most important."

Henry nodded in agreement, but he had a question of his own: "The scientists said that you found how Mr. Televangi sends messages to Mocarsto," he said.

"Yeah," said Jen. We followed him, so we know where he is staying. We saw him send a communication. He was tapping on a machine like a telegraph. Obviously, he's not familiar with the code because he had a cheat sheet in front of him the whole time."

"Fortunately for us, he left the code sitting out," explained Jen. "When he left, we made a copy for ourselves and made a few changes to his."

"So now, only our messages will make sense," added Jon. "When Televangi sends something it will be a bunch of gobbledygook. Mocarsto will assume something is wrong with the transmission. We sent an intelligible one to say that everything's fine and that you're minding your own business here on Earth."

"How does that machine work, anyway?" asked Henry. "How can Televangi communicate with Mocarsto, but Mr. Waddleman and Ms. Engle can't get a message back? It seems like the scientists would have figured that out by now."

"We asked that same question," said Jon. "The scientists are looking into it. However, Dr. Finnegan says he has had some luck identifying the frequency between Sun-Rhea and Earth. The link was always there or else you wouldn't have been able to bilocate here as an infant."

"Dr. Finnegan says that the frequency has gotten much stronger lately," said Jen. "Apparently when you began traveling back and forth to Sun-Rhea, you strengthened the amplitude of the frequency, sort of like wearing a path into the forest floor. Soon after your first trip, Mr. Televangi showed up, right? Mocarsto must have sensed the growing connection between the worlds and found a frequency with which to communicate with him. We still don't know how he got here in the first place, though."

"We assume he took a wormhole," said Jon, "like Waddleman and Engle. Mocarsto has the resources to open a wormhole, but even he lacks the power to sustain it for long."

As the three turned the corner to Henry's street, Jon and Jen stopped abruptly and turned, sniffing the air in the direction of a large oak tree. From the corner of his eye, Henry saw a short, squat man conceal himself behind its trunk.

"Mr. Televangi!" he said with surprise.

Behind him, Henry heard growling, soon followed by a rush of blurry fur. Jon and Jen in their animal forms leapt at the crouching figure on the other side of the oak. Mr. Televangi scrambled up the side of the tree and climbed onto the first branch as the cheetah clawed its way up the thick trunk and the wolf waited below for his prey to fall within his reach.

A loud yelp rang out as the cheetah slid down the tree trunk, her claws digging into the bark. A tranquilizer dart was stuck in her side and she was losing consciousness. Mr. Televangi grinned above her, holding the rifle in his sweaty hands. The cheetah limped past Henry toward a thicket, followed by the wolf, yet unhurt. Mr. Televangi raised his rifle again and took aim at the wolf. Henry heard a loud, quick *phewph* as the dart whooshed and struck its target with a thunk. But Jon had escaped after all. Henry felt the quick sting of the dart, followed by desperate fatigue as he fainted in a heap on his neighbor's lawn.

The commotion brought several people to their front doors, Henry's mother among them. She had arrived home only a few moments earlier. She was upstairs changing out of her work clothes when she heard an animal yelp in pain across the street. She looked out of the bedroom window to see her young son prone on the ground and a creepy man approaching him with a rifle in his hands. Her maternal instincts raging, she bounded down the stairs three at a time and rushed out the front door and across the street. Her intensity frightened Mr. Televangi, who scurried off through the same bushes through which Jon and Jen had disappeared. He hated to leave his prize behind, but there would be other chances. Mr. Televangi rightfully surmised that he would be no match against this mother protecting her son.

Mrs. Harris immediately noticed the animal tranquilizer dart that pierced Henry's upper outer thigh. She pulled it out and read the information printed on its outer casing. She checked Henry's vitals and found he didn't seem to be in distress. The drug had knocked him out, that was certain, but she didn't suppose there would be any toxic effect. She speculated that an animal control worker meant to shoot the wild animal she heard earlier and mistakenly shot Henry instead. Apparently, he was afraid of getting into trouble so he ran away once people had gathered. She could definitely fault the man for his cowardice, but her gentle heart imagined that the man had been coming to check on the boy, and he had only fled once he knew Henry would have help. As the adage goes, it takes one to know one. Mrs. Harris didn't recognize, behind his yellowing eyes, the predator hunting her only child.

Mrs. Harris called a doctor friend who lived nearby. Thankfully, he was home and agreed to come right over to check on Henry. He advised her not to move him until he could ascertain any injuries. She next called Henry's father to come home from the shop. A growing crowd of neighbors collected around Henry's sleeping form as the story traveled to the newcomers, gaining embellishment with each telling.

The doctor arrived and confirmed that the tranquilizer was non-toxic to humans and the dosage was moderate enough to cause the young boy no harm. However, it would leave Henry unconscious for the better part of the night. He sustained no injuries in the fall, and he would be fine once he was able to sleep off the effects of the drug. Henry's father arrived, carried the boy up to his bedroom, and settled him into his bed for a long night's sleep.

His parents called the local animal control authorities and were frustrated to find there was no record of wild animals loose in their area, or an employee by the description given by Mrs. Harris. However, his wife's portrayal of the man who shot their son sparked a sense of recognition in Mr. Harris.

"That sounds like the weird little man who came to the shop last week," he told his wife. The two spent the remainder of the evening speculating on who the strange man could be and why he would shoot their son with a tranquilizer dart. One theory was that he was an animal trainer with the circus whose animals had gotten loose. That story would explain some things. Or, perhaps he was a foreigner from some distant land who brought illegal exotic pets to this country. If he knew that owning them was against the law, it could explain why he had fled the scene and failed to report their escape to the proper authorities. Mr. and Mrs. Harris spent hours inventing plausible stories to explain the day's events, but they never got very close to the truth. Instead, they settled on the most innocuous version of an unintended unfortunate accident that left their son injected with a harmless animal tranquilizer. He would enjoy a deep slumber and wake up refreshed with no real harm done. In the end, we all believe what we want to believe.

Chapter XXXIX
One in a Million, or a Million to One?

"Eulalie!" Henry whispered loudly in the darkness of the rabbit's burrow. He couldn't distinguish anything in the blackness that surrounded him. The smell and feel of fresh dirt reminded him where he was.

"Eulalie!" he said again a little louder. "Are you here?"

A light sputtered in the darkness as Eulalie lighted her wings, casting shadows down the narrow earthen corridors of Miles's underground home. Eulalie rubbed her eyes and said, "I was sleeping, thanks very much. What are you doing back here so soon? I didn't expect you for a few more hours. Did we get it wrong? Is it night back on Earth already?"

"I don't know," answered Henry. "I don't remember going to bed. I don't remember trying to come back here." Henry closed his eyes and leaned his head against the dirt wall trying to recall what had happened.

"I remember now," he explained after a moment. "It was Mr. Televangi; he shot me with some sort of dart. It made me sleep."

"Why would he shoot you with a dart?" asked Eulalie.

"I don't know, really," sighed Henry. "I wasn't doing anything but walking home with the twins. Why would he want to shoot me? Why does it matter what some kid does, anyway?" Henry was agitated, understandably so, having been shot through with an incapacitating poison. The attack, painful and personal, took a toll on his untried innocence and made him doubt his ability to face such evil.

"Mocarsto is building an empire, and it's full of people who don't even want to leave," he complained. "He is some great powerful magician. How am I possibly a threat to him? If he wants to take over Sun-Rhea, what can an eleven-year-old boy do to stop him? Everyone keeps saying I'm some "chosen one" from some "legend" that's supposed to somehow be able to defeat Mocarsto. It doesn't make any sense. How could I make a difference?"

"But Henry," said Eulalie earnestly. "You *are* the only one who can make a difference. You *are* the one of legend. You *are* the child of Sun-Rhea, born in the Wildlands. You *are* born of the marriage between magic and reason. *You* are the one, Henry."

"The one what?" asked Henry dejectedly. "I mean, really. What are the odds that a great evil stronghold that took years in the making will be felled by one kid?"

"Henry," said Eulalie softly. "The odds don't matter, when *you* are the one in a million."

"Don't mean to interrupt," said Miles, hopping down the hollowed-out hallway in his nightcap and dressing gown. "But that's what *yer* doin'—interruptin' my rest. It's the middle of the night. Why don't y'all go on home and come back in the mornin' like proper guests?"

"I don't think I can," Henry answered. "I don't know what Mr. Televangi shot me with, but I don't think I can wake up at home right now. I think that's why I came here."

"Mr. who? Shot you with what, now?" asked Miles, suddenly alert.

"Some lackey of Mocarsto's is loose on Earth and hunting for Henry," explained Eulalie.

"Armed enemy combatants on the offensive!" exclaimed Miles. "Well, then, we don't have any time to lose. What's the plan then, Henry? A covert operation or a direct attack?"

"I don't know," said Henry, a little concerned by the options Miles just presented.

"I think it's time fer you to meet the enemy," said Miles.

"How do we do that?" asked Eulalie. "Walk up to his castle and knock on the door?"

"Kind of," answered Henry. "We could just stroll back into town. It's past curfew. Donegal said the Patrols arrest people who break the rules. He said that maybe they take them to see Mocarsto. At this hour, I don't think we'll need a can of spray paint to get noticed."

"But Henry," objected Eulalie. "Won't he know it's you? Mocarsto wants nothing more than to destroy you. You can't just walk right up to him."

"He won't know it's me," said Henry, reassuringly. "Jon and Jen will send a message, pretending to be Mr. Televangi. They'll verify that I'm still on Earth. It'll be enough to stall him, anyway. I'll pretend to be from the village in Ermintrude Dell."

"What about me?" asked Eulalie.

"Well, you're a fairy who wandered in from the Wildlands. We, both of us, are searching for a better place. We'll say that word of Mocarsto's "commune" has spread far and we teamed up to travel to Cardew to join it."

"I don't know," said Miles shaking his head, "if he buys that, I've got a chocolate teapot he can have real cheap."

Chapter XL
Looking for Trouble

Henry and Eulalie entered Cardew by the same route they had taken earlier that afternoon. All was quiet along the city streets—eerily so. Not even the sound of crickets broke the uncomfortable silence. No sounds of traffic or television sets disturbed the stillness of the night; no din of conversation indicated the presence of human life. All signs of the city's inhabitants were absent, shut up somewhere inside the steel apartments. Cardew was a heavily populated ghost town. A shiver ran up Henry's spine as he felt the void in this cold steel place. Even the Land of Echoes had more life; these people were paler shades than ghosts.

Henry and Eulalie walked deeper into the heart of the city, past the factory where Donegal worked. The cold, motionless machines glinted in the moonlight, lifeless as the inhabitants of the vacant, hopeless town. No one and nothing stirred. A deathlike stillness chilled the stale air. Not even the wind dared to blow. A few small shops, vacant and dark, nestled between the apartment buildings. Henry cupped his hands around his eyes and peered through the windows of a café. Through the glass, he saw the dull silver of steel and aluminum formed into stools, tables, and napkin dispensers. He found the door and tried the knob, and was surprised to find it unlocked. He entered cautiously, leaving the door open behind him. The moonlight, met by the angular efficiency of the café's interior, cast long shadows across the floors and up the walls creating menacing sharp-cornered specters who attended his every movement.

"Look at this, Eulalie," said Henry as he rummaged through bins and shelves arranged in a row like a school cafeteria. He held up a can and read the label: *"Hypnofood: The Happy Food for Happy People."*

"Hmmm, not much of a slogan," Henry continued. "I wouldn't say people exactly seemed happy around here. You'd think he'd call it something else, but I suppose if they're that out of it, it doesn't really matter ...."

"Ummmm, Henry," Eulalie interrupted.

"I mean, they don't seem *unhappy*," Henry continued, thinking aloud, oblivious to Eulalie tugging on his shirtfront. "They don't seem much of anything—it's like they don't even notice what's going on around them ...."

"Henry, look!" said Eulalie loud enough to get Henry's attention. She was pointing toward the doorway, where there stood two large, imposing men wearing official-looking uniforms and heavy police batons on their belts. They stomped into the cafeteria and approached Henry and Eulalie menacingly.

"Good evening, neighbors," said the taller of the two in a pleasantly deep, yet authoritative voice. "How do you happen to be out at this hour? It's well past curfew. All citizens should be home at rest."

The Patrols' imposing presence and obvious strength intimidated Henry. His first instinct was to be obedient and avoid trouble, but he knew he needed to cause a scene so that they might take him to Mocarsto. It would have to be good, too, to make it all the way up to the head honcho. But then he didn't want to get beat up either. Henry thought fast. He knew freedom of expression was discouraged in Cardew. His mind raced as he sought the most offensive, horrible thing he could possibly do in this dismal, predictable world.

Henry jumped up on a sturdy table, gave a big Broadway smile, and belted out a song that echoed against the steel walls:

Somewhere over the rainbow

Way up high

There's a land that I heard of

Once in a lullaby

Somewhere over the rainbow,

Skies are blue,

And the dreams that you dare to dream

Really do come true

If happy little bluebirds fly

Above the rainbow

Why, oh why

Can't I?

Henry added a most expressive dance to his heartfelt rendition of "Over the Rainbow." In the stress of the situation, he could only remember some of the lyrics even though he had seen the Wizard of Oz at least ten times. It was enough, though, to produce the desired effect. As Henry sang, the Patrols winced as if he had released a string of obscenities. They pressed their hands to their ears once Henry hit the very high, and in this rendition, very overdramatic final note.

"Looks like we've got a troublemaker," said one of the Patrols.

"He's not in uniform, either" replied the other. "He must be off his nutrient solution. I've seen this before."

"What should we do with him?"

"Let's bring him to the boss. He takes a personal interest in the loony toons. He likes trying to figure out what makes 'em tick."

The two men grabbed Henry roughly and pushed him toward the door with their batons.

"I'll go quietly," Henry assured them. One of the thrusting batons had come uncomfortably close to squishing Eulalie as she cowered in Henry's front pocket.

Henry walked solemnly between the two Patrols as they led him through the silent city streets, past more factories and apartment buildings. Henry fought the urge to bolt. To his surprise, the Patrols didn't guard him closely. He got the feeling they wanted him to run. Their lackadaisical attitude made him suspicious and a little nervous, but he kept his mind focused on the ultimate goal.

After a few minutes of walking, the buildings thinned and an enormous mansion loomed into view. Mocarsto's palace was the length of a city block, its color of the deepest black. Gold plate, and red, glimmering jewels adorned the entire structure. A black onyx staircase, reminiscent of an old government building, spanned the main entrance. Solid gold snakes with ruby eyes and tongues slithered down massive black marble columns. The ornate ostentation of the edifice stood in contrast to the sleek silver city beyond. Behind the structure, a swift black river churned—its current weighty as though after a heavy rain. The air smelled of river water. Unlike the city borders, the palace was heavily gated and guarded. A spiky-topped black iron gate ran the length of the building. Armed men stood at attention along its perimeter, whether to keep people out or to keep people in, Henry was unsure. As the Patrols escorted him up the marble staircase and the heavy black gate clanked noisily behind him, Henry began to fear it was the latter.

Chapter XLI
The Black Fort

The Patrols prodded Henry and Eulalie through the colossal main doors. Beyond, a large entry hall led into a magnificent great room that shone with radiant opulence. The intensely black marble floors melted across the threshold into a creamy swirl of charcoal and white. A grand staircase flanked the left side and led upward to a balcony hall lined with gold railings. Life-sized statues, suits of armor, and other battle dress stood in recesses along the outer wall.

"Wow," whispered Henry. "This is a pretty nice place."

"Aye," Eulalie agreed. "But it's a little severe. It could use a woman's touch."

"Quiet!" barked one of the Patrols. The company crossed the marble floor as the black and gray swirls melted into a softer palette of gray and white. Another set of great doors swung open and Henry could see that, beyond this threshold, the floor turned a pure, radiant white. The shining whiteness and the reflecting gold produced a beautiful effect in the softened light.

"That is beautiful stone," admitted Eulalie, admiring the floor. "'Tis the first pretty thing I've seen since we got here!"

"Enter!" instructed the tall Patrol who did most of the talking. "He will see you now."

Henry and Eulalie walked timidly into the white room. The red and gold theme was still in play, but an almost impossible whiteness replaced the absolute blackness of the outer walls. The absence of hue in the floor and walls produced a strange swimming sensation, as if there was no point of reference to gain one's bearings. Henry's eyes sought the natural focus. In the center of the room atop a plush red carpet fringed with tassels spun from pure gold rose a great throne at least twelve feet tall. The beauty and richness of the room awed Henry, but Eulalie refused to be impressed.

"It looks like he's overcompensating, if you ask me," she whispered in Henry's ear.

The man himself was dressed simply, yet elegantly, in loose, flowing robes. He reminded Henry of an ancient Eastern prince. Even Eulalie had to confess he was extremely handsome. Mocarsto was not the image of evil that Henry had envisioned. He possessed an air of civility that was notably absent from his henchman, Televangi. As Mocarsto spoke, his words and manner did not belie their first impression.

"Welcome friends," he said to Henry and Eulalie, nodding to each in turn. "Please, be seated," he said, gesturing to two large overstuffed pillows that had been brought in by some guards. Mocarsto nodded to the Patrols and dismissed them graciously.

When the three were alone in the great white room, Mocarsto continued: "I understand that you were caught in violation of the curfew." His voice was rich and velvety like the blood red carpet under his feet.

"Now, I would like to give you the opportunity to explain before the appropriate corrective measures are decided upon."

Henry and Eulalie looked at each other wide-eyed, wondering what to say. After an awkward moment, Mocarsto broke the silence by saying, "It is unusual to see a fairy in these parts." Mocarsto spoke slowly and deliberately and both Henry and Eulalie's hearts quickened from the sense of power and knowledge he conveyed. Henry wondered if Mocarsto already knew everything and was only testing their reactions. He was afraid to lie to this imposing man, yet he knew the truth would condemn them both. His mind raced as he sought words that wouldn't ring false along the magnificent white walls. Eulalie was unusually tongue-tied as well. They had made no plan, for they had no idea what to expect. Henry regretted their poor preparation.

Mocarsto rose and walked toward the pair, forcing them to turn their gaze upward to look at him. "Perhaps," he began, "you are new to town?"

This seemed a plausible story to Henry so he nodded. He was content for now to let Mocarsto do the talking.

"Hmmmm," said Mocarsto, thoughtfully sizing up his guests. "It is rare that we get visitors. But of course, you are most welcome." Here Mocarsto flashed a dazzling smile that sent an odd chill up Henry's spine.

"Of course, Cardew is an orderly society, and we do have rules here, of which you have been found in violation," he continued. "And you were caught singing a song, no less. It is clear you are unfamiliar with our ways. Do tell me, what brings you here to our humble village? Neither of you are from Cardew, that much is clear. A child of Sun-Rhea, if I'm not mistaken," he said, looking at Henry. Then, turning to Eulalie, he continued, "who has grown friendly with the fairy folk. Unusual, indeed." Mocarsto paused for several long seconds before continuing, "As a matter of fact, I have been looking for a particular child, recently from Earth. Perhaps, you could be him? That might better explain your choice of companions."

Henry's eyes grew wide with fright, but he managed to keep his voice from shaking when he said, "No, sir. I came from across the desert, from Ermintrude Dell. I met Eulalie there. She also had heard of your world free of cares. We came because we wanted to join you. We've heard of the happiness you promise your people and we want to be happy too." Henry gulped, hoping that he had not gone too far.

"Is that so?" said Mocarsto, silently processing Henry's answer. Televangi surely would have notified him if he lost track of the boy on Earth. No, much more likely the child was a little soft in the head. The Patrols did say he was singing, after all. Could he be daft enough to have found the way to the Wildlands and befriend a fairy? Or, perhaps, the Federation had become desperate enough to send its children into his lair, equipped with the tiniest of chaperones. The pairing of fairy and mortal was daunting in either case, suggesting some alliance between two of his foes. In any case, it hardly mattered. The outcome would be the same no matter what the case: the boy and his friend would never leave Cardew. Whoever they are, whatever their aim, he will grant their stated wish to join his ranks.

"It could not be that the Federation has sent in two small spies to infiltrate our peaceful village?" said Mocarsto, gauging the reaction of his newest guests. "No, indeed, I would not like to think that."

"No sir," Henry said. He couldn't think of anything else to say, so he sat mutely, waiting for Mocarsto to take the lead.

Mocarsto smiled warily at Henry and Eulalie. "So, your reason and science are not enough for you, boy?" he asked. "And you, fairy. You too have become disenchanted with the wild ways?"

Eulalie had no words either, but she nodded silently. Henry thought she looked mesmerized by Mocarsto's mere presence and he wondered why her fiery spirit had so completely abandoned her.

Mocarsto turned from the two and spoke as if addressing the wall. "Very well," he said. "It is true that I can offer you a happiness unparalleled in your worlds. But you must obey the rules. You must obey *me*. I will not allow insubordination. I will not abide chaos." He turned suddenly on his heels as if to catch the pair unawares and narrowed his handsome, dark eyes. "You will stay here and be my guests. I will give you time to learn our ways and to unlearn the futile yet persistent hope of your previous primitive existence."

"Guards!" yelled Mocarsto, startling Henry and Eulalie with his abruptness. The two men who had brought in the pillows appeared at the doorway.

"Take our guests to their new underground accommodations," he instructed with a suggestion of malicious irony in his smooth voice.

As the guards took Henry and Eulalie in hand and led them toward a side door, Mocarsto spoke casually but with particular emphasis. "And just so you know," he drawled pleasantly, "if in fact you are spies, your mission has just failed." Henry returned Mocarsto's penetrating gaze as his blood turned to ice in his veins.

Chapter XLII
Prisoners

The guards led the prisoners—for there was now no doubt that was what they were—out of the room through a side exit. As the door swung closed behind them, a dingy gloom replaced the cheery brightness of the grand white room. The faint flickering of a distant fire offered the only light. The friends found themselves in an old stone corridor. In one direction, the passageway wound snakily into the deepening shadow, and in the other, it disappeared down a spiral stone staircase. The staircase reminded Henry of tales of gallant knights and gothic frights. He knew, with certainty, the staircase would coil into darkness and the inevitable dungeon below.

Finding himself in an environment so altered, Henry could hardly believe the brilliant white room lay just on the other side of the heavy stone door. He felt a world away from where he had just been only a moment before. Eulalie, however, benefitted from the change of scenery. She was more in her element in these strange shadows than in the dazzling white chambers of the charming, dark man. The guards escorted the pair down the staircase, and to the expected prison cell, complete with cot and crude plumbing. The standard bars were wide enough for Eulalie to fit through, so a large birdcage had been brought in to accommodate her. Eulalie suffered a severe indignity as the guards shoved her roughly inside and locked the tiny door.

To Henry and Eulalie's relief, the guards returned immediately up the stairs without even a word to their prisoners. The friends were glad to be alone so they could formulate an escape plan.

Eulalie's blunt eloquence returned to her suddenly and completely in a stream of obscenity-laden curses for their absent jailors.

"I hate this place!" pouted Eulalie, crossing her arms petulantly. "I cannot abide a cage! This simply will not do!"

"Don't worry, Eulalie," Henry said, trying to calm her down. "We'll get out of here."

"Well, maybe you can," she sighed. "You can bilocate back to your other body, but a fairy's magic doesn't thrive in a pen."

"It's alright, Eulalie," Henry comforted. He sensed her anxiety and knew he would feel the same way if he were as trapped as she was. At least he could bilocate back to Earth where his other body was, even if only for a little while.

"I don't think I can bilocate now," Henry continued. "I'm not sure, but I feel like I can't go back yet. Whatever Televangi shot me with must be strong. I don't think I can wake up yet, so let's make a plan for when I can. I'll find Jon and Jen and have them report to the scientists. They should know what to do next. I'll bring food back for you. You mustn't eat the food here."

"But what will I do when you're away?"

"I don't know ... rest?

"But what if they come for us and you're still away?"

"Now, don't get upset, but I think the plan is to leave us down here for a while. The charm Mirabel put over me will make it look like I'm sleeping. I'll try not to stay away long. If you need me, call for me. Maybe I will hear you."

"And maybe you won't," pouted Eulalie. Captivity did not at all suit the young fairy.

The two sat quietly for a while in the silence of the dungeon, breathing in the scent of the river water that seeped through the stones. The sound and smell of water rushing somewhere outside the cellar walls helped Eulalie feel connected to the wild, natural world beyond her dank prison. Henry kept her company until she fell asleep in the straw at the bottom of her cage. Then Henry, too, slept and dreamt of places he had never before been.

Henry woke with a start. The bright morning light streamed through his bedroom curtains cheerfully. "I'm home," he thought with relief. "What day is it … Tuesday?" Traveling between worlds made it difficult to keep the days straight.

Henry got dressed and went downstairs to breakfast. After another series of his mother's homemade medical tests, she cleared him to go to school. However, she would not allow him to walk the five blocks by himself. Luckily, Jon and Jen arrived just in time to save him from the confinement of the school bus. The thought of his other body lying in the cramped cell in Cardew made him relish the thought of a nice morning walk. Mrs. Harris agreed to let Henry walk the few blocks to school with his friends.

Jen had also recently recovered from the effects of the tranquilizer dart. Jon had pulled her limp body into a thicket and watched over her throughout the night. Mr. Televangi had made a couple of angry adversaries after yesterday's attack. Jon vowed revenge on the man who dared to draw a gun on his twin sister. Jen's animosity toward Mocarsto's toady had also reached new heights, fueled by the personal affront of finding a poisoned projectile in her rear end.

Henry filled the twins in on all that had transpired in Cardew. Jon and Jen promised to relay the message to the scientists and return with their advice. Henry attended his morning classes as usual and tried to downplay the rumors of circus animals and a mad lion tamer on the loose. At lunch, he got a tray of food from the cafeteria and slipped into the infirmary to check on Eulalie.

Bilocation got easier each time he tried it. Mirabel had been right: he struck a resonance with the Annwyn, and that made traveling the worlds easier somehow, as if he were in control of the experience, and not merely at the mercy of some mysterious force.

Now, he was conscious and cognizant of the trip, whereas before he simply woke up at the new destination. Henry sensed their presence as he traded bodies across space and time. They produced a low humming sound and everything seemed to slow down. Once the Annwyn matched the designated frequency, Henry felt as if he were riding on top of a slowly undulating wave, watching space and time stretch out before him in a controlled infinity.

Henry traveled to Cardew and back before the bell rang for English class. Not surprisingly, he found Eulalie bored and irritable. She had had no visitors except for the guards who brought her a little cup of hypnofood, which lay untouched on the floor of her cage. A larger, covered plate sat at the foot of Henry's bed. The charm had worked and they believed Henry to be sound asleep. Eulalie was grateful for the food Henry had brought and he left her in tolerable spirits. He promised to return that evening with word from the scientists on what they should do next.

Chapter XLIII
Guilty

Henry did his best to enjoy a normal day at home, which was not easy considering the circumstances. The neighborhood was abuzz with the goings-on from yesterday. As luck would have it, the circus was in town and the local authorities were harassing its officials, suspecting their complicity in the unleashing of wild animals and errant trainers onto the community. Henry, of course, knew this was not the case, but he could see no way to tell the truth, at least, not now—not even to his parents. For one thing, he wouldn't know where to begin, nor did he have the time it would take to explain the complicated adventures of the past few days.

Mostly, Henry felt guilty about Eulalie. He was sure she was miserable trapped in her cage all alone, but he knew he could do more good here, where his body was at liberty, than confined along with her. He chided himself that he should never have taken her into Cardew with him. She didn't have the same abilities to bilocate as he did. In his defense, though, he hadn't known what to expect. Besides, he didn't think he could do any of this without her. She was Eulalie, after all. Henry suspected she wasn't scared of anything. She would be all right without him. Nevertheless, he promised himself that he would make it up to her; he would get her out of that prison and never let anyone hurt her again.

After dinner, Henry saw Jon and Jen through the front window, coming up the walk toward his house.

"Mom, I'm going outside to play for a while," said Henry.

"Just for a little while," his mother answered. "It is a school night. Besides, for all we know, those animals are still on the loose. Stay near the house!"

"Okay, Mom!" Henry yelled as he ran out the front door to greet his friends.

"So, what's up?" Henry asked as they sat down on the porch. "Did you talk to the scientists?"

"Yes," said the twins in unison.

"They said to wait it out as best you can," said Jon. "See if you can get another audience with Mocarsto. Any information you can get about his plans will help them know better how to fight him."

"No one has ever returned from Cardew," said Jen. "You are the only one who has been on the inside and returned, or been able to return, to report."

"Or the only one who wanted to get out," said Jon.

"That's not entirely true," thought Henry, thinking of Miles. "There is always an exception."

"But you must not let Mocarsto figure out who you are," said Jen. "That would be very dangerous. Keep him thinking you're from Ermintrude Dell."

"'Mr. Televangi' has sent him several messages to verify you have been here all the time," said Jon with a wink. "That should at least give Mocarsto reasonable doubt as to your true identity."

"What if Mr. Televangi figures out what you are doing?" asked Henry.

"Don't worry about Mr. Televangi," said Jon as he and Jen smirked at each other.

"Why? What happened?" asked Henry, trying to decipher the look in their mischievous eyes.

"Let's just say that Mr. Televangi is incapacitated until further notice," said Jen, lightly.

In response to Henry's impatient gesture, Jon explained. "The police might have discovered him on their doorstep severely intoxicated with some incriminating photographs. Considering his fake identification papers were inconveniently shredded, he'll probably be a guest of the local precinct for a few days. But don't worry, we'll keep an eye on him. That's what we're here for."

"Henry!" called Mrs. Harris from the front porch. "It's time to come in and finish your homework."

"Okay Mom," he answered. "I'm coming." He turned to Jon and Jen. "I have to go. I'm going back to Cardew tonight. Mocarsto has left us sitting in the dungeon, so I don't know what I can learn in there, but I have to bring Eulalie some dinner anyhow."

"Mocarsto is probably trying to wear you down," said Jen. "Has he given you anything to eat?"

"Yeah," Henry answered. "Eulalie said they left a plate of the hypnofood, but she didn't eat it."

"Good!" said Jen. "Remember, you mustn't! Bring a sample back with you next time. The scientists want to analyze it."

"And that way it will appear as if you are eating it," said Jon. "The scientists recommend you try to appear to comply with his demands. Act as though you agree with him. Then perhaps, he might let you go."

"Okay," said Henry. "I'll try. I have to go in now. Is there anything else they said?"

"Yes," answered Jon and Jen together again. "They said be careful."

Henry shrugged. He had heard that before. Henry waved goodbye to his friends and went into the house. He finished his homework and got ready for bed. He pulled out a copy of *The Count of Monte Cristo*—the book his English teacher had assigned for this month. It was a long book. Henry had seen the movie last year and thought the intrigue and adventure might appeal to Eulalie. *Maybe I can bring this with me to read to her,* thought Henry as he sleepily leafed through the title pages.

Chapter XLIV
Narratives

"Oh Henry!" exclaimed Eulalie. "I'm so glad you're back! You've been gone a long time!

"I know, I'm sorry," apologized Henry. "But I've brought you a cupcake and a book. I'll read it to you to pass the time."

"A book?" asked Eulalie. "The one about the fairy? Peter Pants?"

"No," Henry giggled at her mistake. "It's not 'Peter Pants.' This book is called *The Count of Monte Cristo.*"

"Who is the Count of Monty Crisco?" asked Eulalie. "Is there a fairy in this one?"

"It's Monte Cristo," corrected Henry. "And no, I don't think there are any fairies in this story."

"Oh, well, I will listen anyway," she answered generously. "It just so happens I have some free time. But I do have a question to ask you. Why is it that you can bring books and cupcakes here and back again, but you cannot bring me?"

"I wondered that too, Eulalie," said Henry. "The scientists say that it only works on inanimate objects." The confused look on Eulalie's face prompted him to elaborate, "Things that are alive. I can't bilocate another consciousness, just mine."

"Well, aren't you special," hummphed Eulalie.

"That's what they keep telling me," replied Henry.

"What else did they say?" asked Eulalie.

"They think we should wait it out for a couple of days. They think Mocarsto will let us go if he believes he's converted us to his way of thinking."

"Well THAT will never happen!" said Eulalie emphatically. "There is no way I would ever concede to such a tyrant. I would rather rot in this jail cell than make nice with that man."

"Just for pretend," Henry coaxed. "We can probably learn more about his operation if we play along. You know, infiltrate like spies. We'll fight the system from the inside."

Henry was learning to play to Eulalie's sense of adventure. She did perk up at the thought of fooling Mocarsto. She hadn't forgiven him for breaking her wings in the crystal cave. In fact, she had grown angrier. She found it easier to despise the man than the boy, even though the boy would grow to be the man. Was it only time that separated the two? The conundrum confused her when she thought about it. Nevertheless, she disliked them both—both creatures who dared to clip her wings, dim her light, and confine her in a murky, windowless basement that smelled of river water.

Henry and Eulalie settled in as comfortably as they could on the little cot and Henry read aloud to her from his book. It was a good story, with many similarities to their own situation. Edmund, the lead character, had been wrongly imprisoned by an evil, jealous, and powerful man. Henry knew from the movie that Edmund would one day be free. He lost many years, but he survived to avenge his enemies. After many hardships, he managed to escape his seaside prison. He uncovered a great treasure left him by his cellmate and transformed himself into the powerful and mysterious Count of Monte Cristo. They read late into the night before drifting off to sleep. Eulalie dreamt pleasantly of Edmund and of acts of revenge suitable to those wrongly imprisoned.

Henry did not dream. He woke up at home in his bed just as day was dawning behind his blue curtains. He lay still for a long time trying to reorient to his current environment. He was having difficulty keeping the days straight anymore. He thought back over everything that happened to him over the past few days, trying to relive every detail and etch them into his memory. He remembered the first time he met the scientists and looked out on the beautiful garden. He recalled the trip to the Wildlands and the Land of Echoes. He thought about Eulalie, of course, and Jon and Jen and Mr. Televangi. Then, there was Miles, whom he met first in a book and then in a dream, and then in the flesh in the deserts of Sun-Rhea.

Henry reflected on his mother and father here at home, and the comfortable life he, until recently, had taken for granted. He mused on beautiful Mirabel—his new mother, his old mother. The thoughts came in a jumbled stream now: Ms. Engle describing particles and waves, Mr. Waddleman explaining space-time curves, Cardew and its shining steel, Donegal and his secret garden, the mysterious Annwyn, and the strange Mocarsto. Where was his place in all of this? What did it all mean?

At length, Henry emerged from his daydream and figured it to be Wednesday morning. He had first met the scientists on Thursday afternoon, nearly a week ago. So much had happened already, and there was no knowing what would come next. Henry remembered what the Tarot Card reader had told him: "You will live to tell the story of your own death."

I guess it's not so bad if I'll live to tell about it, Henry thought. *But the death part ...* He shuddered. *What did she mean by that?*

Henry got out of bed and readied himself for school. He worried some more about Eulalie waking up alone in her dismal cell, as boredom fed her resentment at her lost freedom. He would bring her something nice tonight, he told himself. He wondered how long Mocarsto would leave them in the cell. Part of him hoped he wouldn't have to wait much longer, but another part got chills remembering the ominous words of the gypsy woman. He put the sample of hypnofood he collected from his cell into his backpack to give to Jon and Jen, and reluctantly left the calm of his bedroom. He stopped at the threshold and took a final look at the room he had slept in since he was born.

He had a strange feeling in the pit of his stomach. *A lot has happened already,* Henry thought, *but I get the feeling something big is going to happen today.*

Chapter XLV
Charmed

Henry was in a great mood. Wednesday turned out to be a thoroughly wonderful day, one that he would have thought ordinary, even dull, only a short time ago. Today, however, the peaceful pace of everyday life held a specific and elusive charm. Henry attended his classes and felt genuinely interested in the subjects, particularly English and Science. The day flew by, and before he knew it, the school day was over. Mr. Waddleman didn't call him out of class to bilocate, or even to talk. Henry supposed Jon and Jen had updated him and Ms. Engle on the scientists' plan to wait it out. Henry felt a twinge of guilt about Eulalie, but he knew she could take care of herself. Besides, he was certain he would hear her if she called to him. He thought about checking in on her, but he couldn't bring himself to leave blue skies, sunshine, and the smell of freshly cut grass to return to the dark, dank, moldy jail cell. He would have to go back there soon enough.

Poor Eulalie, he thought. *I'll make it up to her somehow,* he promised again as he ran out to join his friends on the baseball field.

After baseball, Henry walked to his father's shop to practice on the homemade hover-board. When things calmed down, Henry planned to bring home the scientists' version to show his father. He wanted to tell him about it now, but he knew he wouldn't be able to answer all of the questions its presence would raise. Henry wondered if he would ever be able to tell his father the truth about where he got it, or about anything that was happening to him. He wondered if anyone would believe him anyway.

After dinner and homework, Henry lingered in the living room half-heartedly watching television. He hadn't seen Jon and Jen all day, and Henry took their absence to mean there was nothing to report. He was reluctant for night to come when he would have to go back to his prison. Then the guilt grew stronger as he thought of Eulalie alone and upset in her far away cage. He suddenly felt selfish to have had such a great day when his friend was so miserable.

"I should never have let her come with me," Henry sighed. "It was too dangerous, after all. I'll find a way to get her out of there and send her back home. The scientists must have some way to cut through steel bars. I'll pack in some mega wire cutters or something, and then ...."

A new sensation interrupted his thoughts. The Annwyn in his pocket were singing in their swirling way, letting him know Eulalie was calling him. He sensed the urgency in the boiling colors of the tiny world. Henry quickly said good night to his parents and ran upstairs to his bedroom as the Annwyn's resonance began to open the portal that allowed them to travel alongside Henry in their own fashion. Henry had no time to change into pajamas. He flung the covers over his fully dressed body in case his parents decided to check on him. He closed his eyes and searched the universe for his other self, which lay sleeping on the cot in the cell in Cardew.

Within several long seconds, Henry had fully bilocated and opened his eyes with frantic anticipation. The first thing he saw was Eulalie looking horrified as she stared at something outside of the cell bars. She was clearly agitated and her mouth hung open in surprise. Henry followed her gaze to Mocarsto himself standing in front of them. He stared at Henry with eyes full of wild rage. His chest rose and fell with his pronounced breath. His nostrils flared, reminding Henry of a cartoon depiction of a bull about to charge. He wondered what had happened to have them both so upset. Henry sat up on the cot and returned Mocarsto's burning glare.

"So, boy," his voiced boomed. "You are charmed, then?" Mocarsto took a deep breath to calm himself. He clasped his hands behind his back and with bent head began to pace in front of the cell.

"Yes, I know this charm," he continued, not waiting for an answer. "It is no more than a glamour— yet still beyond the skill of your little fairy friend." He motioned to Eulalie in a condescending matter. Eulalie hummphed at him under her breath. "You are touched with the ways of magic. Tell me where a child of Sun-Rhea would come to know such tricks."

Henry looked at Eulalie. He didn't know what to say.

"And to where does he sneak, little fairy, leaving you all alone?" Then, turning to Henry, he said, "What is this trick? Astral projection? Do you wander my little town at night along the astral plane looking for some clue to my undoing? No small magic, there."

Mocarsto paused in his pacing and looked deliberately at Henry and Eulalie. The pair remained mute, waiting for Mocarsto to continue his cross-examination.

"What, you have no defense? No story to convince me of the truth beyond appearances? Well, then, let us continue with the prosecution."

Mocarsto appeared calmer now as he resumed his argument.

"I came down to check on my distinguished visitors to ensure the accommodations were adequate. Specifically, to see how you were enjoying the food."

Mocarsto glared deliberately at the now empty plate. Henry had brought a pocketful of the hypnofood to the scientists so they could decipher its wicked recipe.

"At first, I thought that was good sign—that you would be more … amenable … to my conversation." He turned to look fully at Henry. "Your friend here would have had me believe you were sleeping, but I recognized the charm. I know you left your shell here, while your consciousness traveled elsewhere. Therefore, either your science has advanced significantly, or you, my friend, come from a magic world. Noticing your choice of partner, I would venture to guess the Wildlands."

Mocarsto paused to gauge the effects of his words on the two prisoners.

"Have my old enemies enriched you with their magic and sent you into Sun-Rhea to spy on me? Why would they send a young boy into such peril? Unless it was your idea ... hmmm?" Mocarsto looked at Eulalie. "How else would you come to be in such a world as this?"

"Perhaps," Mocarsto continued, turning back to Henry. "Undoubtedly, you have been to the Wildlands and picked yourself up a fairy tart for company."

Eulalie bit her lip so hard she tasted blood.

"Yes, you have been there, but you are altogether too dull to hail from the Wildlands, and yet, not quite dull enough to come from Sun-Rhea. Although my sources tell me otherwise, I am inclined to believe you are the Earth boy I seek.

Eulalie let out an involuntary gasp. Mocarsto smiled wickedly. Henry knew if Mocarsto were sure of his identity, he wouldn't hesitate to kill them both. Henry took a deep swallow and lied to the tyrant.

"No, s-s-sir," he stammered. "I don't know the place. I came from the valley, where word of your utopia has spread. We came to witness your greatness, sir, to be part of your world." Henry knew this was a cheap shot, but he figured it couldn't hurt to play to Mocarsto's ample ego.

Mocarsto's eyes narrowed around the edges. He waited a moment and then continued.

"Your response is of no consequence. You obviously are not to be trusted. I will have my answers soon enough. In the meantime, I insist you refrain from your parlor tricks. If you leave your body behind again, I cannot guarantee it will be here when you return."

Chapter XLVI
Suspicion

Mocarsto's feet struck a monotonous rhythm as he resumed his pacing across the stony floor. He smiled pleasantly to himself as if reliving a fond memory. After a reflective moment, he addressed Henry, still without looking at him.

"You intrigue me, boy. It may be that I have a use for you, after all. You are obviously in possession of useful talents. You are able to travel outside your own body!" Mocarsto grinned with genuine fascination. "Now, that is not something just anyone can do." Then he looked over at Eulalie with a mischievous grin. She knew he was rubbing it in that she was unable to escape her jail cell like Henry.

"It could be, as you say, that you come from the valley and are in possession of the Federation's impressive scientific advances, grown bored of their reason and 'possibilities.' Or, perhaps, you are that rare wild child who has discerned secret pathways between the worlds, a perpetual wanderer whose curiosity drove you to seek out my camp. Still, a third option, you are the one they speak of: the child of Sun-Rhea, born in the Wildlands, the child foretold to end my reign."

Mocarsto paused to measure Henry's reaction. Henry knew Mocarsto hadn't yet finished his monologue, so he didn't say anything. He held very still and tried not to betray the creeping fear that made the hair on his neck stand on end.

"You see, I have been searching for this child for some time, and I recently discovered his whereabouts," Mocarsto drawled. "Even now, my faithful subject is there, on Earth, to keep an eye on him for me, you might say, which he told me as recently as this morning he is doing with much success. So, you understand, the timing of your arrival here is most interesting. Unfortunately, my subjects lack the ability to travel the worlds in anything but the conventional ways, and communications with them are primitive. Perhaps it is time for a personal audience with my man, so that we can get to the truth amidst these speculations."

"In any case," he continued, "whether or not you are the one I seek, I've little doubt you are both spies. The crime is the same, regardless who commits it, and so merits the same punishment."

Eulalie gasped and Henry reeled a little in his shoes. Henry found his voice to ask, "Why do you think we are spies, sir?"

Mocarsto's laugh was full of mirth. "Oh, come now. There is no need to pretend. Everything about you simply screams 'spy.' For one, nobody walks into Cardew from the free lands. Not that anybody wishes to leave once he joins us, but those on the outside are prejudiced against our ways. Unfairly prejudiced I might add, not that prejudice can be fair. I suppose that was redundant. The point is, the citizens of Cardew are the only ones who could fairly give testimony to the merits of our system, and they never leave it."

"Your zombies?" said Eulalie. "To what could they testify? They haven't a brain in their head, walking around with vacant eyes and no purpose other than to consume more of the poison that binds them!"

"So much for convincing Mocarsto that we are sympathizers," thought Henry in response to Eulalie's outburst.

Again, as if Mocarsto could read Henry's thoughts he said, "Well, now. I do believe your little fairy friend has let the cat out of the proverbial bag. There is really no need to continue with this charade. The company you keep was the next item on my list. Unlike those on your native planet, the people of the Wildlands are not known for their ... acceptance of authority."

Mocarsto had a way of pausing while rephrasing his thoughts. He selected shallow words and trite expressions meant to disguise their true meaning, to divert the careless listener from his malicious intent.

"Come now," continued Mocarsto, "let us stop pretending and be frank with each other. Though you may not have come with the most honest of intentions, I intend you no harm. Indeed, I am happy for the chance to educate you outsiders on the benefits of our little empire. For, you see, they too will be joining us soon enough. And then, the fight is always so tedious. I greatly prefer a peaceable takeover."

Henry shuddered at the thought of Sun-Rhea, so vibrant and alive with color and possibility, falling victim to the sterile silver city and its vacuous inhabitants.

Mocarsto walked across the room and sat down on a low bench by the opposite wall. He seemed strangely at home in the less than royal accommodations of the dank cellar.

"Let us start with the obvious: you are spies come for information. Well, then, I will give you the information you seek. You have been in the city. There are no walls. The people remain of their own free will."

Eulalie snorted with disgust. "You lie!" she hissed. "You force them to eat your drugs that strip their minds of free will. There may be no gates, but their prison is just as binding as this jail cell."

Mocarsto sighed. "Perhaps, but they are happy in their prisons, nonetheless. It was not always like this, but I must admit the hypnofood made it much more ... efficient. We began our first recruitments with the power of our message and a system of incentives, but there were more casualties in those days. The hypnofood has made Cardew safer and more peaceful than ever before." Mocarsto looked at his captive audience and saw the confusion and disbelief in their eyes.

"Very well then," he said. "I suppose I should start at the beginning."

Chapter XLVII
History

"I was a young man when I came to this world," Mocarsto began. "I had been cruelly banished from my boyhood home. I was left to wander through these strange desert lands alone and friendless for too long. The wildness of the barren sands soothed my natural soul. I found an affinity with the scorpion and the rattlesnake, the coyote and the wolf—lone survivors in a hostile environment, masters of their own destinies. Eventually, I tired of the solitude and found myself eager for livelier company than the whispering sands and the silent cactus. I made my way out of the desert and into society.

"I learned of the people here. They are so frail, so pitiful, compared to the hearty stock of the Wildlands. I did not come with a desire to conquer them, but their weakness begged for a master who would relieve them of their suffering. When the rains stopped and the great famine plagued the parched land, these poor ignorant souls were unable to care for themselves or their offspring. Want and violence increased as they stripped the land of its finite resources. They were self-serving like spoiled children, yet unable to fend for themselves, so they turned against each other in battle.

"At this time, I was no more than a wanderer and a witness. I had survival skills enough to weather the transient scarcity. What the Wildlands had not taught me, my time in the desert supplied. I was an excellent hunter and could offer enough food in these trying times to make me welcome wherever I wished to stop. I would return to isolation when I tired of them, desirous again to be lost in the oblivion of the desert.

"One day, a self-proclaimed leader of these pathetic creatures challenged me to fight him, fool that he was. He had correctly surmised that I was powerful enough to threaten his rule, if I had a mind to. He was losing control over his unhappy clan and he sought to prove his strength by besting me in front of his minions. The battle was swift and I, the obvious victor. His followers fell at my feet, calling me master and asking for mercy. This was when I realized how desperately these humans desire subjugation. I neither needed, nor recognized, any master. I was born in the lawless valley of the Wildlands. If these sheep would willingly serve me, would beg me to rule, then I would accept their call.

"Our arrangement was mutually beneficial. The starving people of this wasted place needed relief from their worldly troubles, and I found I needed a kingdom. If, indeed, I could never return to the untamed lands of my youth, then I may as well find my natural place in this world. If these weaklings called out to be ruled, then it may as well be me to rule them.

"Then, as luck would have it, the rains came and the drought ended. The fools gave me undue credit for the rain that fed the thirsty ground. However, I was sage enough not to deny my subordinates' voracious appetite for superstition. Their fanciful and unfounded beliefs nourished them as much as the animals and vegetation that returned to the land after the rains.

"And so my empire began. Abundance returned to the land, the people were happy, and I was a benevolent ruler. But good times bred restlessness in the younger generation. An undue sense of entitlement festers among the children of plenty, those who no longer remember the struggles of the fight or the sting of poverty. These creatures always need an enemy, so when external events do not present a viable cause, they will invent an outrage in order to condemn its perpetrator. They *will* have a reason for blood and mayhem—it is their very nature. The upstarts challenged the ways of their fathers and dismissed the wisdom of age as an archaic sensibility. Soon the rebels organized and sent a formal threat to me, their heretofore munificent leader.

"I do not suffer from the weakness of mercy. My enemy was quickly defeated, but not without some cost to the tender sensibilities of some among my flock. A new day had dawned, and the disillusionment that festered among the young rebels lingered in the perceptions of my once-faithful subjects. Doubt had entered the hearts of my wards and I saw it plague their simple minds. I decided to take action to eradicate this worm of uncertainty that had burrowed into their simple minds and gnawed at their private thoughts. I was displeased with this unrest. I would not have my people challenge my will.

"It was about this time I met a rather interesting man who was skilled in the arts of business and manipulation—two traits of which I found I now had need. He had made a handsome living selling cheap wares and even cheaper promises to the unsuspecting inhabitants of the burgeoning cities. He would move on to the next town before they found him out. When he did overstay his welcome, he was able to confuse an angry mob with the eloquence of his speech. He has an uncanny talent for speechifying. He amused me very much. When his travels led him to our little corner of the world, I chanced to see him speak at the town square. He had a convincing manner about him and I watched him relieve many a fool of his money. This man entered my employ, and I found him very useful indeed.

"I amassed a considerable fortune and found myself quite enamored with money after all—its power is so insidious and complete. As long as I was money's master, I could rule all. Televangi helped me usher in the new age of ever-growing wealth and ever deepening enslavement. We expanded our markets to the neighboring cities by creating and then sating their desires. We dominated the marketplace. The fools bought what we sold them. We grew marvelously rich.

"And yet, there was still unrest. There were still dissenters who would seek a different path, strange ones who diverged from the public taste. They were resistant to the prescribed reality that their peers consumed without thought, individual thinkers who dared to challenge my will, dared to choose against what I chose for them. These fools who would elect to be unhappy, to search for something more than I would give them, vexed me. I was not satisfied without complete subservience. I would not risk another insurgency, another attack on my absolute right as king.

"Soon the answer came to me with a wonderfully simple invention we fondly call 'hypnofood,' and Cardew was born. We built the factories to produce and sell happiness directly to my subjects—a beautiful plan. Consumption and profits climbed to a new high and we all but eradicated civil unrest. These prisons, which you occupy, fell into disuse, for dissatisfaction no longer drove my errant flock from their designed paths. Hypnofood calmed the discontented and quieted the restless. Oh, sure, there were still a few ... anomalies. Some people still required a little more incentive to obey the law. Hence, we have the Patrols. They and key members of my staff alone are exempt from the national food. Their job requires a less sedated mindset. Besides, I secure them to my will through other incentives.

"We expanded our enterprise, bringing peace and happiness to the ever-growing populations along our expanding borders. Hypnofood made it easy for most to embrace the new order. The Patrols subdued those few who resisted until they were successfully acclimated to our ways, or else exterminated. It is a tidy system. We have enjoyed much success over the years. Our numbers have grown exponentially. And now, we intend to welcome all of the children of Sun-Rhea into our blissful little club."

With this statement, Mocarsto appeared to have come to the end of his story. Henry and Eulalie had been listening intently and now they heard the echo of his last words in the profound silence.

Finally, Henry spoke. "But why?" he asked naively. "Why do you care what everyone else does? Don't you have enough?"

Mocarsto chuckled at Henry's foolish question. "My dear boy," he answered, "anything less than total control, complete domination, is never enough. Any element left untethered to my will runs the risk of undoing all I have created. Cardew will never be safe as long as outsiders remain who do not embrace my vision. Some of your 'free thinkers' would destroy this place with the earnest belief that they are helping their fellow man." Mocarsto sneered slightly as he delivered these words. "They could not be more wrong. Their own history proves it. Humans love a tether."

Eulalie sneered back, "No one loves a tyrant!"

"A tyrant!" Mocarsto grinned with a mixture of genuine and mock surprise. "Well, perhaps, my fairy compatriot. Perhaps I am a tyrant. But I help these people, too."

"How do you help them?" Eulalie asked. "By turning their brains into mush and taking away their free will?"

"You say po-tay-to ... I say po-tah-to ...." Mocarsto drawled. "My subjects enjoy a pleasant existence. They have plenty to eat and a safe place to sleep. Crime is practically nonexistent. I provide them with security, entertainment, and nourishment. What more could you ask?"

"Freedom," answered Henry.

Mocarsto looked at Henry as if he had just spoken an obscenity. "Freedom, my boy, is entirely overrated."

Chapter XLVIII
Debate

"Freedom is no more than an itch you cannot scratch," Mocarsto said carelessly.

"What is that supposed to mean?" Eulalie responded, petulantly.

"Of what use is desire that cannot be met?" retorted Mocarsto. "Freedom has no point, no volition. It is entirely without purpose. Freedom is lawlessness, anarchy, disorder, chaos. It is the ultimate undoer, the supreme leveler. Freedom is oppressive with its infinite choices. It is a fool's game."

"And you," he said, turning to Henry, "this freedom you speak of, with such reverence in your voice, is no more than an illusion. Freedom is entirely incompatible with society. Freedom is a concept only applicable to the individual. Free people can never coexist. We all see the world through subjective perception driven by our personal needs and wants. However, these desires require the agreement, nay the subservience, of other people in order to actualize one's will. Free people, truly free people, would never succumb to another's vision. They have their own desires to cultivate, their own will to impose upon others. Whenever free people interact, conflict is the necessary outcome."

"But freedom doesn't mean power over others," Henry objected. "It means no one having power over you."

"Another impossibility," snorted Mocarsto. "Freedom engenders opposing viewpoints. If all are 'equal' under the law of 'freedom for individuals' then nothing will be agreed upon, nothing instituted. All will fall into mayhem, and violence will remain the only means to determine the victor."

"It's not as bad as you make it sound," Henry protested. "People fight and sacrifice for freedom because it's so important."

"Bah! Freedom is too heavy a burden for the human animal. The masses are clearly unable to make choices in their own best interests, so like a loving parent to his inept children, I institute mandatory protection against their own stupidity. I stand as eternal watchguard over the city's maladroit inmates, to save them from the pain of their bitter humanity.

"I take away the painful affliction of choice from my wards, those who have shown themselves entirely incapable and unwilling to bear the responsibility of determining their own fate. They have been such willing slaves, and I have kept my end of the bargain. They do not suffer here, as they do in the free lands. I provide them order and structure and purpose, with no messy emotions to cloud their peaceable enjoyments. Truly, I do not know what you find to object to in Cardew. Your fairy friend's distaste does not surprise me; those from the Wildlands have always honored their unique sovereignty. But you, boy, could be very happy here."

"There is no happiness without freedom," Henry said somewhat sullenly. Mocarsto's speech had strangely affected him because he did see the shades of truth behind his hyperbole. Henry didn't think things were as bad as Mocarsto made them out to be, but then Mocarsto hadn't said anything that was outright false, either.

"Again, you are wrong," countered Mocarsto. "People are happier when the choices are made for them. They are not culpable for any repercussions of the decision. They do not need to trouble themselves with their implications; they do not need to educate themselves as they investigate seemingly endless possibilities. They can simply go about their business knowing that someone else has done the difficult work for them."

"Go about what business?" Henry asked. "I understand there have to be rules and stuff, but not ever being able to decide for yourself, not ever being able to do what you want to do ... that sounds so depressing. How could people ever agree to that?"

"Agree to it? They beg for it. People so readily grow to love their cages."

"But if that is true, then why do you need hypnofood?" Eulalie challenged.

"My dear," Mocarsto smiled. "You do miss my altruism altogether. It is for their own comfort, their own peace of mind that I provide them a serene mental landscape in which to dwell. Without hypnofood, these untidy complex emotions keep them in a nearly perpetual state of suffering and doubt. Trust me, they want the escape I offer them."

"And now, my friends, it is time for you to join them."

Chapter XLIX
Discovered

"What do you mean?' asked Henry. He sensed the finality in Mocarsto's voice and his stomach felt nervous.

"What I mean ..." Mocarsto sighed audibly as he rose to stand imposingly in front of Henry and Eulalie. "What I mean is that it is time for you demonstrate how willing you are to join our peaceful society." He reached into the pocket of his stylish robe and pulled out a small capsule. "You've managed some trick with the food, I see, but here I have a pill full of the same wonderful medicine. I have enough for you both. Take the pill and it need not matter from whence you came or with what purpose. Take the pill and I will release you as free members of Cardew."

Mocarsto ignored Eulalie's harrumph and spoke directly to Henry. "You said you wanted to join us. Here is your chance to show me your veracity, of your own free will." He held the pill out enticingly. Henry walked closer to the prison bars, beyond which Mocarsto stood.

"Nay, Henry! You mustn't!" Eulalie exclaimed.

"Yes, that's it," Mocarsto cooed. He continued to ignore Eulalie. He focused solely on Henry as the boy slowly approached him. Henry's eyes grew wide with apparent fascination for the pill in his enemy's hand.

"Let me release you from your cares," said Mocarsto as he placed his upward palm through the prison bars. "Take the promise of true freedom."

"The promise of oblivion!" hissed Eulalie jumping to her feet with agitation. "Henry! What has gotten into you?"

Henry found himself strangely tempted to take the pill from Mocarsto's hand. It wasn't that he found Cardew, or the lifestyle of its inhabitants, particularly attractive. Still, the lure of ease seemed suddenly palpable to him. Maybe, only curiosity pulled him like gravity to Mocarsto, or perhaps Mocarsto retained some claim to magic. Henry felt in control of his own thoughts. Mocarsto's arguments weren't without merit. How could Henry judge which state was preferable if he didn't even know what Mocarsto offered? But if he did try the hypno-pill, would he ever be able to regain his own mind again, or, like the lotus-eaters, would he perpetually seek the source of his own eradication?

Was it really so wrong to go along with the crowd? Mocarsto did make some valid points. Everyone exists in his or her own subjective reality, but nothing happens without agreement between people. Language itself is a good example. People cannot go around calling things whatever they want. Society must arrive at a common name or else no one would ever understand each other. Who is it that determines the world's definitions? Who decides what things mean? Influence, upon the world and its inhabitants, has always been a matter of power, from the playground bully to the taxman. Human history is the story of violence leading to authority, through corruption and gluttony, overthrown in its turn by a new reigning bloodthirsty vision. Maybe it would be easier to let someone else fight the fight.

Henry was rudely awakened from his reverie as Mocarsto's upturned palm grabbed the boy's shirt, twisting it in his steely grasp. He pulled Henry roughly up against the iron bars. Mocarsto's face was so close that Henry felt his hot breath on his face.

"Foolish boy!" Mocarsto cried. "You are in my grasp now and there you shall remain. Do you think I would give you another chance to escape—a child with your unusual ability to transcend my prison walls? Your friend is contained well enough in her cell, but you need special attention. Now you *will* take that pill. Whoever you are, you will never leave Cardew again!"

Mocarsto shook Henry violently. The force of the blow knocked the Annwyn out of Henry's pocket. The small orb landed on the ground with a thud and rolled along the concrete floor. Mocarsto recognized the object and gasped with surprise. He released his hold on Henry, who quickly scampered to the far wall in an attempt to escape Mocarsto's sudden rage. Now Mocarsto had no doubt about the identity of his captive.

"It *is* you," he hissed at Henry. "It is you after all. The Annwyn could have come into your possession through only one person. I should have seen the resemblance to your puling mother. Televangi has failed me. I see now I had too much faith in the man."

Henry crouched in fear as Mocarsto reached through the bars to pick up the Annwyn that had come to rest near his feet. As he held the swirling world in his hand, an inky blackness pierced the center of the sphere, swirly angrily, mixing with the once vibrant colors until the blackness overtook all. Black churned with ebony streaks and midnight swirls as a throaty humming filled the room.

Henry's heart raced in his chest. He had never witnessed the Annwyn exude such hostility. He remembered what Mirabel said about them—that they amplified wavelengths through resonance in sympathy with their surroundings. The Annwyn made bilocation easier and more pleasant as his consciousness traveled between his two physical selves. They heightened his awareness and sharpened his senses as they sang a song of resonant momentum. The Annwyn had amplified his own thoughts and energy, and now they were in the possession of Mocarsto, surging with the man's own anger and hatred. Henry had not known his comforting singing world could cause him so much fear.

The Annwyn's thrumming grew intense, and the blackness of the orb seemed to seep into the room. Henry stood helpless in the cell corner with nowhere to go. He didn't think it was possible to bilocate with the Annwyn acting in disharmony with his intentions. Besides which, he would not leave Eulalie alone with this monster. Eulalie flew to the back of her cage and lit her wings against the encroaching darkness.

"You may have escaped my foolish henchman, but you will not escape me!" Mocarsto let out a terrific roar and hurled a ball of energy from his clenched palm. Henry instinctively raised his arms to his head to protect himself. An explosion deafened him, and a distinct flash of pain cut through Henry's midsection as the force knocked him off his feet. Rock debris rained down and he realized he was no longer standing. He opened his eyes to a dark night flecked with stars and a crescent moon that seemed to grin at him like the Cheshire cat.

The rock dust cleared to reveal a sizeable hole in the brick wall that had housed his prison. The force of Mocarsto's rage, enhanced by the power of the Annwyn, had also burst the cell door open and crashed Eulalie's cage to the ground. The cage lay in splinters amid pieces of the crumbled wall, but Eulalie escaped unhurt. She flew free through the hole in the prison wall into the night. The seeping smell of river water was pungent on the gentle breeze.

"Oh, Henry, no!" exclaimed Eulalie as she flew over to her friend. Her momentary joy at freedom was quickly quenched by the realization that Henry lay underneath a large portion of the exploded stone wall, which had burst outward into the cool exposed night.

"Fly, Eulalie!" Henry exclaimed. "Get out of here! Don't worry about me. I'm okay."

Mocarsto passed through the bars and climbed over the rock debris to stand over the boy. "No, son," he said in triumph, a wicked smile turning the corners of his mouth. "I do not think that is true."

The heavy rocks had crushed Henry's legs and something sharp had sliced a deep gash in his side. Bright red blood oozed through the gray rubble, and Henry began to feel lightheaded.

"Go," he said to Eulalie, his voice little more than a whisper. "I'll be alright."

"Try your parlor trick, then," Mocarsto sneered. "See if your magic will hold. This shell will perish and you will pose me no threat. Go where you will, go if you can, I will find you wherever you land."

Henry's head swam and he knew he would pass out soon. With his last breath, he yelled at Eulalie to flee. The last thing he saw was the Annwyn still black in Mocarsto's hand. *I hope I can do this without them,* he thought as the blackness engulfed him in its infinite void.

Chapter L
Dead

Henry was nowhere, yet he was everywhere. A great nothingness surrounded him, and yet he felt connected to an unbounded energy. From somewhere above, he saw his mangled body lifeless atop the heap of broken stone that once was his prison wall. Eulalie, weeping, had finally heeded his plea and flown off into the night sky. Mocarsto stood over Henry's inert body, his evil smile radiating hatred for the incapacitated boy who lay half buried under the rubble. Henry felt scattered and disjointed, but he also sensed an undeniable pull toward a nameless something. He remembered the sensation of searching for his body. He tried to recollect where he had left it, but he couldn't remember.

The first few times Henry had bilocated, he hadn't been conscious; he simply awoke in his other body. When he traveled with the Annwyn, time itself stretched out. Yet, even then, the trip was little more than instantaneous. Perhaps he had become too accustomed to the Annwyn. Perhaps he couldn't find the way back without them, or, maybe, there was nothing to get back to. He pondered his situation. What if the second body can't exist without the first? What would that mean for him? Where could he go? Did that mean he was dead?

Henry didn't know if it was possible to have a panic attack without having a body, but he was pretty sure that was what was happening. His vision blurred, and everything in sight became swirly and dark like the inside of the Annwyn in Mocarsto's grasp. He felt as if a large wave had rolled him underwater, tumbling him without control in an endless, airless sea. He could find no bottom and no surface, just unending, unbounded space.

Finally, he heard his heart pounding in his ears and felt sweat cooling on his skin. He opened his eyes to his bedroom in the soft light of dawn. Henry had never felt so relieved in his life. He lay motionless in his bed for several minutes until he could no longer hear the sound of blood pulsing through his veins. Then he lay still for several minutes more, nearly paralyzed. He was in shock.

Henry's heart jumped again in response to his alarm clock clicking on to wake him up for school. He lay unmoving, listening to the music on the radio station, still too shaken to hit the snooze button. Once the song ended and the DJ started to blather, Henry found the will to roll over and turn off the noise. He made his way to the bathroom and took a long shower as he tried to prepare himself for another day at school. He had to admit, he was feeling a little stressed out. The last vivid scene in Cardew still burned in his memory. As he rinsed the shampoo out of his hair and let the warm water stream down his face, he could see it all again, as if a movie was playing on the insides of his eyelids.

From his vantage point above them both, Henry once again saw Mocarsto and Eulalie, as clear as if he were still among the ruins of the prison cell. Every detail was present in his recollection. He saw Mocarsto's fingers protruding from the blood red cuff of his robe, clenching the jet black Annwyn as if he would crush their world in his bared hands. Surely, Mocarsto knew the Annwyn were stronger than that. It was simply his rage pouring out of him, magnified a thousand times by the Annwyn. There was no sign of joy in Mocarsto's face at the demise of his enemy. The very air was thick with black hatred. Henry again experienced the force of his vehemence and shuddered to think of the consequences of unleashing Mocarsto's dark, rage-filled power.

Henry thought about Eulalie. In his memory, she looked as though her heart had broken. She hated to leave Henry there, broken and exposed on the rock shards that would become his gravestone. In the depths of her heart, she believed Henry would survive this catastrophe. Even with this particular body ruined, he had another waiting for him somewhere in space. Eulalie had a narrow window to escape herself, before Mocarsto turned his attention to her. Perhaps he would not bother with the tiny girl. Henry was his focus, his foretold nemesis. Nevertheless, she wasn't eager to find out. Besides, Mocarsto now wielded the power of the Annwyn. She had to tell Mirabel and the scientists what had happened. She would send Jon and Jen to check on him, to make sure he got back to Earth all right. She would do it herself, but she had to go to the Wildlands. She had to warn Thera that Mocarsto had the Annwyn, that he now had the power to return. She would warn Miles of the trouble ahead on her way back to Sun-Rhea. She must hurry. Henry would be all right, he just had to be ....

Henry wasn't sure how he knew all of this. Somehow, as he looked back on the scene in his mind, he knew all of Eulalie's thoughts. He was relieved to know she had escaped Mocarsto's wrath. He saw her disappear into the murky darkness beyond the Black Fort without Mocarsto even noticing her departure. The memory was so vivid; he could almost smell the dank river as it rushed along somewhere just out of sight. Then, Henry turned his attention back to Mocarsto. His ability to understand Eulalie's thoughts applied to Mocarsto as well. Henry focused in on the black thoughts of the evil man and sensed the rage and determination that emanated from the darkness of his mind. Despite the warmth of the shower, Henry felt a chill run down his spine.

"Good luck, Eulalie," he whispered aloud to the shadow of his friend flitting over the darkened landscape of his memory. "I know you can do it."

Henry opened his eyes and turned off the shower. He was halfway dressed when he heard the school bus lumbering down the road. He had one shoe on as it stopped outside his house with the telltale click-hiss of its opening door.

"I'm coming!" he yelled as he hopped down the stairs on one foot, clumsily shoving his shoe on the other. He grabbed his book bag and ran out the front door toward the school bus. The double doors opened to reveal an anxiety-ridden Mr. Waddleman.

"Thank goodness, you're alright," he sighed with relief. Henry slung his book bag in an empty seat three rows back and leaned his head against the window. He could feel Mr. Waddleman's eyes on him in the rearview mirror. Henry closed his eyes and relished the moment of peace during the short trip to school. Today was going to be another big day.

Chapter LI
Perspective

Henry was relieved when Ms. Engle wheeled out the dusty old projector from its closet in the back of the classroom. The children murmured with subdued excitement as she dimmed the lights. Movie days offered free license to pass notes, draw pictures, sleep, or just daydream. Henry was too preoccupied to focus on the mundane rituals of another day at school.

More and more, he felt like an outsider among his peers. He had missed the television show that Kyle and Tommy talked about in homeroom. His friends marveled that Henry had forgotten. The three boys, and much of the school, watched the show every Wednesday night and discussed it eagerly the next morning. Henry little wondered that he had forgotten about the program, even though he never would have missed it before. After all, he had been in a prison cell on another planet with a temperamental fairy while his friends watched television in their living rooms. While they slept comfortably in their beds, Henry was dying at the hands of his mortal enemy.

Henry grew drowsy as the old film flicked through the projector. Its dim light flashed against the wall, lulling him into an almost hypnotic state. High adventure had occupied his sleep for several days now. He craved rest. The scientists had said that his second body rested while his consciousness was elsewhere. Still, he felt the wear of constant stimulation. Besides, his second body had just been severely damaged to the point that it could no longer contain his consciousness. Dying had been a draining experience.

The rhythm of the ancient projector and the drone of the actors' voices lulled Henry into semi-consciousness. He had no idea what the film was about, nor did he care. Ms. Engle was bound to be sympathetic if he fell asleep in her class. She probably planned the whole movie day, anyway, for his benefit. Henry slipped into unconsciousness, glad in this moment that he had no second body in which to wake up.

As he slept, he dreamed. He dreamed he was back in Cardew, but no longer a prisoner in Mocarsto's dungeon. Instead, he enjoyed a bird's eye view, looking down at a mass of people gathered in the heart of the town. Henry felt a strange sensation, similar to the one he had experienced earlier in the shower. The scene was both dreamlike and vivid, as if he were both there and elsewhere simultaneously. Like a bird on the wing, his perspective changed, first swooping in above the heads of the workers, then broadening to a higher view.

He noticed Donegal's face in the crowd of people below, all dressed alike in their gray coveralls and heavy work boots. Donegal was chanting something along with the others, their singular attention focused ahead toward some common object Henry could not make out. Henry could sense the urgency in their faces, the anger in their communal stance. Donegal's expression reminded Henry of the man's outburst the last time he had seen him outside of his ramshackle hut. Only now, Donegal's anger seemed much more menacing. The crowd was already angry, and they were growing furious as they listened to someone speaking up ahead of them. Henry strained to see the object of their attention. His perspective widened as he swung in a pendulum's arc higher in the sky.

Henry noticed a short, greasy-haired man, with dull yellow teeth, speaking animatedly through a megaphone to the growing throng of people. Henry recognized the man at once. Whatever Mr. Televangi was saying radically affected the crowd. Henry could feel the mounting anger like a throbbing pulse. Suddenly, Henry's perspective swung again and he took flight over the crowds. He soared past the factories and steel buildings made dull by the cloudy sunless sky. He swept past Donegal's house, over his desperate, hidden garden and into the desert. As he approached Miles's underground home, Henry espied the rabbit working in his dust-caked yard. Miles looked up toward the approaching wind just as Henry swooped past.

"The fight is at hand, boy!" Miles said, calling up to him. "The winds are changin'! Can't you feel it?!"

Henry's velocity increased as if he were a feather on the gale of a storm. Miles was soon out of sight and Ermintrude Dell was fast approaching on the horizon. Before he could reach the Federation's borders, Henry was swept into another kind of consciousness as a persistent ringing rose up from a far-off land. The bell for third period echoed in his ears as Henry jerked his head off the desk, embarrassed by the drool on his notebook. Luckily, the lights were still off from the movie and nobody seemed to notice him. He felt better when he realized he wasn't the only one who nodded off. Ms. Engle turned on the lights and dismissed the class. She gave Henry a faint, understanding sort of smile, and then wheeled the projector back into its lonely closet and shut the door.

Chapter LII
Trouble Ahead

After lunch, the rain came in. Torrents of vertical rain roared like rapids as they bounced off the tin roof of the middle school. The baseball field was a small pond with muddy, island bases by the time the final bell rang. Coach Kent cancelled practice for the afternoon. Henry opted to take the bus home, rather than walk the few blocks in the downpour. When he got home, he wasn't surprised to see Jon and Jen waiting for him on his front porch. He opened the door and let the pair inside to the welcoming shelter of his living room.

"We heard what happened," said Jen with concern after the twins had settled themselves on the couch. "Are you okay?"

Henry shrugged his shoulders noncommittally. "I guess."

"Eulalie's been very upset," Jon began. "She and Mirabel have returned to the Wildlands. She'll be glad to know you are really okay."

"We have some news for you," said Jen after a pause. "It seems that Mr. Televangi has been released from jail."

"But we haven't been able to locate him," Jon continued.

"We've lost his trail," said Jen.

"I know where he is," Henry told his friends. "He's in Cardew. He and Mocarsto are raising an army to fight the Federation. They have changed the formula of the hypnofood to make the people angry— violent even. Televangi is Mocarsto's Minister of Propaganda and he is, right now, working up the people for the attack."

Jon and Jen sat silently on the couch for a moment with wide eyes and gaping mouths. "How do you know all this?" asked Jen.

"I know because I was there. I saw it," said Henry.

"But how?" asked Jen. "Eulalie saw you die, at least—she saw *one* of your bodies die. You had no vehicle in Cardew to hold your consciousness. How could you have seen all of that?"

"I don't know," answered Henry. "It's true, I couldn't go back to my body, but I was there all the same. I saw them preparing for war."

The twins sat silently for a moment trying to absorb this information.

"How did Televangi get back to Cardew?" asked Jon after a pause. "There's no way he can bilocate, an old grump like him. It takes an enlightened and flexible mind to bilocate."

"Not to mention flexible DNA," Jen added.

"That's why the old folks are here on a one-way ticket," explained Jon, referring to Mr. Waddleman and Ms. Engle.

"I don't know how he got back," Henry admitted. "I think it has something to do with the Annwyn. I think they are more powerful than we know, and they make *him* more powerful somehow. I'm not sure how it works, but Mocarsto and the Annwyn—they're not a good combination."

"What do we do now?" Jen asked Henry.

"Well, I can't bilocate anymore," Henry answered. "I don't have a working second body. You two should return to Sun-Rhea and tell the scientists that Cardew is planning to attack. I don't know when or how ... just tell them to get ready. I'll sneak out of the house tonight and go into the Wildlands by the path in the woods. I'll find Mirabel and Eulalie and together we will prepare for the other battle."

"What other battle?" Jon asked.

"The way I see it, there are two conflicts brewing; this war will be fought on two fronts. Televangi and his zombie army will attack the Federation of Free Minds in Sun-Rhea. Mocarsto, however, will not be with them. He has a more important battle to fight elsewhere. He'll return to the Wildlands."

"But why?" Jen asked. "Why would he go back after all of these years?"

"Because," Henry answered. "After all of these years, he finally can."

Chapter LIII
Three Women

That evening seemed interminable to Henry. Every moment of homework, dinner, and chores stretched and sagged under the weight of his super-consciousness of time itself. He wondered what his new friends were doing in their distant lands, and what lay in store for all of them. He avoided his parents as much as was practical. He was decidedly distracted, but didn't want to draw attention to himself by being too aloof. He spent most of the evening in his room, alternately working quietly on his schoolwork and staring out the rain-streaked windows into the darkening night. The rain didn't let up until nearly bedtime. Henry lay awake in bed listening to water plop in large drops off the eaves and onto the soft grass outside. He stared at the ceiling until, finally, he heard his parents go to bed. Then he lay still for an hour longer to make sure they were asleep. He was eager to get back to the Wildlands, but he knew if his parents caught him trying to sneak out of the house in the middle of the night, he would be in serious trouble.

Henry was cautious as he crept down the stairs and out the back door. The wet, spongy, young spring grass muffled his steps as he slid into the shadows beyond the streetlights. Henry pulled the collar of his jacket high around his ears and his baseball hat low over his eyes and strolled casually along the dark side of the neighborhood streets. He made it to the cul-de-sac without incident and breathed a sigh of relief as he slipped silently underneath the dark canopy of wet leaves. He paused a moment to get his bearings and once more sought the path to the Wildlands. The wet grass under his feet turned dry as he found himself in the verdant, jungle-like woods of the Wildlands. A large and bright moon shone down through the foliage to light his path. Henry continued on to the place where the forest thinned and the path opened out to the gypsy camp. Large fires rolled in stone pits, illuminating silhouettes of the men and women as they moved about in their tents. It was night here, too. The gypsies appeared to be settling down for sleep.

Henry wondered in which direction he should go to find Eulalie. The Land of Echoes was this way, he remembered. He didn't know the way to Eulalie's pond, or where the Tea cup Lady lived. He had come in on the path from Sun-Rhea that time. The pond could be a hundred miles or a hundred yards away. He had no way of knowing. Henry was too agitated to stand still any longer, so he chose a path in an opposite route from the Land of Echoes. He would formulate a plan as he walked. The night was beautiful, warm and crisp and the clear sky twinkled with more stars than Henry thought were visible from Earth. Henry felt free as he wandered across the lonely plains devoid of houses and streetlights. He enjoyed a moment of peace as he trod along the ground in the warm, open space of the Wildlands.

"Ouch!" Henry exclaimed as his foot twisted in a hidden hole. He thudded onto the dusty ground with his arms folded beneath him to break his fall. He sat up and checked his ankle by rotating it back and forth. Thankfully, he wasn't hurt. Henry looked at his surroundings, searching for the object that had tripped him. Gopher holes pocked the ground beneath him. He must have stepped in one and turned his ankle.

I wonder ... Henry thought, *I wonder if this is near where the Tea cup Lady lives.*

Sure enough, up ahead, Henry espied the hillock that concealed the door to her underground chamber. Henry recalled what Eulalie had said about knocking, and not wanting to rattle the delicate teacups, he pulled at the heavy door until it opened with a creak. The sky at his back was bright with stars and an impressive moon, but the light only traveled a few feet down the darkened stairway. Henry walked down several stairs and pulled the door shut behind him. A dim light flickered below from the opening at the bottom of the stairs. As he neared the stairway's end, the shadows danced wildly on the far wall like fire in the wind. He heard murmured female voices rise and fall in the cadence of conspirators devising a plan.

As Henry cautiously crossed the threshold to the great room, his leaping shadow announced his presence to the huddled women who sat with bent heads around a table near the hearth.

"Henry!" squealed Eulalie. "Oh, I'm so happy to see you!" Eulalie flew to Henry and alit atop his shoulder. She threw her arms around his neck and pressed her warm cheek against his.

"Oh, I'm all right, Eulalie," Henry said, somewhat embarrassed by her exuberant display of affection.

The women rose from the table and approached him. Mirabel and the Tea cup Lady stood on either side of another woman clad in gorgeous, flowing robes, decorated by rich colors and intricate designs. She looked like royalty. She was somewhat taller than Mirabel, and considerably taller than the diminutive Tea cup Lady. Her hair was pale and full, and as she stood in front of the blazing hearth, the firelight framing her lovely head in hues of red and gold.

"Henry," spoke Mirabel solemnly. "I'm glad to see you looking so well. Please, come closer. There's someone here I would like you to meet.'

Henry walked over and stood at Mirabel's side.

"This is Thera," Mirabel said by way of introduction. "And this," she continued, placing her arm lovingly around Henry's shoulders, "is my son."

"It is a pleasure to meet you," Thera said in a musical, velvety voice. She smiled sweetly at Henry. She smelled creamy and sweet, like milk with honey. Even as she stood in the dusty gloom of the underground room, she exuded an aura of sunshine and flowers. Henry thought her supremely beautiful, prettier even than Mirabel.

"Please sit," Thera said to Henry, offering him the seat she had just vacated. "Eulalie has had opportunity to relay much of your adventures in Cardew. There is more to the story that you should now know."

Henry accepted her offer and sat down in the chair with his back to the fire. The Tea cup Lady poured him a cup of hot steamy liquid and she and Mirabel resumed their places at the table. Thera sat on the hearth, radiant in the flicker of the fire's glow. She looked kindly at her audience, and in a warm, melodious voice, began her story.

Chapter LIV
Origins

"You have met the man Mocarsto. You know the evil of which he is capable. He's different now from when I knew him. His years of exile have embittered him, yet the seeds that now blossom grew in him then. His desire to dominate all within his sight made him an imperfect child of the Wildlands and a natural enemy to all her freedom-loving creatures. For you see, the Wildlands have always been a magical place full of the mysteries of the universe, where the secret and weird thrive, where dreams walk among us, and pay no reverence to daylight rules. As you know, only certain minds can comprehend our reality enough to cross our borders. Only those capable of some portion of *un*knowing can fathom the magical lands. This is the way it's always been. Mocarsto was never at peace here. Even as a boy, he lacked the ability to *un*know. Despite being born here, he is a creature of another place.

"As Mocarsto grew, so did his rigid desire for power and control. He still had goodness in him, though. He is an intelligent and determined man, and many times, I delighted in his company. But companionship wasn't enough. He wanted to lay claim to me, to own me, to command me. He wished me to marry him, but I would not choose to be bound to a man who would make me feel my bonds, and so I refused him. His fury was unbounded. In his wrath, he broke many delicate treasures, and it was in this moment that I first feared the man. There was no chance of harmony after that display. My daughters and sisters, all of us knew that Mocarsto would not stop until he obtained the object of his desire, and as that object was me, I had little recourse. One of us must leave the Wildlands. We decided it would be him.

"It didn't take long for him to realize the trick I had played him. He would find no prize beyond the Wildlands to win my heart. When he attempted to return, he could no longer find the path. My dear friend, the Tea cup Lady, had brewed him a drink of special herbs that caused him to forget his birthright. When the spell wore off, the barrier had set and the path to the Wildlands was forever closed to him. He was exiled from his homeland and adrift in a strange world. As expected, he was very angry. He was determined to return to the Wildlands, even if he had to blow a hole in the universe to do so. He called upon the Furies, the black witches of the night sky, and made a dark deal to obtain from them the Annwyn.

"It was at this time when Mirabel stole his hard-bought treasure and retreated into the Wildlands to secure it in the one place he couldn't go without it. She was heavy with her child by this time and had grown quite fond of the new world she had found in Sun-Rhea. She wanted her child to know both worlds: the world of magic where she had spent her youth and the new land of reason and science that inspired in her an equal amount of wonder. She feared for the new world and the enemy we had unleashed among them. Since Mirabel loved the inhabitants of Sun-Rhea, we vowed to do what we could to protect them from the menace of Mocarsto, up to the point of allowing his return.

"Not surprisingly, Mocarsto would not accept defeat. He returned to the Furies and demanded they help him gain access to the Wildlands. They chided him for losing the Annwyn so easily and reckoned a steeper price to aid him once more."

"There is one way," the dark sisters said, "to return to the lost land, but only as a child can you revisit. Your spirit is too heavy now to tread the lighter path. You must split yourself in twain and send your shadow-self into the breach. Only he can reenter through the land where the echoes walk. Here your other half must remain, split apart from its lighter element until the selves be reunited and the Furies appeased."

"Mocarsto agreed and the Furies wrung the sparse innocence from his heart and revealed to his child-self the door to the Land of Echoes. As it turned out, the child had a mind of his own. True to character, the child would not be ruled by another. Young Mocarsto did not wish to reunite with the elder. He refused to recapture the Annwyn and return it to the man. Nor did he wish to carry out Mocarsto's desire to wreak revenge on us. He was happy in the Land of Echoes amongst the other shades and half-beings.

"Not long after her arrival in the Wildlands, Mirabel's child was born. We called down upon him blessings of luck and protection. We washed his feet in the basin where meet the Rivers of All Things. The sun and the moon cast their charms upon him and the forest sang him lullabies. Mirabel was planning to leave us to take the child to its father in the new land when trouble befell her.

"As she was making her way to leave the Wildlands and return with you to Sun-Rhea, she espied the boy Mocarsto at the outskirts of the Land of Echoes. None of us knew of his ability to return, even in this half-form. True to his nature, the child sought to secure his place in this new world and protect himself against the elder's return. The Furies had warned of a child made from equal parts wood and glass who will end the empires of both man and boy. The child knew Mirabel had grown sympathetic to the creatures of Sun-Rhea, and if she returned there with the Annwyn, the elder could use their power to return and end his liberation.

"Foolish, darling girl—her desire to protect me from danger enabled the child to fool her. He lured her into the Land of Echoes and trapped her and the Annwyn in the Sky in the Lake. But before he did this, Mirabel bestowed upon you the illusion charm that you still carry. The boy thought the foretold child was with her, but she had had the foresight to leave her newborn son outside the gates of the Land of Echoes. The Tea cup Lady retrieved you and delivered you to your father's people in Sun-Rhea.

"Regretfully, the Tea cup Lady did not share her knowledge of Mirabel's whereabouts. It was wrong of her, but she sought to spare me, and she had faith in the legends. She had protected Mirabel's son, who would grow, one day, to reset the balance and atone for her sin. I assumed the girl had returned to Sun-Rhea as she had planned. I didn't know until today that the boy was still among us. Perhaps we should have known, but we were unaware that Mocarsto was building his own evil empire in Cardew. We should have paid more attention, but with Mirabel gone, the path to Sun-Rhea was rarely traveled. We have neglected our promise long enough. We will not stand idly by while our errant son inflicts his pestilence upon a new land. We will stand and fight him, here, when he comes, for there is no doubt now that he will return to claim us, or kill us. At this point, I know not which alternative he prefers. Either option is unacceptable to us."

"W-what can I do?" Henry stammered slightly. He was awed both by Thera's beauty and by the intensity of her tale. He felt sorry for Mirabel trapped all those years alone and he wondered how the Tea cup Lady had endured her fate on her conscience for so long. As if she had read his thoughts, the small old woman, uncomfortable with the weight of his stare, rose from the table and retreated into the shadows of her underground home.

"According to the legends, you alone can do what must be done," said Thera. "You are the one foretold who will defeat the great evil of our time."

"But do we know for sure that he is the one!?" interjected Eulalie.

Thera smiled at her fairy friend. "Indeed, he is, child."

"Perhaps he is," Mirabel ceded. "But maybe his role was to release me from the Sky in the Lake. Perhaps he has done all he is meant to do. He should return to his world and leave us to fight our brother. Henry has long been removed from our ways. This is not his fight."

Henry was confused and a little hurt at hearing these sentiments. He thought Mirabel and Eulalie believed in the old legends about him being the key to Mocarsto's defeat. He didn't understand why they now began to doubt him. He felt surprised and vulnerable at their misgivings. Maybe he had made a mess out of things by letting Mocarsto get the Annwyn. But in his defense, he was not even aware of their full power. He was doing the best he could! And now, Mirabel actually wanted him to go home—to go home and sit the whole thing out! He knew he couldn't do that, he wouldn't ...

Thera smiled at Mirabel and Eulalie and gave them a long, knowing look that seemed to unravel both the women into discomposure. She turned to Henry next, and her penetrating glance didn't spare him either. It was as if she could read his mind, and Henry soon became embarrassed at the tone of his own thoughts.

"Henry," she said. "Do not be bitter. They do not believe what they say. Their love makes them liars. They mean to protect you, that is all. Let us speak the truth here, so that we may be superior to our enemy. We will not fall to lies even for the sake of love."

Mirabel arose from the table and disappeared into the shadowy recesses of the Tea cup Lady's earthen living room. Henry thought he heard her choke back a sob. Eulalie flitted off after her, leaving Henry alone in the dim firelight with the imposing and beautiful Thera.

"Why are they so upset now?" Henry asked.

"Because the battle is now imminent," Thera answered. "And because ..." Thera sighed and gracefully slid into the seat Mirabel had just left empty. "Because, the legends do not specifically mention that our hero survives."

"Oh," said Henry, a little surprised. "I get it."

"Go home, Henry," said Thera, in her velvet, soothing voice. "Get some rest. We will need you soon."

"Okay," Henry agreed. He slumped out of the chair and headed toward the staircase. He glanced over into the shadows searching for a glimpse of Mirabel and Eulalie, but the room was still and quiet. He slowly ascended the earthen stairs and emerged into the night. Above him, the purple sky twinkled with stars that cheered him as he made his way back through the jungle pathway. He emerged at the cul-de-sac in his own neighborhood and snuck quietly home, where he slept a deep and dreamless sleep.

Chapter LV
Doubt and Deception

"Friday, at last, and a half day, too," Henry thought gladly as he got ready for school. He had slept well and felt more optimistic in the morning sunlight than he had in the doom and gloom of the fire-lit cavern. Not that Eulalie and Mirabel had meant to distress him—Henry understood their intentions were kind. Nevertheless, their concern invaded his peace of mind. The thought had never before occurred to him that he wouldn't be successful in whatever it was he had left to do. Even when he had died in the rubble of his prison cell in Cardew, he hadn't sensed defeat. Even when the Tarot Card Reader had foretold his death, he didn't really believe her. Seeing Eulalie and Mirabel frightened for him was enough to undermine his heretofore unchallenged confidence. It wasn't that he'd never been scared before, but it never occurred to him that, ultimately, he wouldn't win, much less survive.

Still, Henry felt peaceful as he began his day. Perhaps, like calmness before a storm, a rosy light softened the shadows from the coming storm clouds. A serene stillness descended upon the chirping birds. Henry felt vital and alive, for he knew now that the final challenge was fast approaching. He didn't feel anxious, rather an enjoyable tranquility took hold, a sensation that comes with knowing one's place in the universe. One week had forever changed his perspective, and he treasured his new knowledge of secret worlds and hidden pathways.

He wondered if he would ever be able to tell anyone about Sun-Rhea and the Wildlands—maybe Kyle and Tommy, maybe his parents. He wondered if anyone would believe him, or if anyone would be able to follow him to these distant lands. After all, he was supposed to be the only one, the chosen one, somehow. Maybe with the Annwyn he could bring someone with him, or maybe broaden the path so that others could find it—that is, if he could get the Annwyn back. "I'll have to think about that later," Henry decided. "It isn't safe there now anyway." He went downstairs for breakfast, content, for now, with his secrets.

One thing bothered him, though. He took a deep breath to prepare for the lie he was planning to tell his parents. He didn't want to do it. He never lied to his parents before—not about anything important—but he couldn't think of any way around it. Henry rationalized it was only so his parents wouldn't worry about him. Events were leading to crisis. What if he was unavoidably detained the next time he traveled to the Wildlands or Sun-Rhea? He couldn't bilocate anymore. He had only the one body now. Henry knew his friends would call on him soon. It was best to be prepared in case he had to leave suddenly. He knew his parents would believe him. He'd never given them reason not to. He promised himself this would be the last and only time.

"Mom, Dad," Henry began, "Is it okay if I spend the night at Kyle's house tonight?"

***

The day was beautiful, a late spring day without a cloud in the sky. The seasons were just turning from spring warmth to summer heat. By this afternoon, the sun would burn hot in the clear sky, but for now, the temperature was perfect. Squinting through the morning glare, Henry saw Jon and Jen walking down the sidewalk toward him. After greeting each other, the trio decided to walk to school to give them a chance to talk.

"How soon can you get away?" Jon asked Henry.

"I don't know," Henry said. "Do you need me?"

"Cardew's army is poised to attack the Federation," Jen answered.

"Already?" Henry gasped. "I thought we had more time. What can I do?"

"The villagers are building a stronghold at her borders," said Jon. "Mocarsto's forces are mindless creatures, but they outnumber us, nonetheless. Televangi, alone, is commanding the army. Mocarsto is not among them."

"Looks like you were right," said Jen. "We suspect Mocarsto has gone to the Wildlands to wage his own personal war. Dr. Finnegan fears for your mother. She and Eulalie remain in the Wildlands. Mirabel will not leave Thera's side. Nowhere is safe."

"What should I do?" Henry asked.

"Protect your mother, Henry," said Jen. "Mocarsto hates her. He will find her and Thera and seek to punish them for his misery."

"Yes, they need you there more," agreed Jon. "Jen and I will return to Sun-Rhea and help the Federation. Come to us when you can."

At this point in the conversation, Henry realized the three friends had come to the cul-de-sac where lay the entrance to the Wildlands. Henry paused and looked into the shaded grove. "Should I go now?" he asked.

Jon nodded and said, "I would if it were my mother in danger."

"Don't worry, we'll take care of school!" Jen called out after Henry's running figure, but he didn't hear her because he had already crossed over onto the jungle path in the Wildlands.

Chapter LVI
Miles's Story

From atop the lonely stone that marked the entrance to his burrow, Miles watched the horizon where the army of Cardew had assembled along the border. The sun behind him cast his long-eared shadow along the dusty desert ground.

"The natives are getting restless," Miles said to no one in particular. "It's time to join the others."

Miles had seen it for himself, for he had just returned from Cardew. He went as far as he dared, which was just as far as Donegal's garden on the outskirts of the steel city. The garden lay neglected, overrun by errant grasses. Donegal had not visited it these few days. He, like the others, ate only the hypnofood now. When Televangi returned from Earth, he altered the formula to increase the aggression and paranoia in the citizens of Cardew. The new hypnofood was an even more powerful drug, which, coupled with relentless propaganda, induced the entire population to crave the blood of the inhabitants of the free lands.

Televangi told his intoxicated children horrible stories about the wickedness of the free people and the curse of their freedom. He described how their blatant disregard for the natural order threatened the delicate peace the great father Mocarsto had created and bestowed upon his chosen people. Freedom was excess and irresponsible and it threatened the cohesiveness of society, which all individuals serve for the greater good. The masses, not the individual, must thrive, as all are part of the whole. To serve an individual desire is no more than base greed. Personal wants do not extend to the well-being of the masses. All must serve the individual who protects the masses from themselves. Without Mocarsto, the universal soul would dissolve into the chaos and perpetually unfulfilled desire of the free lands. Freedom was a burden that the children of Cardew would lay at the feet of their lord and master.

Miles had listened to this rubbish pumped through the loudspeakers at the factories. He watched as the poor drugged fools substituted Televangi's drivel for purpose. With glazed eyes and compromised brains, they associated anger and resentment toward the Federation with the adrenalized tension mounting in their chemically altered bodies. Televangi was working them up to fever pitch, planning to unleash his chemical warfare upon the Federation in the form of these addle-brained, steroid-ridden zombies. Miles felt sorry for these people, so distant from the truth of things. He was also angry that they had, all of them, fallen prey to Mocarsto's cheap lures of false peace and happiness. Granted, he had starved them and drugged them, but nobody ever said the true path was an easy one. Miles had always seen through the man. He was neither scared nor fooled by Mocarsto, not now and not then.

Miles wondered why so few people had the energy to do the right thing. It had always been obvious to him, but then he had never suffered the pangs of mediocrity. He wasn't easily swayed by empty rhetoric or popular thought. Miles wasn't the sort of rabbit to be frightened of the truth of things. He knew somehow that the entire universe only made sense with a happy ending, but that you could never stop fighting for it.

Miles was a member of a proud race, of which he was the last surviving member. At least they had resisted for a time. Back in the early days of Mocarsto's onslaught, a young Miles had served with his kind in the resistance. They refused to ease their suffering and taste the hypnofood, and so Mocarsto made an example of the rebels. The carnage was terrible and Miles was lucky to escape with his life, but then, Miles did not believe in luck.

Mocarsto captured the rabbit rebels and forced upon them a terrible choice. Shackled and starving, they were offered release on condition of eating a substance proclaimed to relieve all suffering. Miles witnessed the birth of hypnofood. He and his people were the first guinea pigs of the original formula. The other options left to them were slow death by starvation, or a quick death by scythe, which Mocarsto had left for the hearty to prove the strength of their convictions. Rabbit after rabbit succumbed to the hypnofood as the starvation brought madness and despair. Naturally, none chose quick death, but Miles did take up the scythe and cut his paw free from the shackle. No other could stomach the same sacrifice, and Miles limped out of his prison with his bloody stump alone, leaving his countrymen to suffer the effects of Mocarsto's drug.

And suffer they did. The formula was yet imperfect and delirium led to lunacy in all who tasted the tainted food. The once lively race of rabbits were exterminated by a poison that rotted their guts and muddled their minds. From the experiment and its failures, Televangi learned to improve his wicked formula so that hypnofood would claim no more bodily casualties. As for Miles, he retreated into the desert and deep solitude, nursing his wounded paw. He has since grown used to his scars and thinks he wouldn't do without the disfigurement, his hard-won symbol of independence. He had paid a dear price for freedom, as he was now alone in this world, the last of his kind. He left his severed appendage behind him, a personal sacrifice, to wither beside the bodies of his fallen brethren.

Miles shook his head and clucked once more at the weak souls in Cardew. He thought about Henry with a hope he hadn't known in some time. He liked that kid. He had a good head on his shoulders. Still, he was young and untested. Miles wished with all of his heart that Henry would pass muster in the trials ahead of him.

"He shows promise," Miles mused, "but then, look at his father."

Chapter LVII
Donegal's Descent

Donegal stood among the others, dressed for battle, his face twisted in rage. The army wore steel breastplates of the same cold, dull silver as the city behind them. Clouds were forming in the east and the sky mirrored the grayness of the land. A cool wind blew the sparse vegetation at Miles's feet as he peered through his binoculars for a closer look at Henry's long lost father.

"I'll try to spare 'em, for the boy's sake," said Miles to a centipede crawling atop a nearby rock.

He was disappointed in Donegal. Miles had met the man years ago, before Donegal had succumbed to the temptation of false promises. Even then, the man was in a poor state, and Miles had pitied him, for he too had known loss. But now, the man was broken, undone, and pathetic. Miles reflected on Donegal's story and the short time the two had spent in the desert before the lost soul defected to the enemy camp.

Miles knew that Donegal had once been an impressive man, that those who dwelt on the other side of the desert had hailed him as a visionary. He was instrumental in the creation of the Federation of Free Minds, whose purpose, ironically, was to end the rule of the man he now served. The man suffered a blow when his pregnant wife disappeared in a realm he couldn't enter. He cursed the Wildlands and her enchanted heritage. He turned his back on all things magical and turned obsessively to science. When his son was returned to him, Donegal swore the boy wouldn't suffer the same fate as his dear wife.

His work on the bilocator was nearly complete when Mocarsto attacked the city, searching for the boy child. In a panic, Donegal sent his infant son across the universe only moments before the bombs destroyed the building and the bilocator within it. Donegal was badly hurt and lay unconscious for days. His brother, Dr. Finnegan, nursed him back to health. When he awoke, he was distraught to learn that the machine he required to retrieve his infant son was also demolished in the fight. So, too, was his only chance of finding the babe's mother. The child, alone, had potential to enter the Wildlands, and his father had sent him to a strange planet, alone and helpless.

While Donegal lay in a coma, his brother had sent two of their associates through the space-time wormhole to be near the child and ensure his safety. Opening the wormhole took enormous resources and couldn't be attempted again for some time. Donegal would have gone to be with his infant son, but that door, too, was closed to him. He suffered with the knowledge that both his wife and son were beyond his reach.

In despair, Donegal wandered deep into the desert. He wanted to be alone with his overwhelming sadness. His new bride and infant son were gone and he was powerless to find them. Both magic and science had failed him. He, like nearly all reason-bound mortals, could not enter the Wildlands. He was unable to restore the bilocator. He couldn't reproduce the design destroyed in the explosion. His frustration mounted into a debilitating sadness, and he slunk away to mourn in the quiet sands of the desert. Miles had watched him from his own desert home, but he left the man alone with his grief.

Ain't that a shame, Miles thought. *Best to let 'em be; he didn't come out here lookin' for company.*

After some long weeks, Miles thought it time to break the man's solitude. He approached him one night with a bottle of homemade cactus wine. The two enjoyed a pleasant evening around the fire revisiting stories of their adventuresome youths, when the world was no more than a treasure map. Donegal smiled for the first time in many months. But when the stories turned to his recent heartbreak, something seemed to break inside the man. In hindsight, Miles knew it had been too soon. He should have left the man to his sorrow until he came back to life on his own terms. The stirrings these memories evoked brought down upon the crippled man a crushing sense of loss. Donegal couldn't bear the knowledge that he had failed his family, nor the fear that he would never see them again. In the morning, Miles was saddened to see Donegal's footprints still visible in the unmoving sand headed in the direction of Cardew.

That was many years ago. Miles set down his binoculars and spat on the dry ground. He was disheartened to see Donegal prepared to attack his own people. Miles knew he was under the powerful influence of hypnofood, but nonetheless he couldn't forgive Donegal for his submission to it.

"The devil can't take you without your permission," Miles said with feeling, shaking his head. "So far gone, you didn't even recognize your own son when you met him."

Chapter LVIII
Showdown

Meanwhile, Henry and Eulalie made their way to Thera's house. Eulalie met him as he came running out from the jungle path. Their connection was strong even without the Annwyn, and Eulalie had sensed his arrival. The gypsies had decamped, but cold fire pits full of charred wood evinced their recent habitation. Henry wondered where they had gone. He remembered the Tarot Card Reader's ominous predictions. Strange how they had all come true, only in different ways than he had imagined.

I suppose that's part of the trick, he thought.

"This way," said Eulalie, interrupting his thoughts.

"Where are we going?" Henry asked.

"Back to the Land of Echoes," she replied. "Mirabel and Thera are there now."

"Why did they go to the Land of Echoes?" Henry asked.

"Mocarsto will come for the boy first," explained Eulalie. "Now that he has the Annwyn, he will seek to reunite with the boy. He is weaker from the rift. The women have gone to protect the boy from the man. The boy won't join Mocarsto of his own will because he's happy in the Land of Echoes."

"If he does come," said Henry, "how will we fight him?"

"We were hoping *you* would know the answer to that," said Eulalie with gravity.

They walked on in silence. Soon Henry recognized the decaying stone wall that marked the entrance to the Land of Echoes. The air turned chilly as they passed through the heavy iron gate and into the land of ghosts and shades.

"I don't like this place," said Henry sullenly.

"Nor I," agreed Eulalie.

They walked past the field of forget-me-nots, past the lake that had been Mirabel's prison for over a decade. They headed toward the waterfall and the crystal cave where they had first met the boy Mocarsto, when he had almost lured them to their deaths.

"Why are they protecting him again?" Henry asked. "The boy is as wicked as the man if you ask me."

"Aye, I agree," said Eulalie. "But as it turns out, Mocarsto's own worst enemy is himself, which makes the boy an ally of sorts."

"He did try to kill me, you know," said Henry.

"Aye, the boy tried," said Eulalie. "And the man was successful. The man is the bigger foe. It will be worse for us if the two become one again."

They neared the mouth of the cave where Mirabel and Thera stood with the boy. In the perpetually dim light of the Land of Echoes, Henry could make out Thera standing behind him, her hands placed protectively on his shoulders. Mirabel gave Henry a small smile, but there was tension in her eyes.

As Henry and Eulalie reached the others, a deafening roar tore through the dusky sky.

"He is tearing the fabric of the universe to get back here," said Thera. "He has grown powerful, indeed."

In truth, Mocarsto had entered the Wildlands. He emerged from the hilltop where Henry had first seen the boy playing with his shadow friend. Mocarsto was alone. He walked with menacing purpose toward the group, his black and blood red robe billowing out behind him. The wind gained strength and the lifeless air stirred the dead leaves.

Mocarsto reached the cave and looked at the unlikely army of five who guarded the mouth of the crystal cave.

"How convenient," he drawled as he sized up his enemies. "You are all here. I thought I had taken care of *you* already," he said, looking at Henry. "I suppose I shall have to try a little harder next time. Run home to mummy, I see. Well, let us not be all day about it. I would like to wrap this up in time to see the Federation fall." He turned toward Thera and sneered.

"Woman, now that I have the Annwyn, you can never close to the path to me again. You will pay for my years of exile. Each of you will serve me as master of all lands. Sun-Rhea, the Wildlands, even Earth is within my grasp."

He turned toward Henry and pulled the Annwyn out of his pocket. He held it out on his flattened, upturned palm and gazed at it fondly. The orb was swirling violently with ugly dirty browns and purples. Henry could feel the energy it emitted like a surge of electricity. The singing world was pulsating with discord. Henry wondered if the tiny creatures felt pain.

"I suppose I should thank you," Mocarsto said to Henry as he gazed at the orb in his hand. "If it were not for you, I would never have reunited with my friends here, through which all things are once again possible. I find it curious your twit of a mother sent you into my camp with the one thing I needed to end you all, especially after she went to so much trouble to get it from me in the first place."

"That was clever of you, my boy," said Mocarsto addressing his child self, "trapping her here all these years in her wet reflection while her baby boy grew up calling another woman 'mother.' It is a suitable punishment for her impertinence, this thief of what is rightfully mine. You made a mistake, though, leaving the Annwyn with her—such a pity to lock up such power in her watery wasteland. You should have brought the Annwyn to me. It was the only reason I sent you here in the first place."

The boy didn't move or even blink as Mocarsto chided him.

"Come, boy," he said to the child. "Move away from those weak women. Come and join me. I will show you more power than you have ever known."

Young Mocarsto raised his face to look directly into the eyes of the elder and defiantly shook his head.

Mocarsto's face registered surprise at the boy's refusal. He never suspected that the boy had been avoiding him. Suspicion of the boy was as foreign as self-doubt. Would the boy actually sabotage the opportunity to reunite? Mocarsto understood the child was unable to leave the Wildlands, just as the man was unable to enter it. The realization of the boy's betrayal clearly pained Mocarsto.

"What perversion is this?" he hissed at the boy. "You wish to stay here among this ... weakness?"

"I like it here," answered the boy. "I don't want to leave."

Mocarsto smiled and exhaled. "Oh, is that all? Of course, you like it here. This is where you ... we ... grew up. No worries, this place will be ours again. Join me and we will be so powerful that we can go anywhere we want. We can come back here any time we want. You can have this and so much more."

The child appeared thoughtful for a moment. He beheld his female protectors then looked back to the grinning man. In a sudden movement, he bolted into the mouth of the cave.

"I think you have your answer," said Thera. "You repel even the innocence in yourself."

"I have not come here to trade barbs with you, Thera," hissed Mocarsto. "I have grown powerful enough to burst all your charms and bonds. I can unleash the power of the Annwyn and blow a hole in your part of the universe as easily as I blew apart his prison cell." Mocarsto motioned to Henry. "You are a clever one, aren't you? I was certain you were quite dead. A clever trick, that. Perhaps I might make something of you yet."

"I'll tell you what," Mocarsto said as he paced before the mouth of the cave. "Come with me and I will spare you the fate of your female friends. You are young and yet trainable. Your only offense is being born of a betrayer and a thief. Come with me, you and the boy, and we will have worlds at our fingertips."

"It is true, Henry," said Thera. "You can have what he offers. All you must do is serve him—trade your will for his own."

"And why not?" said Mocarsto. "Like a father, I offer protection and prosperity to my children, as long as they obey me. I am smarter and more powerful than they are. It is my right to rule them."

"Your power and your intellect are well met, Mocarsto," said Thera. "No one here accepts your right to rule us. This is yet a free land, and you are not welcome."

"Careful, woman," Mocarsto hissed. "I came only with the intention to tame your wicked willfulness. I assure you, Thera, you and all of the Wildlands will serve me. This, or else I destroy the place. I have lived long enough beyond its borders—you saw to that—not to hesitate to blow you all into oblivion. Test me further and you will know my wrath."

"You know we will never bow to you, Mocarsto," said Thera. "We do not fear you."

"That is unwise, my dear." Mocarsto replied with a smile. He shouted into the mouth of the cave, "Come on, boy! It is time for us to leave." Then turning to Henry, he said, "You had better make your decision as well. Come with me, or stay here and die. We leave momentarily." He then turned and walked into the crystal cave.

Chapter LIX
The Battle of Sun-Rhea

Mr. Televangi stood before his army in the blazing late morning sun. Clouds amassed near the horizon, where his unsuspecting enemy would soon meet their devastation. The day promised to be a hot one in the desert that lay between the steel city of Cardew and the verdant lands of the Federation. The army had gathered at the outskirts of town to await orders to march across the warming sands toward their enemy. Mr. Televangi gave his most eloquent speech yet, filled with hate-fueled propaganda. With false words as his instrument, he painted the free thinkers of Sun-Rhea as the epitome of evil and self-deception. He hardly needed to try so hard. He had altered the hypnofood with such a powerful drug that his army would march to certain destruction at his mere suggestion.

Mr. Televangi enjoyed speechifying. As a diminutive and altogether unattractive man, he found he had to create his own opportunities in life. He had an early gift for talking his way both into and out of situations. He was often surprised at people's gullibility, and their willingness to part with their money. Mr. Televangi's conscience didn't suffer when his lies caused hardships for others. He felt no guilt when fools trusted his silver tongue; he wasn't responsible for their folly, their personal weakness of gullibility. It was every man for himself. According to Mr. Televangi, a man's word was "good" when it brought him good, hard gold. His early career had him dabbling in potions and snake oils to sell at the gypsy camps and rural towns. He hawked his cheap products to the ignorant yokels and lazy dreamers, eager for an easy way to a better life.

When Mr. Televangi met Mocarsto, he knew together they could harness real power. Mocarsto was strong and handsome, a natural leader. He had strange and powerful knowledge from the ancient land. Televangi turned from dabbling in potions to creating a drug strong enough to overpower the human psyche. He worked long nights studying chemistry, alchemy, and psychology. Finally, he developed the formula that became hypnofood. The drug eradicated people's free will and left them vulnerable to suggestion. Televangi could control these fools through his consummate rhetorical and persuasive skill. Televangi didn't mind that Mocarsto was the supreme leader. Televangi was rich, and he had more real power than Mocarsto. He knew that without him, without the hypnofood, Cardew would fall, and so would its great and powerful leader, Mocarsto.

All of this is possible through me alone, thought Mr. Televangi as he surveyed his massive army, worked into a fury by the eloquence of his battle cry. "Now, we attack!" he commanded his drugged soldiers as the bugle sounded the charge.

The army of Cardew stormed the desert with weapons held high. Heavy boots trampled upon Miles's burrow and caved in the hole that led to his underground bunker. Miles, however, was safe in Sun-Rhea. He had gone to meet Henry's scientists and help them prepare for the imminent attack.

"We cannot harm them," sighed Dr. Finnegan. "They aren't thinking clearly. They aren't a true enemy."

"But what else can we do?" asked Dr. Scala. "They attack us with real weapons and force like a true enemy."

"But they aren't responsible for their own actions," offered Dr. Hector hesitantly. "Are they?"

"Poppycock!" said Miles. "Ever'one is responsible for their own selves. It was their choice, ever' one of 'em, to accept defeat at the hands of Mocarsto and his speechifyin' chemist. The lady's right. If they act like an enemy, if they *attack* like an enemy, then there's no sense in layin' out the welcome mat. Ever' war has casualties, and let me tell you, they aim to make a few themselves."

"There is another way," said Dr. Finnegan. "I've been studying the sample of hypnofood that Henry brought back from his prison cell in the Black Fort. I believe I've identified the drug's properties and have developed an antidote. Of course, I haven't been able to test it on a human subject yet. Hypnofood contains a powerful drug, and the antidote could cause unknown side effects. It might be dangerous; it may not even work."

"But we don't have a choice," said Dr. Scala. "Cardew is marching across the desert as we speak. They will be here soon and they come to fight."

"What is this antidote, Doc?" asked Miles. "How will we get 'em to take it? I think it unlikely that these folks will take what you're offerin'."

"Hmmm, yes," agreed Dr. Finnegan. "It is a liquid and it should absorb through the skin. If we could dilute it and wet them with it somehow ..."

"How will we do that?" asked Dr. Hector. "Do we turn the garden hose on them? That hardly seems logical."

"He's got a point, Doc," agreed Miles. "There's too many of them. You can't get them all, unless you plan to fight with water guns."

"I have another idea," said Dr. Finnegan. "If we could make a controlled rain across the entire battlefield, then they wouldn't be able to hide. They would all get soaked at once and their anger would be quelled in an instant."

"If we could only make it rain," added Dr. Scala. "Your brother had success in the laboratory, but his work has gone largely untouched since he ... went away."

"It's high time we put these theories to the test," said Dr. Finnegan. "It's the best chance we've got."

"If the antidote works," said Dr. Hector.

"Well, it's the best plan I've heard all day," said Miles. "Let's make it happen. We don't have much time. What do you need us to do, Doc?"

"Luck is on our side. It's hot and humid out there in the desert. We can introduce a cold front on top of the cloud cover to encourage the rain to fall. If we infuse the clouds with the antidote, then sanity will rain down upon the unsuspecting savages and release them from the power of the drug. We can use the hover bubbles. Pack one with the freezing solution and another with the antidote. Hector, you will infuse the clouds with the diluted antidote mist to form condensation. Then, Scala will introduce the freezing agent to cool the air, and the liquid will fall in drops like a rainstorm. Be sure to work a large enough area to generate a good downpour. We cannot have an isolated cloudburst that only hits a portion of our enemy."

"Prepare the hover bubbles," Finnegan said to Dr. Hector in haste. "Dr. Scala, you come with me. We have to make more of the antidote right away.

"What should we do, Doc?" asked Miles.

"We need a good man on the front line. We must hold off Cardew's army until Scala and Hector can finish their mission. The townspeople are amassed and armed, but we could use a strong leader. We are inexpert in the ways of war. We all knew this day was coming. But we were hoping, that maybe, Henry would prevent it somehow."

"Where is that boy, anyhow?" Miles said.

Chapter LX
The Pit

Henry followed Mocarsto into the darkness of the crystal cave. Eulalie sat on his shoulder, hanging onto his shirt collar. Thera and Mirabel took a couple of tentative steps forward, but lingered by the mouth of the cave.

"Looks like we could use some illumination in here," said Mocarsto. He held out his hand, which held the Annwyn. The tiny world swirled with color and light, growing lighter and brighter with each internal revolution. Soon, the ball began to emanate bright shafts of white light. The light looked fantastic against the walls of the crystal cave and each of the strange company was distractedly delighted with the wondrous optical display. Even the boy emerged from his hiding place to witness the dance of reflected light.

"Ah, there you are," said Mocarsto to the boy. "I have come for you. We will leave now."

The boy stood behind the Rock of Memory, now back on its pedestal. The boy must have rescued it from the Sky in the Lake to preserve the land of lost souls, of which he had grown so fond. Mocarsto noticed the rock as well. He walked to it and set down the Annwyn, still streaming with light, next to the rock on the pedestal so that he could pick up the heavy object with both hands.

"Ah, here it is," said Mocarsto as he smiled at the boy. "You cannot exist here without this, you know. This entire place exists only through the power of this talisman. Not that I understand why you are so attracted to this place. The Land of Echoes is a wasteland of dead time, a land peopled by weak souls who cannot accept their fate. They wander this place trapped in time and their own denial until they wither into shades of what they once were. Your reign here is over, son, and it is time for you to accept that and take the next step toward your future. The past is dead."

"I won't go with you! I hate you!" cried the boy in a passion. In another quick movement, he snatched up the Annwyn and poised his arm to throw it.

"Fool!" hissed Mocarsto. "The Annwyn have enough power to destroy this entire realm. If you unleash it, we will all be destroyed."

"I don't care," said the boy. "Leave the Rock of Memory or else I will smash your toy against the crystal walls."

"Don't do anything rash, boy" hissed Mocarsto. "You do not know what you play at. Here," he said, placing the stone back on its pedestal. "All is well with your pebble. Now hand me back my bauble and we will be on our way."

"I'm no fool," sighed the boy with a look of dejection and defeat. "You'll never leave me be. You'll find a way to destroy the rock and release me from this land, to force me back into your world, into your very self. I won't do it."

The boy Mocarsto looked toward the women who remained near the mouth of the cave. "I mean you no particular harm," he said. "But I don't fear oblivion. I would rather see all ways end than not to get mine."

With that, the boy hurled the Annwyn with all his might toward the back of the cave. Mocarsto's eyes widened with disbelief. Thera gasped as Mirabel looked protectively toward her son. Without thinking, Henry's feet were moving below him. He saw the Annwyn arc as the light faded from its center, and dark gray clouds began to swirl within. Henry knew the pit was there beneath it, the same deep hole he had almost fallen into days before, the same chasm that seemed endless when he and Eulalie had peered into its eerie depths. Henry kept a sharp eye on the Annwyn in the dimming light. As the Annwyn began its descent, Henry leapt and caught the ball midair with an athleticism that would have impressed his baseball coach. He was freefalling now into the pit, too far away to reach either slippery side, even if that would have done him any good. He tucked the Annwyn into his body to protect it from the blow they would both eventually receive whenever he struck the bottom of the unfriendly pit.

Eulalie had still been on Henry's shoulder as he leapt. She flapped her wings as he fell and defied the gravity to which Henry succumbed. She lit her wings and screamed his name in utter panic as she watched her friend plummet into the darkness below.

Chapter LXI
Rainmakers

Drs. Hector and Scala filled the hover bubbles with the necessary equipment and began their ascent to the low-lying clouds above the desert lands that bordered Sun-Rhea. Dr. Finnegan and Miles had sounded the alarm to the villagers, armed and prepared for the fight. They were a makeshift army of peaceable but freedom-loving people, who nevertheless would protect to the death the dignity Mocarsto's minions had sold. Through his binoculars, Dr. Finnegan could now see the approaching army of Cardew as they continued their death march toward the people Televangi had proclaimed the enemy.

Above, in the hover bubble, Dr. Hector zigzagged through the clouds dispensing the diluted, ionized antidote Dr. Finnegan and Dr. Scala had prepared. He made several passes as he sprayed a light mist, molecularly designed to adhere to the moisture already present in the atmosphere. When the clouds were thoroughly seeded, Dr. Scala cooled them quickly with the freezing solution, encouraging the clouds to release their moisture. If all went well, the antidote would rain down upon the murderous masses, soak through their skin and into their bloodstream, and quell their violent passions. Dr. Hector refused to imagine the outcome if their experiment failed.

Down below, Miles had assembled the defenders and led them toward the battlefield just beyond the Federation's borders.

"We must hold them here," he told his troops. "Evil hands must not gain access to the powerful knowledge in these laboratories. Stand your ground until the cavalry comes!"

Dr. Finnegan peered up at the sky and then out across the expanse of desert, darkening now under the shadow of cloud cover. He could see the army of Cardew now without his binoculars. They were close enough to make out their menacing and maniacal faces as they raised their fists and weapons in a battle cry.

"I hope they hurry," Dr. Finnegan mumbled under his breath. He said a little prayer and took his post next to Miles on the front line.

The army of Cardew drew near, brandishing swords and shafts. Their weaponry wasn't sophisticated. Mocarsto had relied primarily on hypnofood to subdue his opposition. Force was a secondary method to secure obedience, and the primitive weapons of the Patrols suited his immediate needs. Nevertheless, Televangi did not fear defeat. He knew the viciousness and brutality his people were capable of in their current state of mind, induced by drugs and vitriol. Televangi rode at the back of the throng, armed with the original, milder concoction of hypnofood. He would use it as a reward to his successful army and an initiation to his defeated opponents lucky enough to survive the onslaught. After today, the free world will collapse in defeat. All of Sun-Rhea will be under the control of hypnofood, and under the control of Mocarsto and Televangi.

Muffled footfalls in the sand turned into a rumble as Miles announced the charge and his army raced out to meet the aggressors. The armies fell upon each other as cold steel and hot tempers clashed in fierce battle.

"Now would be a good time for a rain storm," Dr. Finnegan said to himself, glancing up at the darkening clouds. He quickly returned his attention to the battle as a drug-induced maniac from Cardew attacked him, sword in hand. Dr. Finnegan was no longer a young man; however, he was fit enough to evade the initial blow. He also had the advantage of a clear mind. The people of Cardew suffered noticeably from the mind-numbing effects of the hypnofood. The toxin fueled a blind rage, but distracted their focus from the art of war. Dr. Finnegan coolly tried to fend off the attack without hurting the wayward fool opposite him.

As the swords clashed and Dr. Finnegan came face-to-face with his foe, his heart sank. He recognized the altered man who now challenged him in mortal combat. He had changed significantly over the years. Deep lines of care and disappointment lined his once youthful face. The poisoned hypnofood dulled his eyes like clouded windows. His mouth contorted with anger and illusion as his arms heavily swung his sharpened steel. Dr. Finnegan's joy at reuniting with his brother was easily overcome by the sight of him. Donegal swung again, seeking to connect cold steel with warm flesh. Dr. Finnegan did his best to keep both of them out of harm's way as he silently prayed for rain.

A thunderclap resonated across the desert as the rain began to fall. Fat heavy droplets fell to the thirsty sand as a precursor to a drenching rain that soon soaked them all.

Chapter LXII
Release

"Henry!" Eulalie's scream echoed against the walls of the crystal cave. Henry heard her voice trail him as he and the Annwyn plummeted toward the bottom of the cold, hard pit. Henry felt the Annwyn react to his touch. They seemed almost happy to be back with him. The small orb grew warm in his hand as a crystalline whiteness dotted a midnight blue background like star clusters in deep space. The light grew stronger and blazed outward from the sphere as Henry saw the ground approach beneath him. He closed his eyes and instinctively braced himself for the impact.

Henry landed with a soft thud on the ground. The bottom was not rock hard as he expected, but rather, it gave and shifted under his weight. *What is this?* he wondered as he opened his eyes to his surroundings. Liquid drops were falling on him from overhead. *Is that rain?*

Henry pushed himself up from the ground and felt sand under his fingers. Soft daylight replaced the darkness in the crystal pit. His clothes were wet from raindrops that seemed to be slowing. As the rain cleared and the sun emerged, he recognized some familiar figures. Was that Dr. Finnegan and Donegal in a swordfight? The two men stood facing each other with their weapons at their sides. Donegal's face had softened and he looked like a confused child as he gazed at his erstwhile opponent with wonder and confusion. The antidote had worked and countered the effect of the hypnofood. Memories and feelings long buried washed over Donegal and the sensation was both cathartic and terrifying.

Donegal looked at his brother with recognition and understanding. Then, both men looked at the sand-covered boy beside them.

"Henry?" Donegal said. "Is it really you?"

The Annwyn sang and the worlds pulsed and Henry understood.

"My father?" he asked. "Is that who you are?"

Another pulse and Mirabel was in front of him, standing with Thera and Eulalie in the crystal cave. They each looked around at their changing environment, as waves of energy altered the physical world. They were both in the cave and in the damp desert of Sun-Rhea. The barriers of space eroded under the power of the Annwyn in Henry's hands.

"Mirabel?" said Donegal. "Is it true? You are here, and our son has returned?"

"Donegal!" said Mirabel with profuse joy. "You are well! So many years we have been apart. Our Henry has returned and rescued me from my long imprisonment. And he found you across the worlds."

"The battle is over," said Dr. Finnegan. "The antidote worked. But I would never have been able to make it without Henry bringing back the hypnofood. You did it, Henry. Thanks to you we have won the war."

"But what about Mocarsto?" Henry said. "I thought the legend said I was supposed to defeat him. Where is he anyway?"

Another pulse from the Annwyn and a shifting of the universe brought the group back to the crystal cave where the boy stood peering down into the pit. Henry stood next to the boy to see what he was looking at. Down below in the pit lay Mocarsto in a heap, crumbled atop the broken Rock of Memory.

"What did you do?" Henry asked incredulously.

"Nothing," answered the boy matter-of-factly. "We saw the sand and people, too. We saw you land safely. He went to follow you, to get back his trinket, but it all shifted again and instead of landing in the sand like you did, he hit the rocky bottom. Huh, what was real for you was an illusion for him. He was still holding my rock when he jumped. It's broken now, and he's broken on top of it. He hasn't moved."

Henry was almost moved by the child's wonder and sad resignation. He seemed small and somehow less wicked as he looked down upon his own mangled body and the broken enchantment he so coveted.

The ground swelled and shook and the energy mounted thickly in the air as the Annwyn hummed louder and shone beacons of light through its walls.

"The Rock of Memory is broken," said Thera. "This place can be no more. The old souls who are trapped in the Land of Echoes will be released."

"But where will I go?" asked the boy. Henry wondered at the simultaneous innocence and evil in the child. He almost felt sorry for the lost creature who more than once had tried to destroy him.

"The Annwyn are powerful. With Henry as their guide, the worlds have opened. The lost souls can find their peace where they may. The universe is open."

"But not for long. I feel myself fading," said the boy.

The shades and ghosts that populated the Land of Echoes had amassed outside of the cave. Henry went to meet them with the Annwyn in his hand. The perpetual twilight of the Land of Echoes dissipated in the Annwyn's stunning brightness. Another pulse followed another and the worlds opened to each other. The walls of space deteriorated and physical distance became irrelevant. Henry saw Donegal standing in the desert outside Sun-Rhea. He saw the spirits wandering the Land of Echoes outside the crystal cave. He saw his mother and father, Mr. and Mrs. Harris, at his home on Earth sitting down to dinner, smiling and talking. There were many more worlds, many more images, attached somehow to the shades and people around him. Some were confusing and strange and his mind instinctively focused on the familiar. He saw the reedy grasses of the Wildlands swaying in the wind in the field beside the willow tree where he first met Eulalie. Then, in a blinding flash, it was over.

Chapter LXIII
An End and a Beginning

Henry awoke with the smell of wet leaves in his nose. Brown, sticky leaves stuck to the side of his face as he sat up and looked around. *How long have I been here?* he wondered. It only took him a moment to realize he was in the woods behind the cul-de-sac, near the path to the Wildlands. He pulled the tiny clock out of his pocket. It read three o'clock. The sun through the trees verified it was afternoon. *I should be getting home,* he thought, *before my parents miss me.*

He pushed back the limbs of the trees and emerged into streaming sunshine. Another beautiful day and Henry had a sudden urge to play some baseball. *I think I have practice in an hour.*

He walked to his house, where his parents were busy doing yard work. Their casual demeanor indicated that they had no suspicions about his whereabouts last night. Henry was thankful for their trust in him and he silently vowed never to lie to them again. He cleaned himself up and changed his clothes for baseball. He grabbed his mitt and headed down to the school field to meet his friends.

Henry was at the top of his game. He caught every ball that came near him and hit two home runs before the coach sent the boys home for their suppers. Henry lingered behind to goof around with his friends. They laughed and talked about things pertinent to eleven-year-old boys. Nobody mentioned saving the world.

Finally, he left the field, hungry, but energized. He was looking forward to dinner with his parents. He rushed ahead to find Jon and Jen waiting for him at the first corner.

"Congratulations Henry," said Jen with awe in her voice. "The scientists told us everything."

"Yeah," said Jon, throwing his arm around Henry good-naturedly. "You really did it! Mocarsto is dead and the people of Cardew are free from that horrible hypnofood."

"Mirabel and Donegal are reunited after a decade lost to each of them," said Jen, her eyes beginning to moisten. Despite her bent for the dramatic, Henry hadn't taken her for a romantic.

"Dr. Finnegan is so glad to have his brother back and they're reviving some of the old science projects that have lied dormant these many years," said Jon.

"Even the lost souls in the Land of Echoes have you to thank for their liberation," added Jen.

"Yeah, about that," said Henry. "What happened to the boy Mocarsto? How could the man die and the boy still live? Where did they go anyway?"

Jon shrugged. "I don't know. Mirabel says they went where their hearts would take them."

"Yes. But that boy had a dark heart," surmised Henry. "What about Eulalie? Is she okay?"

"Yes," said Jen. "She's back in the Wildlands with Thera. They went back into Cardew for your other body."

"It's a ghost town now," said Jon. "No one dares go back. The Patrols have fled and the factories are dead. They found your body where you left it, lying under the rubble of your prison cell."

"Eulalie saw that it was brought back to the Wildlands, where Thera can heal you."

"Wow," said Henry. "I hadn't really thought about it. But that certainly is … nice of her."

"Of course, everyone wants to see more of you, Henry," said Jon. "You can keep the Annwyn—they belong to you now—but with two bodies you can bilocate without causing much attention down here."

"I'm glad everything worked out," said Henry. "It was a lot of pressure being the chosen one, and all. But what do I do now? I have two mothers and two fathers now, for one thing. Not to mention the ability to travel to different worlds at will. People on Earth don't usually experience that sort of thing. Well, at least the traveling part."

"Give it time," said Jen with a small smile. "Earthlings are catching on. In some areas they are not so far behind the Federation."

"That's true," Jon agreed. "Besides, it's kind of neat being able to do something that most people can't."

"I guess," said Henry. "But it makes me wonder, 'why me?' you know?"

"Why not you?" asked Jen. "Everybody has their own unique story. So, this is yours. It's a pretty cool one if you ask me."

"Yeah," Henry smiled, thinking it over. "I guess it is. I'd better get home, guys. Tell everyone I will visit soon. Tonight, I think I might just sleep."

"Sure thing," said Jon.

"We'll see you next time," said Jen.

"Good-bye, Henry," said the twins in unison as they both hugged Henry tightly.

Henry walked the last couple of blocks home thinking about the adventures of the past ten days. He knew nothing would ever be the same now that his eyes had opened to these strange and wonderful worlds. He had made friendships that would forever shape his life. With their help, he had dared, he had fought, and he had won. He felt considerably more grown up than he had two weeks ago. He was learning of what he was capable, and he looked forward to exploring the boundless possibilities ahead of him. He walked into his house, with a soft and secret smile, as he thought about Eulalie.

About the Author

Mushin Knott holds Master of Arts Degrees in Literature and Economics from Virginia Commonwealth University and a Bachelor of Arts Degree in English from James Madison University. She has won several Young Author Awards in elementary school for such works as *My Trip to King's Dominion* and *The Day the Zoogies Landed*. *The Adventures of Henry and Eulalie* is her first major publication, with two sequels in the works.

We'd like to know if you enjoyed the book. Please consider leaving a review on the platform from which you purchased the book

CPSIA information can be obtained
at www.ICGtesting.com
Printed in the USA
BVHW031018100223
658278BV00004B/83

9 781682 357118